ONCE REMOVED

CAROLINA WAVES SERIES - BOOK 3

TINA GALLAGHER

Victoria,

I hope you enjoy reading Cal and
Barbara's Story as much as I
enjoyed writing it. :)

Tina Gallagher

GALSALLA PRESS

On the Mend Carolina Waves Series, Book 3

By: Tina Gallagher

Published by Galsalla Press

Copyright © 2020

Cover Design: Lydia Michaels

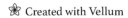 Created with Vellum

Special thanks to:

Cal Chase for letting me borrow his name. I hope I've served it well with this story.

The real Barbara...I wrote the happily ever after you deserved but never had.

And as always...my family.

Chapter 1

Barbara

I stared out my office window, looking down at the factory below. Conveyor belts carried candy in various stages from one station to another, then moved completed confections toward the workers who would package and ship them out.

I used to be one of those workers. One of the packers responsible for boxing perfect chocolate creations and distributing them to the masses. But that was a long time ago. Before Stewart Mack came into my life and I lost myself in his world. Why I'm still in his world three years after the divorce is beyond me.

Not that he's totally to blame. When we met, I wasn't in a good place emotionally speaking, and was ripe for the picking. After breaking up with my college sweetheart, I shifted to team Stewart with minimal sweet talk from the man himself.

Even after all this time, I'm still not sure what put me on his radar. Stewart barely pays attention to the factory workers—or any of the workers, for that matter. He generally lives in his ivory tower and doesn't mingle with the masses.

Before my thoughts could get too Stewart-centric, I spun my chair around to face my desk and the task at hand. Molly Mack Chocolate's expansion and renovation depends on me acing my presentation at the bank this afternoon. If I can convince First Allegiant Bank to loan us an insane amount of money, the company will be able to expand, improve operations, and increase market share. That's the plan anyway. Stewart's plan.

And I have to say, despite the fact that he's a class-A jerk, the man has a good head for business. So far, most of his ideas have had a positive impact on the bottom line. It really pisses me off, too. Not that I want the business to tank, but it would be nice if something bad happened to the asshole. I keep waiting for the karma train to run him down, but he's managed to avoid it so far. He just strolls through life with everything going his way.

Well, maybe not everything. I'm still here. I know if he had his way, I would have been in the unemployment line before the ink dried on the divorce papers. The fact that I live in his mother's pool house doesn't sit well with him, either. I smiled at the thought.

"You look happy." I jumped, knocking my stack of handouts to the floor. "Sorry, I didn't mean to startle you."

My mother-in-law—make that ex-mother-in-law—settled into the seat in front of my desk.

"It's fine. I just didn't hear you come in."

"It's been a long time since I've seen a smile like that on your face. What put it there?"

I chuckled. "You don't want to know."

I love Molly. We bonded the first moment we met and I love her as much as I loved my own mother. But she *is* Stewart's mother so I avoid making any nasty comments about my ex-husband in her presence. It's an unspoken agreement between us that we don't discuss him.

Understanding, she refocused her attention to the handouts, which were once again stacked neatly in front of me.

"Ready for the big presentation?"

"Yep. You?"

"You have the hard part. I just have to sit there and look like I understand what you're talking about."

As usual, Molly is being humble. After her husband died, she started Molly Mack Chocolate in her kitchen. She managed to hold down a part-time job, raise two boys, and build the business into a multimillion-dollar corporation in a manner of years.

"We both know that you understand exactly what I'm talking about. But if it makes you feel better, you can just sit there and look pretty today."

"I'll try my best." She wiped an invisible speck of lint off her skirt.

"Is J.P. coming?" I asked. As head of marketing, my ex-brother-in-law doesn't always attend financial meetings, but I'd requested his presence at this one. Besides his calming presence, he'd also bring a plethora of marketing and industry knowledge in case I need backup.

"Yes, he's driving with us," she said. The fact that she averted her gaze before uttering the next sentence should have warned me I wouldn't like it. "And Stewart is meeting us there."

My ex-husband's attendance at the meeting shouldn't surprise me, but I had hoped something he deemed more important would keep him away. Even though I know the facts backward and forward, Stewart has a way of making me feel and look inadequate.

Squaring my shoulders, I resolved to ignore him during my presentation. And the rest of the time, for that matter.

"Do you know who we're meeting with?"

"Just the usual crew." She looked at the pile in front of me, then turned her attention to my right hand as it obsessively tucked a stray strand of hair behind my ear. "Don't be nervous, Barb. I've been dealing with First Allegiant Bank for almost thirty years."

"I know, but lending is still tight. The expansion is a great idea, but it's not a sure thing—nothing is. My job is to convince them we're worth the risk. I don't want to mess that up."

"You won't." She smiled. "I know you won't."

Tears filled my eyes, but before I could say or do something too sappy, J.P. stuck his head in the door.

"You want to grab some lunch before the big presentation?"

Even though food is the last thing on my mind, I echoed Molly's enthusiastic, "Yes."

CAL

I leaned back in the chair and looked around my office, trying to figure out what the fuck I'm doing here. I've made the thirty-minute commute to this soul-sucking place for the past six weeks and still can't believe this is my life now.

The corner office with its plush carpeting, mahogany desk, and floor to ceiling windows may be someone's idea of paradise, but it's definitely not mine. Grass, dirt, and smelly locker rooms are more my speed.

Sure, my degree is in finance, but I never thought I'd ever actually have to use it. College was only a stepping stone to where I really wanted to end up—the major leagues. Once I was drafted junior year, I figured I'd never have to get a real job. Yet here I am.

Not that I have to work. I was lucky enough to make a great living playing the best game in the world, so I could sit on my ass and do nothing for the rest of my life and never have to worry about money. But since I was forced to retire in what I consider to be my prime, I have to do something.

At thirty-three, I still had some good years ahead of me, but I was old enough to not act like a stupid rookie. I figured if I stayed in shape and kept myself healthy, I'd have at least another seven years in the hot corner. But after chasing a foul ball into the stands, I messed up my neck, and that was all shot to hell.

At least I'd made the catch.

I honestly never planned on having a career past baseball. My goal was to play as long as possible then retire and spend time with my wife and kids. Unfortunately, my marriage didn't work out and I never had kids. I'm blessed with family and friends, but they have their own lives.

The days are awful long when you don't have a purpose. It took me less than a year to realize I needed to work. I sat in the Waves' booth a couple times last season doing color commentary, but realized it's not for me. Not as a regular gig anyway.

My computer dinged and I sat forward and spotted the Outlook notification that filled the middle of the screen. I groaned and rubbed the back of my neck. Another conference call. Thankfully it's only for a half hour, because then I have that big meeting Mr. Robinson has been hopped up about all week right after.

Welcome to corporate America.

Chapter 2

Barbara

I'm glad I went to lunch with J.P. and Molly even though I barely ate. If I hadn't, I would have just hid in my office, obsessing over the presentation. Instead, I was able to relax with two of my favorite people.

Some of Molly's confidence and J.P.'s easy demeanor must have absorbed into my pores, because once we arrived at the bank, I felt uncharacteristically calm. They schmoozed with the bigwigs, while I excused myself to set up in the conference room. I had just finished placing the last handout on the oversized mahogany table when the door opened and my in-laws—make that ex-in-laws—entered, followed by the loan trinity.

I couldn't help but notice that the senior vice-president, Bill Robinson, looked simply smitten with Molly, nor the fact that she seemed to glow under his attention. Tucking those facts away to ponder later, I rounded the table to greet the men who would decide the company's fate.

"Bill, you remember my...uh, Barbara," Molly said. I smirked at the fact that she almost introduced me as her daughter-in-law.

"Of course," Mr. Robinson said, tearing his eyes away from Molly just long enough to shake my hand.

Jim Peters and John Butler, both loan vice presidents, greeted me in turn before we all settled into oversized chairs around the enormous table.

"We're just waiting for our new VP to join us," Mr. Robinson said.

"Oh, I didn't realize you'd added a new member to the team," Molly said.

"He's a relatively new addition to the group. He'll be spending time in both corporate lending and financial planning to decide which suits him best. I'm hoping when he gets up to speed, I'll be able to take more time off and ease into retirement."

Before Molly could comment, the man in question entered the room.

"Sorry I'm late," he said. "I was on a conference call that ran over."

My head snapped in the newcomer's direction as his voice triggered memories of young love and heartache. In profile, his face looked more angular than it had fifteen years earlier. The conservative cut of his black hair, highlighted sharp cheekbones and a chiseled jaw.

I must have made a noise—that or he could hear my heart pounding—because his eyes shifted in my direction. If he was surprised to see me, he hid it well.

"Cal, this is Molly, the president and founder of Molly Mack Chocolate and her son J.P. who heads the marketing department."

Cal acknowledged them, shaking their hands in turn.

"And this is Barbara Mack, Molly's daughter-in-law, the company's CFO," Mr. Robinson continued. "She'll be heading the presentation today."

I knew I should do something, but I stood glued to my spot as Cal rounded the table.

"Barb and I go way back," he said as he took my hand in his. The gesture felt more like a caress than a handshake and the zing that traveled up my arm and to the rest of my body left me even more flustered.

"Nice to see you again," I said, not sure if it was true. My voice sounded ridiculously husky. If that weren't bad enough, I felt a blush spread across my cheeks.

"Yes it is," he said as he slowly let go of my hand.

I frowned, trying to figure out why he looked so happy to see me. After all, our last encounter hadn't been very positive. His answering wink and smile confused me even more.

Tucking my hair behind my ear, I turned to my computer and pretended to do something important. Molly caught my eye and raised her brow. She must have noticed my reaction to Cal. Hell, a blind man would probably notice my reaction to the man.

Great. I don't want to have to explain the whole Cal situation to her. Nor do I want her playing cupid, and from the look on her face and her shifting glances, it was obvious that's exactly what she had in mind.

Oh well, I'll cross that bridge when I come to it.

Everyone settled around the table as I took one last look at my presentation. I felt Cal's gaze on me and fought the urge to look in his direction. Taking a few deep breaths, I finally had myself together when Stewart and wife number two—aka my ex-friend Frances—sauntered through the door.

"I apologize for being late," he said, directing everyone's attention his way. Well, everyone but Cal's. He continued to watch me with those chocolate brown eyes as Stewart kissed Molly on the cheek and shook hands with Bill Robinson. My gaze locked with his while the team assured Stewart that he was exactly on time, which of course he wasn't.

"And I'd like you to meet my wife, Frances," Stewart said. The woman in question held a limp-wristed hand toward Mr. Robinson, who looked slightly confused for a moment. Even though it's common knowledge that Stewart and I are divorced and he's remarried, the fact that Molly still refers to me as her daughter-in-law on a regular basis seems to make people forget.

Peters and Butler shook the couple's hands in turn, then introduced them to Cal. Stewart looked furious as his wife pushed the perfect breasts he had given her as an engagement present out front and center as she tempted Cal to check them out. It gave me a great deal of satisfaction when he didn't take the bait.

Once all the niceties were out of the way, everyone settled around the table. Stewart and Frances sat in the chairs directly across from me and the flush on my ex's cheeks told me that they had either enjoyed a few cocktails at lunch or recently had a quickie. Knowing them, it was probably both.

While they tried to be casual about it, I noticed Mr. Robinson, Peters, and Butler shifting their gazes from Stewart and Frances to me and back. Unfortunately, Stewart noticed too and his reaction left no doubt in my mind he'd had at least a two-martini lunch.

"I know there may be some confusion because unfortunately my mother often refers to Barbara as her daughter-in-law, but I assure you, we *are* divorced. Frances is my mother's only daughter-in-law." He directed a smug look at J.P. before shifting his glossy brown eyes to me, and I knew whatever would come out of his mouth next wouldn't be good. "Barbara over there is what you might call once removed."

Stewart chuckled as everyone around the table remained silent. Frances sat next to him, her Stepford Wife smile firmly in place. A tic appeared in Molly's jaw, but she didn't comment or admonish him. Not that I'm surprised. I know she often doesn't agree with his behavior, but she rarely calls him on it. And, when his bad behavior is pointed out to her, "he's my son" is usually her response. Apparently, that fact absolves him from a myriad of sins.

Over the years, I've learned to not discuss Stewart with her. Molly and I have a great relationship, and if for nothing else, I'm grateful for getting involved with my ex-husband because it brought her into my life as something more than my boss. And, despite letting daily slights go, Molly has stood up for me, even if it wasn't in front of my face. The fact that I hold a high-level position at Molly Mack Chocolate is proof of that.

I know Stewart wanted me gone when we split up. When Molly refused, he wanted me demoted back to the line. Yet, here I am, which I know is Molly's doing. She's also given me a place to live in her pool house and refuses to accept rent.

I glanced over at J.P., and if looks could kill, Stewart would be in trouble, but thankfully he remained silent. In the past, he'd championed for me, only to have his brother verbally tear him apart. We don't need a whole nasty scene to occur in front of the loan trinity—make that quartet—with the addition of Cal.

"Why don't we get started?" Mr. Robinson said, breaking the awkward silence that had settled over the room. Once everyone shifted their focus to him, he started. "As you all know, we're here to discuss funding for a building and machinery expansion at Molly Mack Chocolate. While we've enjoyed a mutually beneficial relationship for many years, current guidelines require that we perform extra due diligence because of the size of the loan and scope of the project. Does anyone have any questions?"

"But this is just a formality, right?" Stewart said. "Molly Mack is a leader in the chocolate industry and this expansion is going to solidify our position at the top."

"Not so much a formality as a formal meeting to discuss the project prospectus and financial analysis." Stewart looked less than thrilled with Mr. Robinson's answer, but surprisingly didn't respond.

"Barbara," Mr. Robinson said. "I believe you're up." While he didn't give me a full-blown smile, his eyes crinkled, softening his normally professional look. I nodded, sending silent thanks.

I stood. "Thank you, Mr. Robinson. First Allegiant Bank has been with Molly Mack Chocolate since the beginning and we appreciate you taking the time to meet with us today so we can discuss our future." I picked up my presenter and brought my laptop to life, projecting the Molly Mack Chocolate logo onto the far wall. "We have some big plans for expansion and renovation, which will make the manufacturing process more efficient and take business to the next level."

While my ex-husband is seated directly across from me, Cal sat next to Mr. Robinson on the other side of the table. Wonderful. If I look one way, I have to see Stewart and Frances. The other direction puts Cal right in my line of vision. Both views are equally distracting.

I stood and shifted to the side of the table so I faced the other attendees.

I clicked through the presentation slides as I spoke, giving my audience something to focus on. Unfortunately, Cal chose to keep his gaze trained on me. Goosebumps trailed across my body and my hand trembled enough that I had to tighten my grip on the presenter.

"Before we go through the financials, I want to direct your attention to the handouts in front of you," I said. "All of the numbers and scenarios I'm about to go over are included in the handouts so you don't have to worry about capturing them."

While everyone around the table opened their handouts and flipped through the pages, I took the opportunity to take a sip of water. I glanced over at Molly, who smiled and flashed a discreet thumbs-up. So far, so good.

"Why don't we take a look at the initial expenditures first? They're on page nine of the handout."

Engaging the built-in laser pointer on my presenter, I directed a red dot onto the first line of numbers and explained what they stood for. Line by line, I went through the budget we had carefully laid out for the new machines and warehouse space.

"Does anyone have any questions?" I asked, looking first at Mr. Robinson, then at the other bank officers, lifting my gaze as I turned toward Cal, so I viewed the wall behind him.

CAL

Of all the banks in all the world…

Barbara Murphy, after all this time. I've fought the urge to cyberstalk her through the years. I figured it would have been pointless anyway. She made it perfectly clear my lifestyle wouldn't work for her and I couldn't have imagined giving up baseball back then. It's bad enough now, but at least I lived my dream for more than a decade.

I should be focusing on her words, but it's not easy. She's very distracting with that beautiful face and those baby blue eyes. Not that they've looked directly at me yet. Instead, her gaze skims the top of my head when she turns in my direction.

The fact that I still affect her so much she can't look at me must mean something, right?

I shake that thought out of my head and again focus on her words. Based on what I see in her charts and what I've actually heard her say, the plan looks solid. Between that and the bank's relationship with Molly Mack...both the woman and the company...this deal seems like a no-brainer. I'll be curious to hear what the others have to say.

Barbara wrapped up her presentation and opened the floor for questions.

"Everything you've shown looks solid," Mr. Butler said, echoing my own thoughts. "But as you know, best laid plans often fail. What is your contingency plan if this doesn't follow course?"

Before Barb could answer, her asshat of an ex-husband stood and put on what I assume was supposed to be a charming smile. To me, he just looked constipated.

How did someone as amazing as Barbara marry this douchebag?

"Mr. Robinson, you know Molly Mack Chocolate. You've been there with us since the beginning. My mother built a multi-million-dollar corporation using mixing bowls in her kitchen. If that's possible, then it's impossible for this to fail with our current market share and reputation pushing us forward."

I didn't like the way he just took over or how he addressed Mr. Robinson with an answer to Mr. Butler's question. And I especially didn't like the way Barbara seemed to shrink with him in the room. What the hell is the deal here?

While Mr. Robinson explained the current lending climate and stringent guidelines First Allegiant has to follow, I looked around the table, trying to figure out the Mack family dynamic. Molly's face looked pinched as she watched her son, Stewart, take the stage away from Barbara. J.P. massaged his temples, his gaze focused on the table. Frances watched Stewart with fascination, as though every syllable he uttered was gospel. And Barbara got smaller and smaller as the meeting went on.

"We appreciate you all coming today," Mr. Robinson said as he stood and buttoned his suit coat. "Barbara, your presentation was wonderful. Very informative." He held up the folder that sat in front of him. "We'll go over this and get back to you by the end of the week."

"I'm not sure what there is to go over," Steward said. "It's pretty cut and dried. Either our relationship is worth something or it's not." He took a breath as though he was fortifying himself to go on a tangent, but before he could do anything, Molly stood and cut him off.

"Thank you so much for meeting with us today, Bill. Take all the time you need and if you have any questions, give Barbara a call," she said, with an emphasis on Barbara's name.

Stewart puffed up his chest and looked like he was going to say something, but Molly narrowed her eyes in his direction and he deflated. Walking over toward Frances, he took her hand and said, "We'll await your answer." They left the board room in the same dramatic fashion as they'd entered.

I watched Barbara methodically stack papers into a pile and unplug her laptop from the projector. After placing everything in her case, she stood and glanced at J.P. who was talking with Mr. Butler. She tucked her hair behind her ear twice before shifting her gaze to Molly. Her eyes widened and she shook her head. For the first time since I entered the room, her eyes met mine. Before I could evaluate the panic I saw in her blue depths, I felt a tap on my shoulder. I turned and found Molly Mack standing right behind me, a wide smile engulfing her face.

Even though the top of her head barely reached my shoulder, the woman held an air of authority. I guess you don't build a business like Molly Mack Chocolate without being tough, especially as a single mother back in the eighties.

"Ms. Mack," I said. "It's nice to meet you. I'm a big fan of your chocolates."

"Mr. Chase," she responded as she shook my hand. "I'm happy to hear you're a fan. So..." Her gaze darted around my shoulder for a second before returning to my face. "...how is it you know our Barbara?"

Chapter 3

Barbara

Crap! What is Molly saying to Cal? Or just as troubling...what's Cal saying to Molly? I fought the urge to cross the room to find out.

Turning my back to them, I tucked my laptop and files into my tote, struggling to listen to their conversation. Unfortunately, besides low murmurs and a few chuckles, I couldn't hear a thing. I glanced over my shoulder and cringed. Both Molly and Cal were looking in my direction. I turned back around nearly giving myself whiplash.

As I zipped my tote, my mind whirled, trying to think of what to do next. I'm all packed and ready to go. I can't just stand here like an idiot. Taking in a deep breath, I shrugged my bag over my shoulder and turned, trying my best to look nonchalant.

Unfortunately, my heel snagged in the carpet causing my foot to stay in place while the rest of my body turned. I felt myself falling and grabbed onto the thing closest to me, which was a chair. That would have been great if it didn't have wheels. Instead of helping me stay on my feet, it rolled forward and I slid to the floor, seemingly in slow motion. My knee hit the carpet first, then my hip, and I was able to slam my hands down to prevent smashing my face.

"Barbara!" Molly yelled.

"Holy shit!" I heard Cal say before I felt him kneel next to me. "Are you okay?" he asked.

Taking in a deep breath, I dropped my forehead to the floor and nodded, trying to ignore the pain in my ankle and figure out how to stand gracefully. Realizing there was no dignified way up, I placed my palms flat on the carpet and pushed up my shoulders, planning on shifting to my knees, and standing from there. But you know what they say about best laid plans.

Instead of effortlessly lifting myself, a blinding pain shot from my ankle up my leg and I screamed, falling back to the floor.

"What's wrong?" Cal asked, his hand resting on my waist.

I couldn't speak. I was too busy practicing my yoga breathing hoping it would help stop the painful throbbing that had settled into the lower half of my right leg. Cal and Molly's voices floated around me, but I couldn't make out their words.

Cal's hand moved from my waist and I felt him leave my side. The words *ambulance* and *now* pulled me out of my semi-fog.

"I don't need an ambulance," I said and tried to lift myself up again. The groan that escaped me belied my words.

Molly's hand rested on my head as I set it back on the carpet.

"Try to relax. Help is on the way."

I heard Cal and Molly speaking, then other voices flowed into the mix. I'm mortified, humiliated, and embarrassed and a whole thesaurus of words that can't begin to truly describe how I feel.

I'd just finished praying for the floor to open up and suck me in when Mr. Robinson knelt next to me and said, "I'm so sorry this happened, Barbara. The ambulance will be here soon."

I want to lift myself up and tell him I'm okay. I want to get up and walk out the door, go home, have a drink or three, and wallow in self-pity. But once again, when I try to move, pain shoots from my ankle and takes my breath away.

"Honey, the ambulance just pulled up. The paramedics will be here soon," Cal said, at my side once again. I'd be lying if I said the slow strokes of his hand on my back didn't offer comfort. "Mr. Robin-son, would it be okay if I accompany Barbara to the hospital?"

"Of course, of course," Mr. Robinson replied.

Before I could object, I heard a commotion that signaled the arrival of the paramedics. After clearing the room, they settled on either side of me, checking my vital signs.

"Barbara, we're going to have to roll you over," the one on my left said. "But before we do that, I need to remove your shoe. The heel is stuck in the carpet so I'm going to have to wiggle it free." He put a hand on my calf. "Ready?" I nodded. "Here we go." I felt my shoe shift from my heel and groaned as agonizing pain shot through my leg once again. "Just breathe and try to relax," he said.

Yeah, easy for him to say. Every time I move, I feel like someone is driving an ice pick into my ankle. I've twisted my ankle many times before, but this feels a thousand times worse. As I was wondering about that, I felt pressure on my calf then a tugging on my foot that turned up the pain quotient to a million. I screamed and as the tugging sensation happened again, everything went black.

CAL

Barbara's scream had me running into the conference room. I know the paramedics are professionals, but I have to see for myself that she's okay. They'd strapped her to a plastic board and lifted her as I entered. Barbara looked like she was asleep, but I can't imagine that's the case considering the twisted mess her ankle had been.

When I asked, the female paramedic confirmed that Barbara had passed out when they removed her shoe. I sucked in deep breaths and let slowly let them out in an attempt to stave off the waves of nausea that rolled through me at that thought.

I followed as the paramedics carried Barbara out of the confer-ence room and placed her onto the gurney they had stored in the hallway. Molly, J.P., and Mr. Robinson stood near, surrounded by curious bank employees.

"Is she all right?" Molly asked, her voice a strange combination of shriek and whisper.

"She passed out when we removed her shoe, but her vitals are fine," the paramedic said.

"I'll go with her," J.P. said.

"I'm going," I said.

Under any other circumstances, I would have found J.P.'s look comical. But right now, I'm worried about Barbara and nothing else matters.

"Why—"

I'm sure he's wondering why some guy they just met is going to the hospital with Barbara, but Molly interrupted her son's words, so I'll never know for sure.

"J.P., I'd like to go home and lie down for a bit," she said. "Cal offered to go with Barbara so she's not alone right now. We can meet them at the hospital once I get my bearings. I hate to admit it, but this whole day has taken a toll on me."

He didn't look totally convinced, but Molly flashed what could only be described as puppy dog eyes at him and he nodded. Placing his hand on her elbow, he escorted her to the elevators.

I followed the paramedics and Barbara, still out cold on the gurney, into the elevator, leaving J.P. and Molly to wait for the next. On the first floor, bank employees stopped in their tracks to watch as we left the building and the paramedics rolled Barbara into the waiting ambulance.

I'm sure this will be the talk of the water cooler. Anything out of the ordinary is generally fodder for gossip, and someone being taken away in an ambulance definitely qualifies as unusual. The fact that I'm climbing into the ambulance with her will only fuel the fire.

The paramedics settled the gurney into the ambulance, making sure it was secured and directed me to sit on what looked like a shelf. One climbed into the back while the other slammed the door next to me before reappearing in the driver's seat.

Sirens roared to life and I nearly fell off my seat when we pulled away from the curb and took a corner on, what I'm sure was, two wheels. Holding Barbara's hand, I prayed she'd be all right. I've seen a lot of injuries throughout my career...once a come-back line drive hit Joey Collins in the face and shattered his eye socket and the whole right side of his face collapsed...but I've never seen anything like Barbara's ankle. Her body had faced one way and her foot pointed in the completely opposite direction. I can't imagine the pain. No wonder she passed out.

The paramedic finished hooking an IV to Barbara's left hand and sat back, pulling two cards out of the pocket on his thigh, then proceeded to fill out a multitude of forms attached to his clipboard. The ambulance came to an abrupt stop and the paramedic stood, handing me the cards.

"Can you hold on to these for her?" he asked.

I looked down and saw her license and insurance card. Molly must have given them to him. Good thing because I'm clueless beyond Barbara's name and birthday.

They rolled her out and I climbed down from the ambulance and followed them through the sliding doors into the emergency room.

"Someone will find you once they examine her," the paramedic said over his shoulder as they disappeared through the double doors.

With nothing else to do, I settled onto a couch in the waiting room and watched a Seinfeld rerun, hoping to distract myself from the mental image of Barb's ankle. One episode ended and another began, and still no word. I stood and paced the corridor, stopping at the vending machine. I'd missed lunch thanks to that damn conference call, but I'm too amped up to eat anything now. Instead of food, I fed a dollar into the machine and selected a ginger ale. As I bent to retrieve the green bottle from the tray, I remember Barbara teasing me about my drink preference when we first started dating. I'm not sure why she thought it was so unusual, but by the time we were through, it was her drink of choice, too. I wonder if it still is.

"Mr. Chase?"

I turned and spotted a nurse peeking out from the door Barbara had disappeared behind gesturing me in her direction. No one had asked my name, so I can only assume someone recognized me.

"Ms. Mack is back from X-ray and settled in. You can go back now."

She held the door open wide and I slipped inside.

"She's in room ten," she said, pointing to the right.

"Thank you, Nurse..."

"Shannon," she said. Placing her hand on my bicep, she added. "If you need anything at all, just let me know."

I shook off her hand and headed toward Barbara's room, throwing a quick "thank you" over my shoulder. While I'm definitely not interested in what Shannon was so obviously offering, I normally would have handled the situation more gently. But right now, I can't focus on anything beyond making sure Barbara is okay...a fact I don't want to examine too closely just yet.

A nurse was exiting the room just as I reached the door. I looked over her head and saw Barbara asleep on the narrow bed.

"Is she all right?" I asked.

She nodded. "We gave her something for the pain so she'll probably be a bit groggy. The doctor will be in to talk to her once he reviews the X-rays."

"Thank you."

I pulled a chair from the corner next to the bed and sat, feeling like I'd run a marathon. Weaving my fingers through hers, I rested my chin on our joined hands and watched her sleep. How can a woman I haven't seen in fifteen years affect me like this?

Then again, besides my ex-wife, Barbara is the most significant relationship I've ever had. She actually might be more significant than my ex-wife in that she was as invested in me as I was in her. Then she was just...gone. Even at the time, I understood her reasons for ending our relationship, but understanding didn't erase the pain.

I've often wondered if I would have been as successful in my career if we hadn't split up. I'd always given it my all, but after she ended things, I became obsessed. I worked out like a madman, trimmed down, muscled up, and spent hours honing my reflexes. The hot corner has its name for a reason, and I was determined that nothing would get by third base on my watch. My hard work earned me a rookie of the year status as well as three Gold Gloves. Would any of that have happened if I'd had something else to focus on besides baseball? If I hadn't poured all my misery into training in the beginning?

Before I could dig into that too deeply, bleary blue eyes fluttered open. She blinked repeatedly, struggling to focus. Once she did, two adorable lines appeared in her brow, right above the bridge of her nose.

"Cal?" Her gaze shifted to our joined hands and she disentangled our fingers, resting hers on her stomach. "Why are you here?"

"Here in Conway or here at the hospital?"

"Both." She shifted herself higher up on the bed and cringed.

"I'm here at the hospital because I wanted to make sure you're okay," I said. "And I'm here in Conway because, as you know, I went to college here, and I like it."

"Why are you working at First Allegiant Bank? After your baseball career, I can't imagine you need to work."

"We'll save that story for another time," I said. "For now, how are you feeling? Have they told you anything?"

"It's broken, but the doctor hasn't been in yet to let me know the extent of it."

Her mouth turned down. I'm not sure if it's because I evaded her question or because she didn't like the answer to mine.

"The nurse told me I passed out."

I nodded. "When they removed your shoe."

She closed her eyes and swallowed.

"Please tell me Stewart and Frances didn't see." Her small voice echoed how she had shrunk next to her ex-husband. What the hell is the story with those two?

"No, they were already gone."

"Thank God." Her eyes popped open. "But everyone else did?"

"The only ones who witnessed the actual fainting were the paramedics. They kicked everyone else out of the room when they started working on you."

"I guess that's something."

"The important thing is that help arrived and got you to the ER as fast as possible."

She snorted. "Easy for you to say."

"It really wasn't that bad," I assured her. "You fell, but it's not like you had a dress on and it flew up over your head or your pants ripped and you were commando."

Her chuckle brought back memories of happy times. One thing Barbara and I did a lot of was laugh together. I never realized how important that is in a relationship until I didn't have it any more.

"I still don't know what happened," she said.

"Your heel got stuck in some loose threads in the carpet."

She rolled her eyes. "Seriously? Who else would that happen to?"

"You should buy a lottery ticket. Might be your lucky day."

Resting back on the pillows, she closed her eyes, rubbed her temples, and sighed.

"Are you okay? Do you need me to get the nurse?"

I was halfway out of my chair when she answered.

"No." She shook her head and slowly opened her eyes. "They gave me something for the pain, and it's making me a little fuzzy."

I settled back into the chair.

"Close your eyes and relax," I said, patting her hand. "I'll be here if you need anything."

Glossy eyes glanced down to our hands, then back to my face.

"If only that was true," she said, then closed her eyes again.

I wanted to push her to continue, to talk about the past, and more importantly, a possible future. But I couldn't. It wouldn't be fair to take advantage of her vulnerable state. But mark my words...when she's not drugged, we *will* talk.

Chapter 4

Barbara

How on earth am I going to stay off my feet for six weeks?

I'll go insane.

According to my orthopedist, if I'm good and follow his orders, there's a 97% chance my ankle will heal properly on its own. If I don't stay off it or it doesn't heal right, he'll have to fix it surgically. Neither option makes me happy, but at least if I sit around for six weeks, the odds are in my favor that I won't have to go under the knife.

So here I sit on my couch, my right leg propped up on two pillows. The black boot covering me from foot to knee feels bulky and foreign. Molly pushed me forward and plumped the pillow behind my back before letting me settle back against the arm of the couch again. She tossed a fleece throw over my legs and stood back to study her handiwork. Seemingly satisfied, she looked around my living room/dining room/kitchen combo. Nodding as though I'd passed some kind of test, she perched on the edge of my coffee table.

"I feel so awful about this," she said.

"If I wasn't so klutzy, this wouldn't have happened."

"Bill said they have someone scheduled to fix that carpet. He noticed the loose threads last week when the wheel of his chair got caught on them. He's horrified that this happened." Her gaze shifted, as it tends to do when she's about to say something I don't want to hear. "Also, you were distracted because I was talking to your young man."

I've never told Molly about Cal. Why would I? I'd been with Stewart. Why lament about my lost college sweetheart to my mother-in-law? But based on the gleam in her blue eyes, she obviously knew something and she wasn't going to let this go. Molly may look sweet, but you don't accomplish everything she has without being part hard ass.

"I don't know what you mean," I said. "I don't have a young man."

Which, of course, wasn't a lie.

"Maybe not now, but he was very important to you at one time."

That wasn't a question.

I looked down at the blanket on my lap, and traced the geometric pattern with my index finger.

"Barbara." Molly's voice was barely a whisper, but it still commanded me to look at her. "Talk to me."

Her kind expression pulled me in. I'd drunkenly recounted my heartbreak to Jess and J.P. one night and they'd both given the supportive "fuck him, it's his loss" speeches as friends are inclined to do. Other than that, I've never really spoken to anyone about the relationship, and I try to avoid ever thinking about it, and I've been pretty successful for the most part. But now with Cal's reappearance, something tells me he's going to be front and center in my thoughts whether I want him there or not.

I don't know if it's the leftover painkillers in my system or if my fall jarred the box I'd stuffed everything Cal related into, but suddenly he's all I want to talk about. I want to tell Molly about our relationship and how it ended, and how I'd felt so empty afterwards.

"Cal sat behind me in English 101 our freshman year in college," I said. "For two weeks, no matter where I sat, he'd be in the row behind me." I settled further into the couch and got more comfortable. Molly sat silently, her small smile urging me to continue. "Of course I noticed him. How could I not? He's gorgeous...and that smile." I trailed off, lost in the memory. "I remember the first time he spoke to me. I nearly fainted." Molly chuckled and I said, "Seriously, I'm not kidding. My heart skidded to a stop, then pounded, and I heard a buzzing noise in my ears."

"What did he say to you?" she asked.

"He asked me if I had a pen he could borrow."

"Did you?"

"Of course," I said. "You know what a pen snob I am. I always carry extras in case one dies. God forbid I have to use some kind of basic stick pen."

"So, he borrowed your pen and you fell madly in love?"

"Sort of. We started talking in class, he asked me out, and then we fell madly in love."

"What happened?"

I swallowed. "Cal got drafted."

"You broke up because he got drafted?"

"No, not then. It was after..." I swallowed and rubbed at the ache in my chest. "...after my mother died."

I looked down at the blanket and toyed with its edges, needing to escape the sympathy in Molly's eyes. She didn't say a word, yet somehow I felt compelled to continue.

"Cal was playing in Texas. Between practice and games, getting together was tough, but we were determined to make it work. I was able to meet up with him a few times and we talked on the phone constantly," I said. "You know that my mother died from pancreatic cancer." Molly nodded. "She'd been in remission, but at the end of my sophomore year in college, something showed up on one of her scans during a routine check. We thought it would be the same as before...a few rounds of chemo and she'd be good again." I opened my mouth to speak, but instead of words, a shuddering breath came out. I closed my eyes and swallowed. "She died the following year."

"Honey, I can't even begin to imagine how difficult that time was for you. To be so young and so alone." She blinked away tears and shook her head. "Continue with your story before I get too verbose."

I'm amazed I've never shared this part of my life with Molly. But honestly, when I met her, I was really trying to move on. So while she knows how and when my mother died, she doesn't know all the details...and I obviously never told her about Cal.

"I felt so alone. I didn't have any close family and the friends I had didn't know how to help. Cal tried to be there, but he was just starting his career, and wasn't able to take a lot of time off. He did come to my mom's funeral, but he could only stay for the day. Then he was off playing ball again. He'd call every day like always, but it was different. At least it felt different to me. Looking back now, I'm sure I was depressed. It started to bother me that he couldn't be with me when I needed him. Part of me understood...after all, he was chasing his dream. But another part wanted him with me."

"So you ended it."

I nodded and said in a small voice. "I ended it."

"What did he say?"

"He was upset and tried to talk me out of it." I shrugged. "We'd been together three years at that point and had talked about the future a lot. It had always included him playing professional baseball and me working around that. But for some reason, I didn't want that anymore. With my mother gone, you'd think I would have been more open to a life on the road since I had nothing to tie me down, but I felt more inclined to stay in one place and grow some roots. So when he asked me to reconsider and go on the road with him, I said no. Plus, I still had a year left of college and I promised my mom I'd graduate."

"And that was that?"

My sad chuckle ended on a small sob. I swallowed three times, attempting to dislodge the lump that had settled in my throat. "That was that," I finally said.

I opened my mouth to tell her about the weeks of misery that followed. How I'd cried all the time and seriously considered calling Cal and begging him to take me back. Before I could get the words out, three quick knocks sounded just before my front door opened and my best friend, Jess, strolled through followed by J.P.

The two had dated for a couple years but had split when J.P. came out of the closet. They remained best friends in a true Will & Grace fashion.

"Oh my God," Jess screeched and rushed to my side. "How are you feeling? I can't believe this happened. J.P. said you can't move for six weeks. What do you need me to do?"

J.P. placed his hands on her shoulders and backed her a few inches away from the couch. "Give her a chance to answer one question before you ask another." He chuckled.

"Sorry," she said. "Hi Molly. I didn't mean to ignore you." She walked over and gave Molly a kiss on the cheek. J.P. followed and did the same.

"I understand," Molly said. "Our girl gave us quite a scare."

"What did the doctor say?" Jess asked. She and J.P. settled into the love seat across from me.

"Basically that I can't put any weight on my ankle for six weeks. Hopefully the bones will heal properly so I don't need surgery."

"Is it really painful?"

"It was, but it's not so bad now." I nudged my chin in J.P.'s direction. "I'm sure he told you that I passed out when they took my shoe off."

"Yeah, and he also said that your foot was totally turned around and facing the wrong direction." She scrunched her nose. "Thank God I wasn't there. I probably would have hurled," she said. "Or passed out right beside you."

"On that note, I'm going to leave you kids alone to talk," Molly said. She walked over and kissed me on the forehead. "Don't you worry about anything but getting better. We'll bring you food and anything else you need."

"Thanks Molly," I said. "I'll need my laptop. Is it still at the bank or did one of you grab it?"

"Oh no, you're not working. I want you to concentrate on getting better."

"It's really not an either-or thing. I can sit here and work without putting weight on my ankle."

"Don't argue," she said. "Just relax right now. We'll discuss it again in a couple weeks and see how you're feeling."

Hopefully that discussion will be more diplomatic than this one.

"Will you sneak my laptop to me?" I asked J.P. when she left.

"Are you serious?" he asked. "You want me to go against my mother and face her wrath?"

"Wimp," Jess said around a chuckle.

"Then you do it," he said.

"Nope, I'm good. Sorry Barb, you'll just have to lie around eating bon-bons and watching movies. Or maybe make a dent in your to-be-read pile." Jess sighed and held her hands to her heart. "Sounds like my idea of heaven. Except you'd have to come feed me the bon-bons," she said to J.P.

"I'd expect nothing less," he said.

"You guys are crazy," I said. "But seriously J.P., is Mark going to be able to handle doing his job and mine?"

"You're always so far ahead of whatever needs to be done, I'm sure he'll manage."

"Will you have him call me if he needs anything or has questions?"

"I'm not sure if that's allowed. I'll have to check."

I rolled my eyes. "Seriously? I can't talk on the phone with a coworker?"

"You know my mother."

"What about Stewart?"

"What about him?" J.P. asked.

"What's he going to say about this?"

"If Stewie gives you any shit, or says one negative word, I swear I'll throat punch him," Jess said.

Did I mention that Jess hates Stewart?

Besides the fact that he can be a total ass, she hates the way he treats J.P. and me. After all these years, I'm still not sure what happened between the two brothers. Molly said they used to be close. By the time I came along, there was a hostile sarcasm between them.

Now, they can barely be in the same room together. I don't know what's going to happen when Molly isn't around to keep the peace.

"He won't say anything that will piss mom off," J.P. said. "It's not like you did this on purpose. Things happen."

I rubbed my forehead. "Thank God he wasn't there when I fell or passed out. As bad as it was, that would have made it a hundred times worse. What did he say when he found out?"

"He just laughed." J.P. had stopped sugarcoating his brother's words and actions a few years ago.

"What a fucktard," Jess said. "Tell me again why you married him?"

While I'm sure it was a rhetorical question, I felt compelled to answer.

"He really was sweet when we started dating, and even when we were first married."

And that's the truth. Over the years, I've tried to pinpoint exactly when things changed between us, but can't. Our marriage just slowly eroded. It got to the point where we only spoke about work issues and even then, he treated me like I'm an idiot. Nothing I did was good enough and no matter how hard I tried, I couldn't please him. Couldn't get it back to how it was in the beginning. Sad to say, if he hadn't started seeing Frances I probably would have stayed despite all that.

"Don't go there, Barb," Jess warned. "I know they say it takes two to both make or break a marriage, but you are the exception to that rule. He treated you like shit and still does. You don't deserve it."

"I still don't understand why he pursued me in the first place," I said. "I'm definitely not his usual type and it's not like we were friends before he asked me out."

J.P. sat forward and looked down at his clasped hands. The tips of his ears turned bright red and when he looked back at me, I noticed his whole face was flush as well. He started to speak, then closed his mouth and shook his head.

"Don't waste your time trying to figure out my brother. It's time you'll never get back, and you sure as hell won't figure out that puzzle."

"Let's stop talking about Stewie," Jess said. "He's not worth it." She wiggled her eyebrows. "But I would like to talk about the tall, dark, and handsome stud who accompanied you to the hospital."

Chapter 5

Cal

I pulled to the side of the road alongside the driveway that would lead me to Barbara's house. I've talked myself in and out of coming a hundred times...yet here I am.

What the hell am I doing here?

Why, after all these years, do I still feel so connected to her?

And how am I going to play it cool when all I want to do is pick up right where we left off?

I glanced over at the purple peonies on the passenger seat resting on the giant box of Hot Tamales I wrapped in purple paper. Her favorite color and her favorite candy. The flowers are extra...my girl had never been a huge fan. I paused. I wonder if she is now. Guess I should go find out. After all, I've come this far. What have I got to lose?

I turned into the driveway and followed it to the pool house around back, just like Molly told me. When I saw her at the hospital the night of the accident, the older woman had been very willing to share details and mentioned more than once that I should stop in to see Barbara. I get the feeling she's playing matchmaker. Not that I'm complaining.

When I spotted Barbara in that conference room, my gut had twisted into knots. It's the same feeling I got back in English 101 when she sat in front of me that first time. After that, I made a point to always sit a row behind her. For weeks, I tried to figure out how to approach her, what to say. I wasn't exactly a stud in high school, but I'd held my own. And I'd never been afraid to talk to girls. But I knew she was different, that once I made contact with her, I'd never be the same. And I was right.

I parked next to a silver Audi SUV, turned off the ignition, and took a deep breath. I'm not sure how Barbara is going to react to my just showing up like this. She hadn't seemed thrilled to see me at the bank, or later at the hospital.

I've thought about that a lot over the last couple days. Sure, our relationship had ended, but it hadn't exactly ended badly. There wasn't any cheating or fighting. We just wanted different things. I'm hoping her reluctance to be in my presence has to do with the fact that she still has feelings for me.

Only one way to find out.

Grabbing the flowers and package, I climbed out of the car and walked across the sidewalk to her threshold. I was just about to ring the bell when the door flew open.

"Well hello."

The woman in the doorway nearly looked me in the eye. Since I'm 6'3", that doesn't happen too often unless I'm hanging out with models, which I haven't done in years.

"Hi, I'm Cal Chase," I said. "I'm here to see Barbara."

"I'm Jess Asher, it's nice to meet you." She opened the door wide and stepped aside. "Come in. As you can see, Barbara is resting on the couch. We're just trying to keep her amused."

I recognized J.P. Mack from the meeting the other day and walked over to shake his hand.

"It's good to see you again," he said.

Turning around, I found Barbara's gaze on me. Those cornflower blue eyes have always been mesmerizing.

"Sorry to stop by unannounced, but I don't have your phone number and I wanted to see how you're feeling."

"Yet you know where she lives?" I heard the smile in Jess's voice.

"Molly mentioned where I could find you." I directed my answer to Barbara.

"Of course she did," J.P. said. I heard a slap, but didn't turn away from Barbara to see its source.

"Whatcha got there?" Jess asked.

At that question, I realized I'd just been standing in front of the couch, gazing into Barbara's eyes. I'll take it as a positive sign that she hadn't looked away either.

"Here," I handed her my bounty. "These are for you." I gestured toward the flowers. "I know you're not a huge fan of flowers, but it's kind of tradition to bring them when visiting someone who's hurt or sick, and they are your favorite color." Her sweet smile tugged at my heart.

"Thank you. They're beautiful." Holding them out to Jess, she said, "Would you mind putting these in water?"

Jess jumped up, grabbed the flowers, and headed toward the kitchen, a few steps away.

Barbara picked up the wrapped box and its contents rattled. She frowned and slid her finger through the gap in the paper, revealing the red box.

"Oh my God," she said, ripping the rest of the wrapping away. "You got me Hot Tamales?"

Her smile had my heart pounding like I'd run up ten flights of stairs.

Jess placed the vase on the coffee table and sat back in her spot next to J.P.

Barbara ripped the rest of the paper off in true Christmas morning style.

"Thank you," she said, blinking back tears.

Kind of an emotional reaction to a box of candy, but I chalked it up to the fact that she's had a rough couple of days.

"Uh, Barb, we have to get going," Jess said.

I looked back as she grabbed J.P.'s elbow and pulled him up beside her. He didn't look like he wanted to leave, but when he started to protest, she silenced him with an elbow to the ribs. They both walked over to Barb and hugged and kissed her in turn.

"Do you need anything before we go?" J.P. asked.

"No, I'm good. I have three different drinks here and Molly is bringing dinner over later."

He kissed her on the forehead and said, "Call if you need anything."

"I'll stop by tomorrow," Jess said. "Make sure you take it easy."

"I will," Barbara said.

Jess leaned down and whispered in Barbara's ear. I watched a blush rise up Barbara's neck and flow over her face. She glanced in my direction and the color intensified.

"See you later, Cal." Jess waved as she dragged J.P. out the door.

I looked over at Barbara. Her eyes were trained on the box of Hot Tamales that rested in her lap.

"So," I said, breaking the silence. "How's the ankle?"

Barbara looked at me with startled eyes, as though she'd forgotten I was there.

"Okay," she said and shrugged. "It's bearable anyway."

"Just be sure to take it easy. You want it to heal right."

"I know."

"I'm serious. Once you start feeling better, you're going to be tempted to push it, but don't."

She snorted. "Says the man who taped his sprained ankle game after game despite what the doctor said."

"Yeah well, I was young and stupid," I said. "Just promise me you'll listen to the doctors."

She took in a deep breath and let it out slowly, then looked me right in the eye.

"Why are you here, Cal?"

"I wanted to make sure you're okay," I said.

"You brought me Hot Tamales."

Her whispered words tugged at my heart. I didn't have a lot of money back in college and couldn't take her on fancy dates like I'd wanted to. Pizza once a week was pretty much the extent of it. But, thanks to the Dollar Store, I could afford to buy boxes of her favorite candy on a regular basis.

I nodded. "I did."

"Why?"

"Why not? They're your favorite," I said. "At least they used to be."

"I haven't had them in a long time."

"No?" She shook her head. "Why not?"

"They were kind of our thing. After—" She gestured toward me then settled her hand back in her lap. "They reminded me of you and it was just too painful."

"I'm sorry I took them away from you," I said.

I was sorry for so much more when it came to her. Why hadn't I been there for her? Looking back, I should have tried harder. Figured out a way to make it work. Put her first or at least even with my career. But as I said before, I was young and stupid.

BARBARA

I thought I was over him. But seeing Cal again brought it all back, especially when I unwrapped the damn box of candy. They say it's the thought that counts and that's as true now as it was back in college.

Despite my reassurances that it didn't matter, the fact that he couldn't afford to wine and dine me on a regular basis back then had bothered him. But once he'd discovered my weakness for a certain cinnamon-flavored candy, he'd gifted me a box at least once a week, with a sweet note written on each one in black marker. Dinner at a five-star restaurant could never beat that.

It's obvious from the look on his face that he'd gotten pulled back into the memories, too. That's dangerous territory. Too many what-ifs and what-could-have-beens. Time to change the subject.

"So how did you end up working at First Allegiant?"

He snapped his gaze toward me then blinked several times.

"I'd talked to Bill Robinson at a few Waves events. After I retired, he called and offered me a job."

"That easy?"

"Pretty much."

"Do you like it?"

He shrugged. "It's not what I thought I'd be doing at this point in my life, but it keeps me busy."

"Did you know I was going to be in that meeting?"

"No." His smile revealed straight white teeth and dimples that only make rare appearances. "But it sure was a nice surprise." His smile dimmed. "Something tells me you don't feel the same way."

I shook my head. "It was just a shock. Once you took the baseball path, I figured you'd stay there."

"And you avoided that path?"

His smirk told me he knew the answer to that question.

"Like the plague." I chucked. "So when you walked through that conference room door, I nearly fainted. I'm not sure how I pulled myself together enough to make it through the presentation."

"You were amazing," he said.

"Are you officially telling me something?"

"Nope, nothing official. That's up to Mr. Robinson to relay," he said. "But unofficially, I'd say Molly Mack Chocolate is going to be busy with expansions in the near future."

"That's good to know."

Pain shot through my ankle as I shifted to get more comfortable, taking my breath away.

Cal jumped out of his seat. "Are you okay?" I nodded and felt him at my side. "What can I do?"

I breathed through the worst of it. I may not be a full-blown yogi like Jess, but at least I'd learned how to breathe through pain...or *discomfort* as they refer to it in yoga class.

"Nothing," I said once the searing ache reduced to a dull throb.

"Are you sure? Did the doctor prescribe anything for the pain?"

"He did, but I don't want to take one until after dinner." I glanced at the clock. "Which Molly should be bringing shortly."

"Are you sure?"

"Positive. It's good now." His brow furrowed as though he was trying to decide whether to believe me or not. "Seriously. Once I settle in, it's barely noticeable. It only really hurts when I move too fast."

Cal nodded and sat back down.

"What were we talking about?" he asked.

"Your job."

"Then I think it's time for a new topic. That one isn't very interesting." He smiled. "Tell me how you ended up as CFO At Molly Mack Chocolate."

Not something I really want to discuss with him, but he asked.

"After my mother died, I needed money. Life insurance had paid for her funeral and there was enough left to cover most of my tuition, but I needed money to live. So, I got a job working on the line at Molly Mack. It was second shift, so I was able to go to class early in the day and work from three to eleven."

I didn't like the look that crossed his face...a mixture of regret, sorrow, and anger...so I spoke quickly, hoping to erase it.

"It wasn't an ideal situation, but it's where I met Jess, so I consider it fate," I said. "At the time, she worked as an assistant in the HR department. We hit it off immediately, despite the fact we have absolutely nothing in common."

I couldn't keep the smile from forming as I told Cal about her relentless pursuit of my friendship, despite my attempts to keep her at arm's length.

"It wasn't that I didn't like her, I was just so busy I didn't think I had time. And looking back, I think I was a little depressed. But she told me she was going to smother me with her love until I realized I couldn't live without her. And she did, and I can't."

"You've been best friends ever since?"

"Pretty much."

"Is she the one who recommended you for your current position?"

"No, like you, I kind of fell into my position," I said. "After graduation, I had started dating Stewart, which put me in direct contact with Molly. Before that, my only interactions with her had been during her daily walks of the floor." I took a sip of water and continued. "One of their accountants had resigned, leaving a gap in the department. Molly offered me the position. Over the next couple years, I started taking on more and more responsibility and they eventually changed my title to CFO." I held up my hands. "And here I am."

"Do you like it?"

"I do. I love working with Molly and J.P. and the rest of the staff is great."

"What about Stewart?" he asked. "It doesn't seem like he'd be easy to work with."

Before I could figure out what to say, the back door opened and Molly breezed through with a shopping bag.

"Dinner's here," she said just before she stopped short. The thing is, I've known Molly long enough to know when she's acting. Besides the fact that she had to walk by his car to get to my front door, I'm sure Jess let her know Cal is here. "Oh, hello Cal."

"Ms. Mack." He stood. "It's nice to see you again."

Molly set the bag on the coffee table.

"Please call me Molly," she said as she started unloading the bag.

Amazing aromas filled the small space of my living room as my coffee table was soon covered with take-out containers from my favorite restaurant.

"How many people are you feeding?" I asked.

"You need to keep up your strength," she said in full Mother Hen mode. "Besides, you have company. Will you be able to stay, Cal?"

He seemed unsure whether he should or not, but honestly with Molly, he didn't have a choice.

"Stay," I said, pulling his attention to me. "I don't eat this much food in a week and I'd hate for it to go to waste."

The corner of his mouth kicked up. "Okay, I'll stay."

The man in front of me should seem like a stranger, but he doesn't. We've lived very separate lives for the past fifteen years, but his smile, those eyes, and that sexy voice with just a hint of Virginia make me feel like we haven't missed a beat.

Chapter 6

Cal

"Cal, Molly Mack is here to see you," my assistant said through the intercom.

"Um okay. Send her in."

What else could I say? She's one of the bank's oldest customers. Besides, she kind of scares me.

I stood and walked around the desk to greet her as she entered my office.

"Molly, this is a nice surprise."

"I'm having lunch with Bill Robinson and I'm a little early so I figured I'd stop by and say hello."

"I'm glad you did," I said, not sure if that was true or not. It seems like she's trying to play matchmaker with Barbara and me, but don't know if that will help or hurt my chances. "Have a seat."

"Thank you, but I can't stay," she said. "I just wanted to mention that I have somewhere to be tonight so Barbara will be on her own. If you're not doing anything, maybe you can stop by and keep her company."

For the past week, I've fought the urge to go see Barb. That first time, I said I'd wanted to see how she was doing right after the injury, but now I'm afraid it would just seem creepy if I just kept showing up uninvited. Yes, we were close in the past, but I'm not sure what our relationship is now.

Are we friends?

I think I'd like to be...and maybe even more than that...but I'm not sure how she feels. I guess this is my chance to find out. The worst she can do is say she's not interested. It's not like she can run away.

"It just so happens that I'm free after work."

"Perfect," she said.

"Any suggestions on what I should bring for dinner?"

"We had Italian last night, so anything else would be fine I'm sure." I nodded, acknowledging her words. "And I'm sure she wouldn't mind another box of those candies. She seemed to enjoy them, although I'm not sure if it was more because of the taste or the sentiment."

I opened my mouth to speak then closed it, at a loss for words. Stuffing my hands in my pockets, I rocked back on my heels, shook my head, and chuckled.

"I'm not really sure what to say about that."

She patted my arm. "You don't have to say anything. It's just something to think about. Barbara told me about you and the Hot Tamales and it's one of the sweetest things I've ever heard." A sad smile crossed her face. "I love my son, but I will never forgive him for what he did to that girl or how he treats her now. I raised him better." She straightened, her normal confident exterior back in place. "I'm a pretty decent judge of people, and I believe you're one of the good ones. I also believe that what you and Barbara had all those years ago is lingering below the surface just waiting to be rekindled," she said. "I've never seen her react to someone the way she did to you. Not even Stewart when they were first together. Maybe your story didn't have a happy ending all those years ago, but this could be your second chance. Life doesn't give us too many of those, so when it does, you have to make sure to not let it slip by."

Part of me wants to tell her to butt out and the other part wants to beg her for advice. Before I could do either, two quick knocks sounded on my office door just before it opened and Mr. Robinson peeked his head inside.

"I heard you were in here," he said to Molly. "Ready for lunch?"

"Yes, I am." She hiked her purse onto her shoulder and looked back at me. "Thank you for chatting with me, Cal."

"No," I said. "Thank you."

She gave me a knowing smile, then let Mr. Robinson usher her out the door.

I DROVE UP MOLLY'S DRIVEWAY AND CIRCLED AROUND TO THE POOL house. This time the only car parked outside is Barbara's Volkswagen. Back in college, she had an ancient Beetle. I wonder if she's ever driven any other make of car.

Reaching over into the passenger seat, I retrieved the bags I'd stashed there. I thought about cooking dinner instead of grabbing takeout, but figured I'd save that for another time. Because if I have my way, there will be another time.

I approached the door and knocked twice before turning the knob and opening it. Molly told me she'd let Barb know I was coming and leave the door unlocked. It's not like she can get up and let me in. And at least my showing up isn't a total surprise.

"Barb?" I stepped inside and closed the door behind me. I walked through the small foyer and spotted her curled up on the couch sleeping, an open book resting against her chest.

Tiptoeing through the living room, I made my way to the kitchen and placed my bags on the counter. After pulling out the individual containers, I debated whether or not I should put them in the refrigerator. I prefer my sushi not refrigerated, but I don't want it to go bad either.

Glancing at my watch, I decided to give it another fifteen minutes. If she's not awake by then, I'll refrigerate everything.

I grabbed the other bag I'd brought and walked into the living room, and set it down next to the couch. Then I took the opportunity to check out Barb's space. I hadn't had a chance to do it last time I was here.

The far wall has built-in shelves filled with books and pictures. One of the first things we bonded over was our love of reading. Pretty funny since we both had math-based majors.

I smiled when I spotted some military thrillers scattered throughout the women's fiction and romance novels. Back when we were together, we'd often read the same books, even though our personal preferences were for two very different genres. It was nice to share our interests and even broaden each other's horizons. I found that I liked some of the romance novels and to this day, still read certain authors. Obviously, Barbara took a liking to my kind of books, too.

My stomach twisted at the pictures of Barbara and her mother. Janet Murphy was a sweet woman who was taken from her daughter way too soon. My family drives me crazy at times, but I love them dearly and can't imagine life without them. Barbara is the only child of an only child. She never knew her father and her grandparents died before she entered high school. At twenty years old, she was totally alone.

I'd wanted to be there for her and had even asked her to come on the road with me, but she'd refused. She could have gone to live with my family, but she didn't want to do that either.

Settling into the same chair I sat in last time I was here, I watched Barb sleep. She looked so peaceful until she shifted. Her face twisted into a mask of pain then she let out a long groan and sat up. The book hit the floor with a loud bang.

BARBARA

I wrapped my hands around the brace over my ankle and focused on breathing. Logically I know touching the brace doesn't do anything to ease the pain, but for some reason it makes me feel better.

"Is there anything I can do?"

If I wasn't dealing with the pain radiating up my leg, I probably would have jumped off the couch at the sound of his voice. Molly told me Cal was stopping by, but I didn't hear him come in. I glanced at him and shook my head before closing my eyes and breathing through the last of the pain. Once it was over, I settled back against my pillow exhausted.

I felt Cal watching me and slowly opened my eyes.

"Are you okay?" he asked.

"I'm good, thanks." He looked me up and down, then seemingly satisfied, nodded and sat back down in the chair across the room. "When did you get here?"

"About ten minutes ago. You looked so peaceful, I didn't want to wake you."

"I wish you had."

"Why?"

"You don't think you sitting here while I'm sleeping is a little strange?"

He shrugged. "It's nothing that hasn't happened before."

"True, but that was a long time ago," I said.

A lot of things happened between us before that are off limits now, but I don't want to lead the conversation down that road. Unfortunately, that didn't stop my thoughts from taking the journey.

I'd had boyfriends before Cal, but he was my first true love. And he'd been absolutely perfect. It's true he couldn't afford to take me out all the time or lavish me with expensive gifts, but I didn't care about that. He gave me all the things that really mattered...his time, attention, and consideration. Not to mention my first orgasm.

Being young and naive, I'd actually believed we'd live happily after. Then again, I'd also thought my mother would beat cancer. I guess neither of those things were in the cards.

"Barb?" From the tone of his voice, I figured it wasn't the first time he'd said my name.

"Sorry. What did you say?"

"I asked if you're hungry," he said. "I brought sushi and should probably put it in the refrigerator if we're not going to eat it right away."

"You brought sushi?" The corner of Cal's mouth kicked up and he nodded. "Sounds great. I could definitely eat."

He walked to the kitchen and I heard him rummaging around, taking lids off containers, opening and closing doors and drawers, and placing dishes on the counter. I twisted as far as I could without pain and observed him moving around my space. I'll admit, he looks good, natural.

My lower back protested its current position, so I turned back around and settled against the pillow. Minutes later, Cal appeared at my side carrying two plates full of sushi with chopsticks resting across the center. He handed one to me, and set the other on the coffee table then straightened and rubbed his hands together.

"What would you like to drink?"

This is so surreal. Not only is Cal here in my home for the second time, he's also waiting on me.

"Water please." I pointed toward the tumbler on the coffee table. "I'm not sure what else is in there to drink. I know I don't have any ginger ale."

]"Water is fine. I have to limit my soda intake now that I'm not training all the time." He patted his stomach. "Gotta keep in shape."

I bit my tongue and enjoyed the view as he walked back into the kitchen. There is nothing wrong with that man's shape. Back in college, Cal was the living epitome of tall, dark, and handsome, but age and maturity have taken that to a whole other level.

He came back and placed my tumbler on the coffee table within reach, then picked up his plate and settled into the chair, setting his drink on the floor beside him.

I picked up a piece of spicy tuna roll with my chopsticks and dipped it in soy sauce then shoved the whole thing into my mouth, chewed, and swallowed. I was about to eat another piece when I noticed Cal watching me. "This is delicious. Thanks for bringing it."

His eyes were focused on my mouth, then he blinked and picked up his chopsticks.

"You're welcome. I remember sushi used to be one of your favorite meals."

"Still is."

I'd emptied more than half my plate before either of us spoke again. Cal was the one to break the silence.

"So how's the ankle? Feeling any better?"

I shrugged. "For the most part it's okay, but when I move certain ways or stand, it hurts. But it's nothing like it was when I first did it."

"When will you know if you'll need surgery?"

"Not for a few more weeks," I said. "But I'm being good, so fingers crossed it won't come to that."

Cal nodded at my words then reached down and picked up his water. I watched him swallow, fascinated by the motion of his throat. He set his glass back down on the floor and shifted back in the chair.

I focused on eating my remaining rolls, mostly to avoid looking at him. Unfortunately, that didn't stop me from picturing him in my head. A mental slideshow played as I cleaned my plate. His eyes, his smile, his...*everything.*

Yes, I went there. And my heart beat faster just thinking about it.

Cal is undeniably attractive, but the most beautiful thing about him is his heart. He really is a good person and so unbelievably sweet. At least he had been. And I have to admit, it seems he still is. Considering he not only accompanied me to the hospital then stopped by to make sure I was okay after my injury. Not to mention the fact that he's here tonight.

Watching him eat, I couldn't help but note the differences the years have brought. He wears his hair shorter now, so the curls I used to love to dig my fingers into are gone. The cut makes his jaw look stronger, more angular. And even through his button-down dress shirt, it's obvious his body is leaner and more defined.

I popped the last roll into my mouth and chewed, my mind drifting back to Cal in various states of undress. He'd had an amazing chest back then, I wonder what it looks like now. He's definitely bigger and broader.

Is he bigger and broader *everywhere?*

I was mid swallow when that last thought invaded my brain and I started to choke. Cal was at my side instantly, which didn't help the situation because the area I'd been pondering was right at eye level as he stood next to me.

"Are you okay?" I nodded. "What can I do?"

I shook my head, grabbed my tumbler, and took a long drink of water. That pushed most of it down. I coughed a couple more times, then took another drink and cleared my throat.

Settling back against the pillow, I said, "Thanks. I'm good now."

"Are you sure?"

"I'm sure." I offered a watery smile. "Wrong pipe."

He took my dish, then grabbed his and brought them into the kitchen.

"Need a refill?" he asked, at my side once again. Picking up my tumbler, he shook it. "Might as well top it off so you have a drink for dessert."

"You brought dessert?"

Cal rolled his eyes and chuckled. "Of course I brought dessert. It's the best part of the meal."

Guess he still has a sweet tooth.

He disappeared into the kitchen again, then came back carrying my tumbler in one hand and two small dishes with a huge brownie on each. After setting my drink on the coffee table, he handed me one of the plates.

"These are from a coffee shop not too far from my house. I also brought some chocolate chip cookies. And of course, these." He reached behind him then held out a box of Hot Tamales.

I looked at the box then back up at those brown eyes. Shared history flowed between us, the bittersweet memories forming a lump in my throat.

"Thank you." My voice sounded thick as I took the red box from his hand.

He just nodded in response as he sat back down, making me wonder if he had the same issue.

Looking down at the box, I spotted the picture he'd drawn of a foot encased in a brace along with *Feel Better Soon*. Back in the day, he'd written a message every box of Hot Tamales he'd given me, sometimes a doodle. In three years, he never repeated himself.

I tucked the candy between my thigh and the back of the couch to save for later. Right now, I have a brownie to concentrate on. My mouth watered at the thought. Picking up the fudgy dessert, I took a big bite and groaned.

It's amazing. The texture is perfect and the taste is sweet, rich, and intense.

"Good?" Cal asked.

"Good doesn't even begin to describe it," I said and took another bite.

I finished my brownie in record time. Glancing over at Cal, I watched him shove the last morsel into his mouth, so I don't feel too embarrassed about inhaling mine.

"Mmm, I think that was better than sex." As soon as the words were out, I wished I could pull them back.

Cal raised his brow as he chewed and swallowed that last bite, then slowly shook his head.

"The brownies are delicious, but better than sex? I don't think so."

I can't have this conversation with him, even in jest. He's too hot and it's been way too long for me. That last fact hadn't bothered me until Cal came into the picture again. Now all kinds of inappropriate thoughts about him pop into my head at random times. The fact I'm home all day with nothing to do doesn't help the situation.

Cal must have sensed my lack of desire to pursue the topic because he changed the subject.

"There are four more in a box in the kitchen along with some chocolate chip cookies." Standing, he walked across the room and took my plate. "They're just as amazing. Do you want me to grab one for you?"

I clutched my stomach. "God no. I'm stuffed." Reaching down, I grabbed the Hot Tamales and held them up. "And I still have these to eat. I don't want to go into sugar shock."

He walked into the kitchen and I heard the faucet turn on. The man even washes dishes. I held back the sigh that wanted to escape. The water turned off and I had just enough time to collect myself before he appeared at my side again.

"Need anything else?"

"No, I think I'm good for now."

I shifted on the couch, trying to get comfortable. Which he noticed, of course.

"I almost forgot." He kneeled next to me and pulled over a shopping bag. "I brought this for you."

He pulled out a black cylinder.

"What is it?"

"It's a foam roller. Normally you use it to roll out sore muscles, but when I was laid up after my surgery, my lower back got really sore and this helped when I leaned against it. I thought you might be having the same problem, so I figured I'd bring it along."

Sushi, desert, and now this. If I didn't know better, I'd think this man is too good to be true. But I know for a fact that he's everything he seems to be and more. I blinked, stopping myself from traveling down memory lane again.

"How does it work?"

"Can you sit forward a little?"

I did as he asked. He shifted closer and tucked the roller between my back and the pillow.

"Now sit back and just kind of settle against it," he said, holding it in place. "What do you think?"

I wiggled my butt down a little to shift the roller into a better position then arched so it pressed against my lower back, helping to give it a much-needed stretch.

"That feels really good."

"Yeah?" That one word and the sweet smile that accompanied it nearly melted my heart.

"Yeah," I said and smiled.

"It vibrates, too. Want to give that a try?"

"Sure."

He looked down.

"Crap. The button is on the other side." He looked me in the eye and held up his arm, indicating that he wanted to reach around me. "Do you mind?"

"No." The word came out as a tiny squeak.

Cal leaned closer still and reached across my stomach. His forearm rested against me and soon I felt a slight vibration in my lower back.

Pulling back slightly, he rested his hand on my hip. "How's that?"

"G-good." Hopefully he'll think my stutter is a result of the vibration and not his nearness.

"This is on low. I don't recommend any higher until you've used it a couple times."

I nodded, hoping my eyes don't look as wide as they feel. I also hope the state of my nipples isn't too obvious.

"Give me your hand," he said. I hesitated just a second before dropping the box of Hot Tamales I'd been clutching to my lap and placed my hand in his. "To turn it on, just push this." He rubbed my fingertip against a tiny button, then shifted it to a small switch. "This turns the power off if you want to totally shut it down. The cord is in the bag, but it's fully charged right now so you should be good for a while."

His words barely registered as I struggled to focus on what he was telling me instead of his jaw mere inches away. His five o'clock shadow is heavier than it had been back in college and I couldn't help but wonder how it would feel against my skin.

"Barb?" I shifted my gaze and found those milk chocolate eyes focused on me. As compelling as they are, it didn't stop my eyes from dropping to his lips just for a second. "Oh hell," he groaned when I looked at him again.

Cal's mouth was on mine before I took my next breath. The quick, powerful kiss was both familiar and new and I wanted more. He must have read my mind because, in the next instant, his mouth opened over mine, taking the kiss to a whole other level. Chocolate lingered on his palate, but as our tongues tangled, I finally got to taste him. He's as delicious now as he was fifteen years ago.

He broke the kiss and looked directly into my eyes, seemingly asking permission to continue. The corners of my mouth lifted in a small answering smile.

Sliding his right hand across my jaw, Cal wrapped his long fingers into my hair and tilted my head back and to the side. I had expected a full-blown, tongue-tangling kiss, but instead he nibbled at my bottom lip before placing his mouth over mine and applying a wonderful suction that nearly melted me in place. The foam roller he brought continued to vibrate behind my back, adding to the sensory overload.

It really has been a long time.

Long and hard, soft and gentle, our tongues tangled in a hot, sexual duel. He was literally making love to my mouth and I didn't want him to stop. A groan emerged from Cal's chest and he pulled back just far enough to drag in a deep breath.

"Christ Barb," he whispered before dipping his head and starting all over again.

He moved his hand behind my back and the vibration stopped, then I felt the roller move just before I heard it bounce to the floor. Cal's strong forearm took its place, and somehow he managed to push me deeper against the pillow and pull me into his chest at the same time.

I wasn't complaining about either. Especially since he did it without breaking the kiss.

"Barb?" I heard Jess's voice through my sensual fog. "Whose 4Runner is parked outside?"

Cal broke the kiss, but didn't shift away, his burning brown eyes focused on mine. In their depths I saw his desire so clearly, I couldn't turn away. Couldn't speak, either.

I heard the door slam, then shoes clattering against the floor in the foyer and I knew Jess would be stepping into the living room any second.

Cal moved away slowly and I immediately missed the feel of him.

"Wait until you hear what Stewie did to J.P. today."

That last word faded as she spotted Cal and me in our semi-compromising position.

"Oh. Uh, sorry." Jess stood frozen in place for a second, then she gestured toward the door. "I'll just go now and we'll talk later."

Before she took a step, Cal stood.

"No, come on in. I should probably get going anyway." He looked down at me and winked. "I want to get in a run before it gets dark."

I couldn't hold back my laugh at his words. Back when we were dating, he once told me that he used to go running to get rid of pent up sexual energy. He then joked that after we started doing the deed, he was out of shape.

"Thank you for dinner and the brownies. Everything was delicious."

"You're welcome." Looking at Jess who still stood on the other side of the room, he said, "There are some brownies and chocolate chip cookies in the kitchen. Sorry, we ate all the sushi."

"You are a prince among men, even if you ate all the sushi," she said and walked into the kitchen. I'm sure she's on the hunt for a brownie, but knowing Jess, she's also giving us privacy to say goodbye.

"Enjoy the rest of your night." Cal seemed to hesitate, then he leaned down and kissed my forehead. Before straightening, he picked up the discarded roller and stood it up next to the couch. "The charger for this is in the bag right behind you. There's also another little treat in there for you. Let me know what you think."

I frowned, confused by his last words.

He smiled. "I'll talk to you later."

Chapter 7

Barbara

"Holy fuck, Barb. I'm so sorry." Jess walked out of the kitchen carrying a half-eaten brownie. "By the way, this is the most fantastic brownie I've ever had."

"I know. They're from a bakery near Cal's house. I didn't get the name of it though." She settled into the loveseat adjacent to the couch and folded her legs onto the cushion. "What were you saying about J.P.?"

"No way." Jess shoved the last piece of brownie into her mouth and shook her head as she chewed and swallowed. After licking her fingers clean, she said, "Don't think you're going to distract me from what I walked in on."

I had no idea what to say, so I just sat there tracing a pattern in the creases of my slightly crushed Hot Tamales box.

"What exactly did I walk in on?" she asked. "I mean, I obviously know *what* I walked in on, but how did it happen? What led up to it? Tell me all the deets." She bent her legs in front of her, wrapped her arms around her shins, and rested her chin against her knees.

I took a deep breath and slowly let it out. "I have no idea. One minute he was showing me this foam roller..." I pointed down to the object in question. "...the next we were going at each other like teenagers."

Jess didn't move but a smile slowly spread across her face.

"Stop that, you look like the Grinch."

She dropped her feet to the floor and sat forward.

"So how was it?"

The brain is truly an amazing thing. All you have to do is think of something, and you can picture it, smell it, taste it, and remember the way it felt all in your mind. At Jess's question, I relived every single detail of my make-out session with Cal. I reached up and brushed my index finger against the tingling skin where his bristly chin had probably left beard burn.

"Woah." Jess dramatically fanned her hand in front of her face. "You don't have to answer my question. The look on your face says it all."

"Yeah, it was pretty great. Cal was an amazing kisser back in the day, but holy hell, now it's at a whole other level."

"Why did you guys break up again?"

"He got drafted after junior year and my mom died later that summer." I shrugged. "Things got so messed up. Cal was off playing in Texas. He could only come home for the funeral...not even a whole twenty-four hours. And in my head I understood why he couldn't be with me, but my heart was broken."

I opened the box of Hot Tamales the topic of our conversation had given me, popped a couple in my mouth, and chewed, trying to collect my thoughts.

"He asked me to join him on the road so we could be together, but I wanted to finish school. His mom told me I could go live with his family in Virginia, but for some reason I didn't want to leave. So I stayed here, alone and depressed."

I shoved more candy into my mouth. This conversation is hurting my heart. I've tried not to think about all this through the years because whenever I did, I couldn't help but wonder if I made the biggest mistake of my life back then.

"So that was it? You broke up and he went away?" Jess asked.

"He called a few times, trying to get me to reconsider. After the first couple conversations, I stopped answering. Eventually he stopped calling."

"And he played for the Waves all this time and you never ran into him?"

"How often do you run into any of the Waves?"

"True." She stood. "Those chocolate chip cookies are calling me. Want one?"

"No thanks. I'm concentrating on these." I held up a handful of Hot Tamales before shoving them into my mouth.

Jess returned with two cookies in one hand and a glass of milk in the other and settled back onto the loveseat. Taking a bite, she chewed then took another quick bite.

"These are just as yummy as the brownies. Perfect texture, not too sweet," she said then finished the cookie with one big bite. Between chews, she asked, "So what are you going to do now?"

"What do you mean?"

"Now that this perfect man is back in your life, what are you going to do about it?"

"I'm not sure it's like that."

Jess laughed. More dramatically than the circumstances warranted, in my opinion.

"Barbara, that man is obviously wooing you, in case you didn't notice." She pointed to the box of candy in my hand. "Those Hot Tamales should be your first clue. That hot kiss I walked in on is the last. I'm sure if you think about it you'll figure out all the others in between."

She finished the cookie and chugged the last of her milk, then stood and walked into the kitchen. Her version of a mic drop after her last comments.

I'm not an idiot. It does seem like Cal is at least semi-interested in picking up where we left off, but I'm not sure what I want to do about that. I do know that I feel alive around him in a way I haven't felt in a long time.

"So what are you gonna do?" Jess asked from behind me.

"I'm not doing anything for the next few weeks, in case you forgot."

She stood next to the couch, hovering over me.

"Doesn't tonight show that you don't need to go anywhere to take action?" I tossed the empty Hot Tamales box onto the coffee table and shook my head. "Just promise me that if he does pursue something, you'll be open to it."

"Okay, I promise," I said because if I don't, I know she won't quit.

She patted my arm. "That's my girl." Reaching down, she picked up the bag Cal had put next to the couch. "What's this?"

"Cal carried the foam roller in that."

"There's something still in it."

"The charger."

Jess pulled out the cord and placed it on top of the roller. She peeked back into the bag and smiled then reached in and dramatically pulled out another box of Hot Tamales and handed it to me.

"Looks like the ball's in your court," she said. "Or, considering Cal's former profession, maybe I should say that you're up to bat."

My heart pounded as I looked at the box. In his usual style, Cal has scribbled a message with a black Sharpie. But this one left no doubt of his intentions. He'd drawn a plate, fork, and knife along the top and a phone at the bottom with the words *May I come over and cook you dinner Saturday night?* along with his phone number in between.

Jess handed me my cell.

CAL

I finished the last of my water in one long chug then tossed my empty bottle into the sink. Toeing off my running shoes, I left them near the foyer then reached down to peel off my sweaty socks. I threw them and my previously discarded T-shirt into the laundry room as I passed it on the way to take a much-needed shower.

My lungs hurt from the strain I put them under and I know my calves and thighs will be stiff tomorrow. But it will be worth the pain if I get some sleep instead of tossing and turning all night.

Hey, it worked back in college. For the most part anyway.

I stripped then stepped into the shower and turned the spray on full blast. The cold water shocked my system, but felt good on my sweaty skin. I turned the knob all the way to the left and soon scalding hot water pounded against my chest. Turning around, I lowered my head and let the spray loosen my stiff muscles.

Tonight had been just like old times with Barb. And I know she felt it too when she wasn't too busy overthinking things.

I'd felt a connection to her the minute I spotted her in class all those years ago and it seems it's still there even after so many years apart. When I saw her in that conference room a couple weeks ago, it was like no time had passed. Like we could just pick up where we left off and move forward.

I reached for my all-in-one wash and lathered up then did a quick rinse.

Kissing her hadn't been in my plans tonight. I figured I'd save that particular move until after I impressed her with my stellar culinary skills. Assuming she accepts my offer to cook for her.

I turned off the water and stepped out of the shower, wrapping a towel around my waist as I walked into the bedroom. Grabbing my phone from the nightstand, I sat on the bed and rested against the pillows.

No missed calls.

I'd hoped she would have called by now. I even left my phone on during my run in the hopes she would. Normally I put it on do not disturb when I exercise so I can focus, but I didn't want to miss Barb's call.

I thumbed through the scores for the day. New York won this afternoon, giving them a solid five game lead in first place. The Waves are playing out west this week, so the game doesn't come on for another hour.

When I first stopped playing, I tried to ignore all things baseball, but the game is in my blood and without it, I'm just not me.

Besides, my best friends still play so it's not like I can totally stay away.

My phone vibrated then started to ring, a local number displayed on the screen.

"Hello."

"Hi, um Cal?"

"Hi. Uh, yeah. Hey Barb."

Smooth. Real smooth.

"I wanted to thank you again for dinner tonight. It was delicious and so were the brownies," she said. "I haven't tried a cookie yet, but Jess scarfed down two and gave them a thumb's up. She left one on the coffee table for me. As soon as I'm not so stuffed, I'll eat it."

"You're welcome, but you can't still be full from the sushi. It's not that filling."

Hell, my stomach is growling now. I plan on having a snack while I watch the game.

"It wasn't just sushi," she said. "Don't forget that huge brownie. And of course the entire box of Hot Tamales I ate after you left."

Her last sentence made me smile. Especially since she told me she hadn't eaten them since we broke up. Before I could comment, she spoke again.

"Speaking of Hot Tamales, I saw your message on the second box."

"And?"

"And..." I held my breath during her pause. "That sounds nice."

"Great! Chicken marsala okay?"

"It's one of my favorites."

"Perfect. I'll come by around five?"

"I'll be here. Do you need me to do anything beforehand?" she asked, then chuckled. "Not that I can actually do anything, but I can always put Jess to work."

"Nope, I'll have it all under control."

There's so much I want to say to her, but it can wait until Saturday night.

Chapter 8

Barbara

"You look amazing, if I do say so myself."

Jess had insisted on doing my hair and makeup for my dinner with Cal. Honestly, I was going to be happy to just take a shower and put on fresh clothes. That's where my standards have sunk to after being couch bound for three weeks.

"Your hair looks so good."

"Thanks for taking the time to curl it."

She settled onto the loveseat. "You should wear it like that more often."

"It just took you nearly an hour to get my hair to submit to the curling iron. I don't have the patience for that."

I swiped my phone to selfie mode and checked myself out again. I'll be honest, while Jess was doing my makeup, I was afraid she was putting it on too thick, but it looks amazing. Just a hint beyond the natural look, it makes me look put together without seeming like I'm trying too hard.

"Do you need me to do anything else?" she asked.

I looked around. "I don't think so. Cal said he's bringing whatever he needs. Did you put the ginger ale in the refrigerator?"

"Yep. And the dark chocolate salted caramels are in a bowl on the table."

"Thank you so much, Jess. I feel like such a lump just sitting here all the time."

"You're supposed to be just sitting there so your ankle heals the right way. And hey, you just passed the halfway point. You'll be up running the world again before you know it."

"I wish Molly would let me work. At this point, there's no reason I can't."

"Because she knows if you were working, you'd get stressed about whatever is happening with the company then even more stressed that you're not at the office to handle it." She looked at her watch and stood. "Your hot baseball player will be here to cook you dinner soon so I'm gonna take off. If I didn't love you so much, I'd be jealous as hell."

"Don't turn green yet. I have no idea what's happening with Cal and me."

"You don't have to know. Just be sure to give whatever it is a chance. He seems like one of the good ones."

After dispensing those words of wisdom, she left. Before the quiet could settle in, I picked up the TV remote and clicked the Pandora app, setting it to shuffle through all my classic rock channels. The soft strains of The Eagles filled the air and I picked up the book I'd been reading before Jess had arrived, hoping to finish it before Cal got here. I only have a few pages left, but unfortunately, my brain wouldn't shut off long enough to let me get into it.

Maybe I shouldn't be getting so stressed out about a date, but I can't help it. Tonight isn't what I'd consider a conventional date, considering our history. And the fact that I won't be able to do anything but sit here will drive me crazy.

Cal Chase was the love of my life and breaking up with him is the hardest thing I've ever done. Which is pretty funny considering I ended a ten-year marriage. Of course, by the time my marriage ended for good, it had already been dead for a long time. Through the years, Stewart had started treating me more and more like an afterthought and when I found out he was sleeping with Frances, divorce was the only option.

It wasn't like that with Cal.

Things were good until my mother died and then they weren't. For me anyway.

At the time, I couldn't imagine dealing with a long-distance relationship. And I didn't just want to chase Cal from city to city while he followed his dream.

A car door slammed outside, pulling me from my thoughts. I glanced at my phone. Five o'clock on the dot. I heard a quick knock, then the door opened.

"Barb?"

"I'm here, in the same place you left me four days ago."

He walked in, carrying a big box.

"We'll see if we can give you a change of scenery tonight," he said, then stopped and stared at me.

"What's wrong?"

He blinked then shook his head. "You look beautiful." Walking the rest of the way into the room, he placed the box on the loveseat. "Don't get me wrong, you always look great, but it's really kicked up tonight."

"Jess insisted on putting makeup on me."

"She curled your hair, too." He smiled. "It looks really nice."

"Thanks. I love curly hair but it takes forever to make mine look like this."

"You love it because you don't have it."

"So I've been told." By him, many times. Time to change the subject. "What's in the box?"

"Everything I need to cook dinner." He opened the box and held up a pan then a pot. "And the ingredients."

"I do have pots and pans, you know."

"I'm sure you do, but I wasn't sure exactly what you have and I'd rather bring the ones I use all the time."

He placed the items back inside then picked up the box.

"Let me get a few things started, and I'll be back," he said then walked into the kitchen.

I should've sat the other way so I could watch him work, but that puts my bad ankle on the edge of the couch. I'm always afraid it'll drop to the floor if I move the wrong way. This damn boot is so heavy, it wouldn't take much.

Glancing over my shoulder, I watched him move around my kitchen like he's done it a hundred times before. I'll admit, it's sexy as hell. *He's* sexy as hell. No man should look that good in khaki shorts and a polo shirt.

Turning back around, I picked up my phone and opened the wordplay app. I'd cleared one screen when the smell of garlic filled the air, and it only got better from there.

"My mouth is watering out here," I yelled, loud enough for him to hear.

He walked out of the kitchen drying his hands on a towel, which he slung over his shoulder when he was done.

"So I was thinking," he said. "It's a beautiful night. Why don't we eat outside?"

As nice as that sounds, it takes me forever to maneuver myself around on my crutches. Jess went through so much trouble making me look date ready, I don't want to ruin the effect clomping around like a drunken gorilla.

"What's that look?" he asked.

I shook my head and decided to only share part of my thoughts with him.

"I'm not great on my crutches, so I only move when absolutely necessary."

"I can carry you."

"You're not going to carry me."

"Why not?" He pointed toward the French doors that led directly to the pool area. "We're only going right there."

"I'm too heavy and this brace is awkward." He swiped the towel from his shoulder and tossed it onto the coffee table then took a step toward me. "Seriously Cal, this is ridiculous."

He leaned down. "Wrap your arms around my neck."

When I hesitated, he pulled back slightly and raised his right brow. I rolled my eyes and did as he said. He slid one arm behind my back and the other under my knees.

"Let me know if I hurt you."

He slowly straightened, taking me with him. I held on tight as he stood to full height, fighting the urge to stick my nose in his neck and inhale. And even though I resisted, I could still smell his clean scent. It's like fresh spring air combined with the ocean breeze.

"Do you want to sit in a lounge chair or at the table?"

Cal turned his head when he spoke, putting his chin precariously close to my lips. I pulled back slightly, away from temptation.

"I'll sit at the table. It will be nice to be upright for a little while."

He kicked a chair back from the table and set me down. Then he pulled another chair over, leaned down, and gently lifted my leg, setting my foot on the cushion.

"Is that good or do you want me to get you a pillow?"

"This is perfect. Thank you."

"I'm going to check on dinner. I'll be right back."

Tilting my head back, I took a deep breath and slowly let it out. I haven't ventured outside since my injury and it feels nice to be in the fresh air. It also feels nice to have Cal here with me.

"Looks like everything is ready. Would you like some wine with dinner?" he asked "I brought red and white."

"White sounds good. Thank you."

He disappeared inside again then came back out carrying a bottle of wine in one hand and two glasses in the other. It seems he's found his way around my kitchen with no problem. Setting the glasses down, he filled one then the other before placing the bottle in the middle of the table.

I took the glass he offered and smiled. "Thank you."

"You are very welcome," he said. "I'm going to make our plates. I'll be right back."

Raising the glass to my lips, I took a small sip then a bigger one. This wine is amazing. Slightly fruity, it's not too sweet, but not too dry either. Stewart would probably comment about how crisp and elegant it is and talk about notes and use other words non-wine snobs wouldn't understand.

I shook my head. There's no room for Stewart tonight. Or ever for that matter.

"Everything okay?" Cal asked as he placed a plate in front of me.

"Yeah. Why?"

He sat in the chair next to me and shrugged. "You looked upset."

"No, I'm good. Just annoyed that I'm just sitting here while you're running back and forth. I wish I could help."

"I know not being able to do things is aggravating especially for a Type-A like you, but it'll be worth it." He picked up his fork. "Dig in."

The plate in front of me could have come from a five-star restaurant instead of my kitchen.

"Cal, this looks amazing." I used my fork to cut off a piece of chicken then speared it and a mushroom and popped the bite into my mouth. "Mmm, this is delicious."

"Yeah?"

"Oh yeah." I chewed another piece of chicken, this one topped with the fluffy mashed potatoes. "It's perfect." I swallowed. "Honestly, it's the best chicken marsala I've ever had."

Looking relieved, he picked up his fork and started to eat.

"So what made you expand your culinary skills beyond eggs, pancakes, and French toast?" I asked.

"Necessity. Going out to eat gets boring and I got sick of breakfast for dinner so I had my mom teach me some basic stuff."

I smiled. "How are your parents?"

"They're doing well. My dad is enjoying semi-retirement and my mom splits her time between keeping his business organized and chasing grandchildren."

"How many little Chases are there?"

"Five total. Jamie and Ben each have two and Alex has one."

"Please tell me there's a girl in there somewhere."

He nodded as he finished chewing. "Two. And my mom is having a ball shopping in the pink aisles as she calls them."

"I'm sure she is. She was outnumbered by boys for years."

"She's still outnumbered," he said with a wink.

"True, but it's a little more balanced than it was before."

"It is, especially with my brothers' wives added in. But we like to tease her that we're still in the majority."

"I don't know how she ever survived in a house with so much testosterone." I took a drink of wine. "This is really good." I spun the bottle to check out the label. "I'll have to pick some up."

"I can give you a few bottles. My friend Jack's soon-to-be father-in-law is a silent partner in the vineyard and he gave me a case." He shrugged. "I'm not much of a wine drinker, but this stuff is pretty good."

Out of the corner of my eye, I saw someone walking across Molly's porch. I cringed when I spotted Stewart and realized that he was moving in our direction.

CAL

One minute we were discussing wine and the next Barbara's whole demeanor changed. She stiffened and folded in on herself just like I'd seen her do at the bank meeting.

"Barb?"

Before she answered, I heard another voice.

"Do you know where my mother is?"

I looked over my shoulder and watched her douchebag of an ex-husband storm through the pool area to where we're sitting.

"I haven't seen her since last night."

"Oh please. She's been hovering over you day and night since you broke your ankle."

"Not today. I don't know where she is."

"She was supposed to meet Frances at the Werner Foundation dinner but she's not there and she's not answering her phone," he said.

I stood and faced Stewart before Barbara could answer because something tells me she was about to apologize to this asshole. For what? I have no clue.

"Like Barb said, Molly isn't here."

He blinked and looked surprised to see me standing there. Then he looked down at the table and back at me. I knew the exact second he recognized me because a fake smile replaced the sneer on his face.

"Aren't you Cal Chase?" I nodded. "What are you doing here?"

"Before I was rudely interrupted, I was having dinner with a beautiful woman."

He opened his mouth then closed it again, looking back and forth between Barb and me.

"I didn't realize that was you at the bank meeting a couple weeks ago," he said. "Is that where you two met?"

"Barb and I go way back," I said. "And if you don't mind, I'd like to get back to our date."

"Your date?" Narrowing his eyes at Barbara, he nodded then smiled at me. "Well, if you happen to see my mother, tell her to call me."

That said, he stalked away.

I sat back down. "Is he always like that?"

She shrugged. "When things aren't going his way, yes."

"Should we be worried about Molly?"

"I don't think so."

"Then why didn't she show up at that dinner?"

"Stewart probably told her about the dinner and that he wanted her to go with Frances. He wouldn't have taken her no seriously. And what you just witnessed is his reaction to her not doing what she said she wouldn't do in the first place."

"Somehow I followed that," I said. "I'm guessing Molly isn't fond of Frances."

"She never has been. Even before—" She shook her head and took a sip of wine.

I pushed my plate away and picked up my glass. "Sounds like there's a story there."

"Not really." She shrugged. "I met Frances about six years ago when we were seated next to each other at a fundraising event. She'd just moved to town and was looking for a friend, so we ended up hanging out once in a while. Molly never really cared for her. She once described her as a vapid opportunist."

Barbara finished her wine and let out a sarcastic chuckle.

I refilled her glass and mine then set the empty bottle off to the side.

"So you two were friends and now she's married to your ex-husband."

"Yep," she said, popping the p. "Turns out Molly was right. Frances saw an opportunity to sleep with my husband and took it."

"Seriously?"

She nodded. "It was going on almost a year before I found out. Things hadn't been great for a while but it wasn't anything I wasn't willing to deal with. But I couldn't handle cheating so I left."

"Understandable."

"I stayed at a hotel for a few nights and when Molly found out, she told me I could stay here so I didn't have to rush into finding a permanent place." She held her arms out. "And here I am three years later."

"Well, if it makes you feel any better, I lived in my friend's pool house for about a year after my divorce. And honestly, if he hadn't gotten married, I probably would have stayed there longer. But after his wedding, it seemed like it was time to move on." I stood and picked up our plates. "I'm gonna throw these in the sink and bring out dessert. Would you like more wine?"

"No, just water please," she said.

I went inside and quickly washed the dishes then set them in the rack next to the already-cleaned pot and pan. Grabbing the Black Forest cake I'd brought out of the refrigerator, I cut two large slices and put them on the plates I'd set out earlier. I left them on the counter and filled a glass with water for Barbara and another with ginger ale for me. She'd obviously gotten my favorite drink special for tonight, since she didn't have any earlier in the week.

"You're better than a waiter," Barbara said when I walked outside carrying two plates in one hand and two glasses in the other.

I set everything on the table and sat back down.

"I'm all about doing things in the least amount of trips."

"On that we can agree," she said then took a big bite of cake and chewed. "Oh my God, this is amazing."

Digging into my own cake, I tried not to focus on her sexy little moans or the way she licked whipped cream off her fork. I finished my slice in record time and took a long drink.

"I told you mine, now it's time to tell me yours," she said. I looked at her and raised my right brow. "What happened with your marriage?"

"Not to sound totally clueless, but I thought things were fine until one day Marsha told me she couldn't deal with my schedule and that she wanted a divorce." I chuckled. "But I guess you wouldn't find that as surprising as I did."

"How long were you married?"

"Just about six years."

"So weren't you already playing for the Waves when you met?" I nodded. "Then I don't know why the schedule would have been surprising."

"That's what I said, but it didn't get me anywhere. Once she asked for a divorce, that was it. She didn't want to talk about anything or go to counseling, and after the lawyers got involved, things got messy." I took in a deep breath and slowly let it out. "For a while I tried to figure out what happened, but don't waste my time anymore. I guess it just wasn't meant to be."

I hadn't meant for things to get this deep tonight...or ever, really. But I suppose it would have all come up eventually if we spend time together, like I'm hoping we will. Thankfully she seems willing to let the subject go for now.

"Would you like anything else? More cake?"

"No, I'm good. I would like to go back inside though. My leg is starting to fall asleep in this position."

"Sure thing." I stood and picked her up.

This time she wrapped her arms around my neck without protest. I walked slowly, wanting to savor the feel of her relaxed against me as long as possible. Just before I set her down on the couch, I swear she inhaled against my neck just like she used to back in college. I stopped and turned my head until we were nose to nose. Looking into her wide eyes, I recognized all the same things I've been feeling since I saw her in that bank meeting and it made me ache. For two college kids who were madly in love but just couldn't keep it together. For what they could have been. For the time they lost. And for her. Always for her.

I lowered my mouth and kissed her. I'd meant to just brush her lips with mine once or twice to seal that connection, but it quickly turned into something else. Just the feel of her soft lips had me needing more. I shifted my grip and pulled her closer, then opened my mouth over hers to deepen the kiss. She threaded her fingers through my hair as our tongues tangled together.

I inched my way to the couch and sat, settling her across my lap. Pulling back slightly, I felt her shuddered breath against my chest.

"Are you okay?" She nodded and looked at my mouth then leaned in for another kiss. That's definitely on my agenda too, but I need to make sure I don't hurt her. I reached up and cupped her jaw, slowly breaking the kiss. After kissing her nose, I rested my forehead against hers. "Is your ankle okay?"

She wiggled against my lap and I shifted so her butt sat on the couch instead of so close to my raging erection. Her calves rested on my thighs and I reached over and grabbed a pillow and placed it under her ankle.

"That good?"

"Yeah." The word came out on a soft sigh.

Barb licked her lips, inviting me to take another taste. Threading my fingers through her hair, I angled her head and kissed her, long and hot and sweet. I dragged my hand along her thigh, stopping to squeeze her hip before moving up and dipping my fingers under the hem of her shirt. With my palm flat against her waist, my thumb rested just under the lacy edge of her bra.

I curled my fingers in and cupped her breast, rubbing my thumb over her nipple. Her answering moan vibrated against my chest and I wanted more. I squeezed and kneaded her plump breast as the kiss turned even more hot and almost desperate. She dug her fingertips into my scalp when I pinched her nipple between my thumb and forefinger.

At least I know I'm not the only one affected here.

My dick throbbed against my zipper as we continued to make out on the couch like horny teenagers. I wanted to shift between her thighs and thrust against her to alleviate the ache. Then drag my mouth down her neck to nip at the curve of her breast and kiss my way to its center to lick and lave her hard nipple. And definitely move this beyond second base. But I know I can't do any of those things right now. I need to slow this down before I risk hurting her.

I shifted my hand back to her waist and slowed the tempo of the kiss. Thankfully she followed my lead because at this point, my control is hanging by a thread.

After placing one last kiss against the corner of her mouth, I pulled back just enough to see her face. Her nostrils flared as she took in deep breaths with her eyes still closed. She let out a soft hum as her swollen lips curved into a small smile.

"Barb?"

"Hmmm?"

I removed my hand from her waist and cupped her jaw, softly stroking her cheek. She slowly opened her eyes and met my gaze.

"As much as it kills me to say this, I should go."

She blinked and those little lines formed between her brows just above her nose.

"Do you really have to?" she asked.

I let out a chuckle that was half moan.

"You're killing me, Smalls."

"Still quoting that movie?"

"The Sandlot is a classic. It deserves to be quoted."

I slid out from beneath her legs, making sure not to bump her ankle. Resting her foot on a pillow, I sat at the other side of the couch.

If I stand up right now, it's going to be really obvious how much I'd love to stay.

The air still crackled between us and when she licked her lips, it took all my willpower to stay on my own side when I really want to slide between her legs and make every dirty thought in my head become reality.

Barb looked down at her lap and tucked her hair behind her ear, a sure sign she's either nervous or overthinking something. I don't want her doing either of those things.

"Thank you for tonight," I said.

She looked up at me and smiled. "I think that's my line. After all, you did all the work."

"I had a great time, and I'm hoping we can do it again. Maybe Tuesday?"

"I'd like that," she said. "But you don't have to cook. We could just order out."

I stood, finally confident that I won't embarrass myself.

"I'll see how Tuesday goes. Either I'll make something and bring it along or grab takeout. Does six o'clock work for you?"

"I'll be here."

Chapter 9

Barbara

"Knock. Knock." Molly peeked around the corner of the foyer into the living room. "Are you alone?"

"Yes, I'm alone."

She walked in and sat on the love seat.

"So, how was your date?"

It's almost noon. I'm surprised she waited this long to come over.

"It was really nice. Cal made the most amazing chicken marsala with mashed potatoes and green beans. Since it was such a beautiful night we ate outside. Oh, and he brought Black Forest cake for dessert. There's over half the cake left in the refrigerator if you want a slice."

"Don't try to get me off topic by mentioning dessert."

I should have known she's going to want play by play details of the night.

"There's not much else to say on the current topic. Cal came over and made dinner. We hung out for a little while, then he went home."

"Nothing else happened?"

I literally laughed out loud when she wiggled her eyebrows.

"I don't kiss and tell."

"Wonderful." She clapped her hands and laughed. "I was surprised his car wasn't in the driveway when I got home."

"Which reminds me," I said. "Stewart was here looking for you. He said you were supposed to meet Frances at some dinner."

She pursed her lips and took in a deep breath through her nose. "He's my son and I love him, but that boy is going to drive me crazy. I told him I wasn't going to that dinner every single time he mentioned it to me."

"That's what I figured, so I wasn't worried that you were abducted or something."

"I hope he didn't harass you too much."

"He probably would have gone off on his usual tagent about how I need to step back so you have room for Frances, but Cal kind of put a stop to it."

"Cal was here when Stewart showed up?"

I nodded. "We were outside and had just finished eating dinner."

"Stewart was surprised when he learned Cal was at that meeting."

"He seemed even more surprised to find out that Cal and I know each other."

"You never told Stewart about your relationship?"

"We never really discussed exes and at that point, I just wanted to move on. Our breakup hadn't been overly dramatic but it had been extremely painful."

Before she could ask, I filled Molly in on the basic details.

"I want you to know that I wasn't carrying a torch for Cal the whole time Stewart and I were married. I did love him." I shrugged. "I don't know. Maybe if we'd had children, things would have been different."

Despite the fact that we hadn't used birth control for years, I'd never gotten pregnant. We'd both been checked and according to the doctors, there was nothing physical preventing us from conceiving. After I found out about Stewart and Frances, I considered the fact that we never had children divine intervention. I'd go crazy if I had to share custody with those two.

"I never doubted that you loved him. And I know he loved you, too. I'm not really sure—" She shook her head. "There's no use playing the what if game. You'll just drive yourself crazy."

I'm surprised she said that much. Molly and I rarely discuss my relationship with Stewart. I know she doesn't approve of his actions a lot of the time but as she always says, he is her son.

She waved her hand. "Never mind all that. Let's talk some more about Cal. He's so tall and handsome. Reminds me of my John with those kind brown eyes."

"You're not gonna make a move on him, are you?"

Even though the question wasn't serious, Molly's answer was.

"It wouldn't matter if I did. That man only has eyes for you." I couldn't stop the smile from spreading across my face if I wanted to. "You really like him too, don't you?"

I nodded. "When Cal asked me out in college, I couldn't believe it. There wasn't a girl on campus who wouldn't have killed to be in my shoes. And after that first date, we were inseparable." Shaking my head, I stopped myself from going too far down memory lane.

Molly stood and walked toward me. She rested her hand on my shoulder and squeezed.

"This is your second chance. Not everyone gets those, so be sure to grab onto it with both hands and hold on." She smiled down at me. "Now I'm going to have a piece of that cake. Care to join me?"

CAL

I grabbed the bakery box from the passenger seat and stepped out of the 4Runner, glad I'd decided to drive it today instead of the R8. My neck is killing me and the seats in the car are less comfortable despite the fact it cost twice as much. Or maybe after driving it for so many years, the Toyota's seats have just molded better to my body.

"Hey Cal."

It's an off day for the Waves and my friend and former teammate, Dan McMullen, invited me over to hang out with the guys. I hadn't noticed his daughter sitting on the front steps when I pulled up.

"Hi Lexi. How've you been?"

"Good. I'm just out here waiting for my friend Megan." She looked at the box in my hand. "What'd you bring?"

"Brownies."

At this point, I think I may be single-handedly keeping my neighborhood coffee shop in business.

"I can carry them in for you if you want," she said around a big smile.

"Like I'd trust you with a whole box of brownies." Lexi's sweet tooth rivals mine. I stepped closer and lifted the lid. "You can take one each for you and your friend." She looked at the contents of the box for several seconds before reaching inside and pulling out two brownies. Probably the biggest ones.

"Thanks."

"Is everybody inside?"

"Daddy, Uncle Jack, and Dale are out back and Mommy and Hannah are in the kitchen talking about the wedding." She pointed toward the double doors behind her. "This door is unlocked if you want to walk through."

"I don't want to interrupt wedding talk. I'll just go around back. See you in a bit."

Walking around the side of the house, I stepped through the gate and spotted the guys across the yard. Dan manned the grill and Dale, aka Monte, and Jack relaxed in lounge chairs.

"Yo!" I yelled, turning their attention my way.

Each of the guys shouted their own greeting. Jack's hand moved to his side then a red playground ball came sailing my way. Thankfully the reflexes I'd honed playing third base for more than two decades didn't fail me. I picked the ball out of the air with one hand and threw it right back at him without dropping the box.

"He's still got it." Jack laughed and tucked the ball under his arm.

I made my way around the pool to the covered patio and placed the box on the table then pulled out a chair and straddled it, resting my arms on the back. This position is usually the most comfortable when my neck is acting up.

Dan set his spatula down and lowered the grill lid.

"Hey stranger," he said. "Glad you made it."

The guys have made a point to let me know when they're getting together but my newfound banker's hours don't always mesh well with their crazy schedules.

"I'm surprised you didn't cancel."

"Why?" Dan asked as he sat in the chair next to me and propped his feet against the edge of the seat across from him.

"The game ended pretty late last night. I figured you'd want to relax."

"I am." He gestured toward his feet. "See, my feet are up." Then he pointed at Jack and Monte. "And those two haven't moved since they got here."

"Not true." Jack pointed toward the back door with his beer. "I went inside to get the last round."

"That's just because you can't go more than fifteen minutes without seeing Hannah," Monte said.

A slow smile spread across Jack's face. "Guilty." He waggled his eyebrows then took a long draw on his beer.

If you'd told me a couple years ago that Jack Reagan would be getting married, I'd have laughed in your face. Through most of the years we played together Jack avoided real relationships. He carefully chose the women he spent time with based on their willingness to go away quietly at the end of the season.

That all changed when one of his carefully chosen women decided she didn't want things to end and took her revenge by writing a tell-all book. It was pretty tame as those kinds of books go, but the owner of the Waves decided Jack needed to do some extra image work and had him work closely with Hannah Adams from the public relations department. Once they started spending time together, Jack fell hard and fast. It was a lot of fun to watch. They're getting married in November. A smallish event right here at Dan's house.

"Speaking of drinks. What can I get you?" Dan asked.

"I'm good for now," I said. "But you know you don't have to wait on me. I'll grab something in a bit."

He reached out and nudged the lid of the box open enough to peek inside.

"Those look awesome," he said.

"Wait 'til you taste them."

"Lexi will be thrilled."

"She already is. I saw her out front waiting for her friend and gave her a couple," I said. "She said Sabrina and Hannah are discussing the wedding in the kitchen, which is why I decided to sneak around the side." I looked at Jack. "Shouldn't you be in there with them?"

"You've met Hannah, right? The princess of planning. The queen of organization. For the most part, I just have to show up," he said. "Besides, it's her day so whatever she wants is fine with me."

Before we could bust his ass about how he's totally whipped, the back door opened and the women walked outside.

"Hey Cal," Sabrina said. She placed the platter of steaks she'd been carrying on the table then leaned down and kissed my cheek. "It's good to see you."

Dan reclaimed his place in front of the grill and soon the scent of searing steaks mixed with aroma of the potatoes and vegetables that had already been cooking. My mouth watered in anticipation.

Hannah settled onto the lounge with Jack and said, "Cal, how are you feeling?"

"I'm hanging in, thanks."

"Great!" She smiled. "Then you'll be able to make it to the end of the year meet and greet."

She raised her voice at the end turning the sentence into a question, but her tone said she'd only accept one answer.

"Yeah, sorry I haven't gotten back to you on that. I wasn't sure if I had anything going on the days you mentioned."

"I'd hoped with enough notice you'd be able to make it work," she said. I opened my mouth, still not sure what to say, but she must have read the reluctance on my face. "Cal, you have to come. You were really missed last year."

My neck surgery was three days before last year's event, so I'd had an exemption. But to be honest, I would have been reluctant to go then, too. I don't want to be one of those retired players who lives to hang out at all the team events reliving his glory days. Instead of saying that, I decided to keep things light.

"With these clowns there to keep everyone entertained? I doubt anyone noticed I wasn't there."

My three former teammates flipped me off with such synchrony, it seemed like they'd practiced the move.

"Behave." Hannah slapped Jack's hand down. He wrapped his arms around her waist and pulled her in for a quick kiss. She settled into his embrace then turned her attention back to me. "So can I count on you to be there? You have the potential dates." She smiled. "We're counting on it being the last one because that means we're in the Series."

How did I think I'd bow out of attending with Hannah in charge? She's a force to be reckoned with.

I shook my head and laughed. "Sure, I'll manage to be there whenever it is."

"Great!" Hannah said. "I'll email you the daily schedule. That will stay the same regardless of what day it's held."

Before I could comment, Hannah's phone buzzed and she looked down at it. She leaned closer to Jack and tilted the phone so he could see. They shared a smile, then she pulled the phone closer and her thumbs flew across the screen.

"Hey Monte," Jack said. "You'll get a chance to strike out with Karen Walsh again when we're down in Tampa next week."

Hannah dropped her phone on the chaise lounge, rolled her eyes, and sighed. "Do you guys ever stop?"

Dan, Jack, Monte, and I looked around at each other then laughed.

Sabrina shook her head and said to Hannah, "It's like dealing with children." She looked at her phone. "Speaking of, it looks like Gavin is waking up from his nap. I'll be right back."

She and Dan had a little boy toward the end of the season after I was injured. Now he's about to turn two. Lexi came along shortly after I met Dan, so he always seemed a little more settled than the rest of us, but with the addition of Sabrina and now Gavin, that's been multiplied. That doesn't mean he's above acting as juvenile as the rest of us when we get together.

"So are you gonna ask Karen out again when you see her?" he asked Monte.

During one of Jack's PR events, he met Jeremy Walsh and his mother Karen, and invited them to a spring training game. Since then, they've been regular attendees. Monte took an instant liking to her but she's turned him down every time he asks her out. Which is pretty much anytime the Waves play in Tampa.

"I'm going to say no." Monte said. "She's obviously not interested."

Of the four of us, Monte had what I'd call the most active dating life. Between Lexi's mom and Sabrina, Dan only dated once in a while, and Jack had his "seasonal girls" until he fell for Hannah. I've always had full-blown relationships, no matter how short-lived. It's never been my style to date a bunch of girls at once. But for most of the years I've known him, Monte had women scattered throughout the country that he'd spend time with when he was in their town. That must have gotten old because a few years ago, he started hanging out with the guys and me more when we were on the road.

The funny thing is, I've heard Monte talk more about Karen Walsh than he ever did about any of those women. I guess he's really fallen for her. First Dan, then Jack, and now Monte. And I guess I can include myself now that Barbara is back in my life.

"I've heard that before," Jack said around a smug smile. "I'm sure once you see her you'll change your mind."

I sat back and enjoyed the verbal shots being fired back and forth, mostly between Jack and Monte. Dan and I got in a comment or two, but for the most part, we just watched the show. I'll admit, I miss this almost as much as baseball itself.

That is until Monte decided to deflect the conversation my way.

"If you're done busting my ass, don't you think we should find out what's going on with Cal?" he said. "We haven't seen him in a few weeks. He could be engaged by now." That bomb thrown, he stood. "I'm going to get another round."

Dan smirked and raised his right brow. "*Are* you engaged?"

I shook my head and laughed. "Nope, not engaged."

"Is there someone *special* you'd like to tell us about?" Jack asked.

Before I had to answer, Sabrina came back outside with a still sleepy Gavin on her hip, followed by Lexi and her friend, Megan, putting an end to my interrogation. Hannah took the baby while Jack followed Lexi to the pool to watch the new dive she just learned. Dan opened the grill and checked the steaks while Sabrina debated with him over whether or not they're done enough.

Monte came back outside carrying four bottles of beer and two waters. He walked in my direction and handed me a bottle then placed the rest of his bounty on the table behind me, keeping a beer for himself. Dropping into the chair Dan had vacated earlier, he looked at me and saluted with the bottle before taking a drink.

If I was still playing, these guys would already know about Barb. When you're in each other's pockets like we were during the season, it's hard to keep things like that secret. But I'm not with them like that anymore, and for now, I'd like to keep her all to myself.

Chapter 10

Barbara

I tucked a bottle of iced tea into the waistband of my yoga pants, shut the refrigerator door, and slowly made my way back to the couch. I'm getting better with the crutches, but moving around is still a struggle. My house just doesn't have the extra space needed to accommodate using them. Plus I'm always afraid I'll bump my ankle on something. So it's definitely a slow go anytime I have to get up.

Hopping my way in front of the couch, I slowly lowered onto the cushion and shifted sideways to put my leg up. I placed the crutches on the floor next to me for easy access then removed the bottle from my pants and set it on the coffee table, grabbing the remote before settling back against the pillows.

My eyes need a break from reading, so TV is going to have to help pass the time today. I turned on Netflix and decided to check out Outlander. I read the books years ago and have been meaning to watch the series but never really had the time. That's obviously not an issue now.

I got sucked into 18th century Scotland and before I knew it, Netflix was judging me and asking if I was still watching. Of course I'm still watching, I have nothing better to do. I picked up the remote and resumed streaming. My phone buzzed just as the opening song ended. Yes, I can skip it, but I kind of like listening to it. I may even sing along with the parts I know. Don't judge.

Pausing the show, I picked up my phone and smiled when I spotted the text from Cal.

Cal: I'm looking forward to tonight.

Barbara: Me too.

Cal: Do you need me to pick anything up for you?

Barbara: No, I'm good, thanks.

Cal: I'm sitting in the most boring meeting ever and I swear the clock is moving backwards. But if it ever moves forward again, I'll see you around 6pm.

Barbara: I'll be here, probably still watching Netflix, which is what I've been doing all day.

Cal: Anything good?

Barbara: Outlander.

Cal: Sing me a song...

Barbara: You've watched Outlander?

Cal: You'd be surprised what ball players get up to during rain delays.

Barbara: You're just full of surprises.

Cal: Gotta keep you on your toes, Murphy. ;) See you later.

I pushed play on the remote and rolled onto my side, hugging the phone to my chest. The latest episode was more than halfway over when I realized I had no idea what's going on. Instead of paying attention, I've been lying here with a silly smile on my face thinking about Cal.

Last time he made me dinner, the night had ended with the most delicious kiss. I'm hoping that will happen again tonight. Or maybe it will even go farther. I clenched my thighs at the thought.

It's been a long time since I've had sex, or even wanted to. Full disclosure, Stewart is the last man I've been intimate with and that was a few months before I left him. You do the math.

And I honestly haven't missed it...until now anyway. At first, I was devastated by the divorce and probably a little depressed. After that, no one really appealed to me and I've never been one to just randomly hook up. But since Cal walked back into my life, sex is all I can think about. Specifically, with him.

The fact that we've already had sex makes it even worse. I have actual experiences to fantasize about...and they were very, very good experiences.

Maybe tonight will put an end to my dry spell. It's been so long, I just hope I don't embarrass myself.

CAL

I studied Barb from across the table as she twirled spaghetti onto her fork. She caught me looking and paused with her fork halfway to her mouth.

"What?"

I shook my head and smiled. "You're beautiful."

Her cheeks turned pink and she shoved the pasta into her mouth and chewed, her eyes locked onto her plate.

Last time I'd cooked her dinner, Barb had looked stunning with her hair curled and full makeup. Tonight she looks just as amazing with her face bare and hair in a messy bun. But what keeps catching my eye is her v-neck t-shirt that shows just a hint of cleavage.

Barbara has amazing boobs and I know for a fact they're super sensitive. At least they used to be, and I don't imagine that would go away. I shook my head clearing *those* thoughts from my mind and shoved a half of a meatball into my mouth and chewed.

"This is delicious, Cal," she said just when the silence was getting a bit awkward. Probably because I've been mentally reciting baseball stats, trying to not think about her perfect pink nipples.

I swallowed. "Thank you. Another one of my mom's recipes. I tweaked it a little bit...added more garlic and parmesan cheese."

"I really like it." She took a sip of her wine. "I'll have to cook you dinner when I'm up and about again."

My mouth curled into a slow smile. "Barbara Murphy, are you asking me on a date?"

She blinked and seemed to hesitate, then the corner of her mouth hitched up. "I guess I am."

"I accept." I took a bite of fresh, buttered Italian bread punctuating my words.

I know that technically her name isn't Murphy anymore...I haven't even seen signs of a hyphen anywhere in her bank paperwork...but I can't think of her as anything else.

"So how was your day?" I asked.

Since I'd brought the meatballs and sauce heated in my crockpot and the salad ingredients chopped, it hadn't taken me too long to get dinner on the table. Until now, our whole conversation had revolved around her shock that I actually own a crockpot. I figured I'd change the subject.

"Today just blended with all the rest. I'm sure your day was much more exciting."

I rolled my eyes. "I wish I could say it was, but honestly, sitting here watching Netflix was probably more riveting than my day."

She placed her fork on her nearly-empty plate and her blue eyes locked onto mine, filled with concern. "Do you like your job at all?"

Sitting back, I dragged my fingers through my hair and shook my head.

"It's fine, it's just not what I thought I'd be doing with my life."

"Cal, you're so smart, you could do anything you want."

Anything but play ball.

I bit back the words that would make me sound like a whiny pussy.

Instead, I smiled. "It's just a big lifestyle change. I'll adjust eventually." Wanting to shift the topic off of me, I asked, "What about you? You said you like your job. Is that really true?"

"I do." She shrugged and picked up her fork, playing with the remaining spaghetti on her plate. "Sure there are things I'd change if I could, but I work with some great people and get to play with numbers all day."

I thought about asking if her asshat of an ex-husband is one of the things she'd change, but decided against it. Before I could continue the conversation, I felt a couple drops on my forearm. I looked up wondering when the sky had gotten so dark.

"We'd better get inside. It looks like the sky is going to open up any minute."

She looked up, and I smiled at her surprise at the change in weather. It's nice to know she's as distracted by me as I am by her.

I stood and held out my arms.

"Your chariot awaits, milady."

I raised my brow when she hesitated. She shook her head and rolled her eyes, then lowered her ankle from the chair it had been propped on and pushed her good leg against the patio to shift her chair sideways.

Leaning down, I slipped one arm under her knees and the other behind her back and stood straight when she wrapped her arms around my neck. I carried her to the couch, resisting the urge to sit and settle her onto my lap. Instead, I set her gently on the cushion.

"I'll be right back," I said. "I'm gonna go clear the table."

Walking back outside, I put our dirty dishes into two neat stacks and carried them inside, just as the sky opened up.

"Good thing we came in," I said as I placed the dishes in the sink. "It's really coming down now."

"Thankfully you were paying attention. I was drunk on great food."

I turned on the faucet and squirted detergent onto a sponge, then washed the dishes and stacked them in the wooden strainer. Barb has a dishwasher but there are only a few things and I finished the task quickly, then turned off the water, grabbed a towel, and dried my hands.

"Would you like more wine? I can open another bottle."

"No, but some water would be great."

I pulled two glasses out of the cupboard and dropped in some ice cubes. I filled hers with spring water and mine with ginger ale. Grabbing the glasses off the counter, I walked into the living room and handed Barbara hers then sat in the chair.

"Thank you," she said and took a long drink. Setting the glass in her lap, she slowly dragged her index finger along the rim. I watched the motion, mesmerized until she spoke, drawing my gaze up to her face. "I'm sure I can Google it, but I'd rather get the facts from you." I took a drink and raised my brow as I swallowed, urging her to ask whatever she wanted to know. "I know you retired because you got hurt. But what exactly happened?"

I did a mental *whew*. I'd expected her to ask a probing question about my divorce or maybe even about the baseball groupie scene. For the record, I only have second-hand knowledge of the latter. Besides the fact that casual hookups were never my thing, my first Minor League coach did a good job scaring the hell out of me. He told tales of girls who did whatever was necessary to hitch their wagons to potential future stars. A child, support payments, and having to deal with a baby mama for the rest of my life seemed like a steep price to pay for a one night stand.

"Do you mind if I sit over there while I tell this tale?" I asked.

She hesitated then shook her head and shifted to move her legs to the floor.

"No, stay that way," I said and walked over to the couch. As carefully as possible, I lifted her legs and slid onto the cushion underneath, resting her calves across my lap. "Okay?"

Barb nodded, eyes wide. I know I'm invading her personal space, but I can't help myself. She stiffened when I rested my hand on her shin and I heard her quick inhale. Time to lighten the mood.

"What was the question again?"

Barb chuckled and wiggled her butt, relaxing further into the pillow.

"How did you get the injury that forced you to retire?" she asked.

Forced. That word sums it up perfectly.

Barb's small smile urged me to tell her what she wanted to know.

"We were playing in New York and it was the last game of a road trip. So of course, there was a rain delay and then the game went into extra innings. The score was tied in the thirteenth and my buddy Jack hit a two-run homer giving us the lead. You'd think that would have sealed our win, but as usual, New York wasn't going down without a fight. Their first batter hit a homer. That rattled our pitcher just enough to walk the second hitter. They put in a pinch runner and he stole second on the next pitch. I got the next guy out, but that still left us in the bottom of the thirteenth with one out and the tying run on second."

I broke eye contact and shifted my focus to my thumb as it stroked her soft skin. This is the part I've been replaying in my head since that night. I have so many *what ifs* and it's a daily struggle to not get sucked into them. I can't go back and change things, so I force myself to focus on moving forward.

"The next guy hit a popup off the third base line. I saw the ball from the second it left the bat and I had a good angle on it. Running at full speed, I dove over the wall and into the stands. I made the catch a split second before I crashed into the seats, banging my head against the base. My body kept moving forward and my neck twisted, which is probably what caused the most damage. I ended up with two herniated discs in my neck." I let out a sarcastic chuckle. "At least I got the second out and we ended up winning the game."

My gut twisted when I looked over and met Barbara's shiny eyes.

"Couldn't they fix them?" Her voice sounded thick.

"Not so I could play," I said. She looked at me with wide eyes, urging me to explain. "After it happened, I took it easy then rehabbed for a couple months before joining the team again. At first it seemed okay, but after a few weeks, it was a struggle. The pain was constant and by the end of the season, it radiated through my shoulders to my elbows and my fingers tingled sometimes so I'd have trouble gripping the ball. That's not ideal when you have to make the throw from third to first." I took in a deep breath and let it out slowly, focusing on my fingers again. They look good wrapped around her shapely leg. "I finished the season pretty strong, all things considered and we won the Series that year. I'm thankful I was able to hold on long enough to be part of that. It was definitely a dream come true.

"My friend Dan's wife, Sabrina, is a physical therapist and I worked with her during the off season to strengthen my shoulders and neck. I had a steroid shot before spring training and another a couple weeks after the regular season started, but the relief was short-lived. The third injection didn't help much and by August, I knew I had to make a decision. I could't keep getting injections and if I kept playing through the pain, chances were I'd do some serious damage eventually." I squeezed her calf and glanced over at her. "I finished the season, but I only played half the games toward the end. We didn't make it to the Series that year and once the playoffs were over, I had cervical fusion surgery. After that, playing professional ball wasn't an option."

Barbara bent her legs and nudged herself closer to me. I watched a tear run down her cheek and drop from her jaw onto her shirt leaving a wet spot. She placed her hand over mine, threading our fingers together.

"Cal, I am so sorry," she said. "I know how much you love the game. I can't imagine how hard it's been for you."

I leaned my forehead against hers and breathed in her sweet scent before placing a soft kiss on the corner of her mouth.

"Thank you for understanding." I kissed her again, this time longer and full on the lips. "But I have my health and someone's idea of a dream job. Not to mention I'm sitting here with a beautiful, amazing, sexy woman." Reaching up, I rested my fingers along her jaw, wiping away a stray tear with my thumb and smiled. "Things could be worse."

Chapter 11

Barbara

I Googled yet another version of what I want to know then scrolled through the ads for law firm sites until I found something legit. I've been doing this for the better part of an hour and based on what I'm reading for the fourth or fifth time, I think I can safely say I have my answer.

The more time I spend with Cal, the more I can't stop thinking about this. Well, this and sex, but he's pretty adamant about not taking things past the kissing stage until I'm out of this damn boot. I mentally shrugged. I guess turnabout is fair play. Now I know how he felt those first few months when we were dating back in college.

Since our first dinner, he's made it a point to come over a few times a week and we talk or at least text every night. In some ways it's like we've picked up right where we left off. I'm not sure what will happen once I'm back on my feet and we're out of our little bubble, but after five weeks of getting to know him again, I definitely want to find out.

"Hello." Jess yelled from the doorway. "Your own personal Grub Hub is here."

She walked into the living room carrying a bag in each hand.

Tonight's dinner is a bacon cheeseburger and fries from a local bar. I'm pretty sure none of my clothes are going to fit me when this is all over.

She dropped the bags on the coffee table and said, "Beer?"

"Sounds good."

She disappeared into the kitchen and I placed my iPad on the coffee table and grabbed one of the bags. My mouth watered at the thought of biting into the juicy burger.

Jess came back carrying a kitchen chair and two bottles of Blue Moon. She handed me one of the bottles and set the chair next to the coffee table. Picking up her own bag, she looked at my tablet then back to me.

"You're not working are you?"

"No, just doing some research."

After shooting me a look of disbelief, she glanced at the screen.

"What's this?" Angling the iPad closer to her, she read exactly what I've been researching. "Are you serious about this?" she asked around a big smile.

"I think so." Opening my container, I lifted the burger with two hands and took a big bite.

Surprisingly she did the same and seemed content to eat in silence until I was ready to talk. I was about halfway through my burger and a good portion of fries when that happened.

"Cal has this habit of calling me Murphy or Barbara Murphy," I said. "At first, it took me a second to remember that's me...or at least it used to be." I picked up a fry and nibbled on it, taking some time to collect my thoughts. "I haven't thought of myself as Barbara Murphy since I married Stewart. But since meeting up with Cal again, I feel more like the old me, and the last name Mack just doesn't fit her."

When I left Stewart, I never even thought about changing back to my maiden name. In fact, I was shocked when he brought it up during the divorce proceedings and even tried to have the judge tell me I had to stop using the name Mack. I'll admit now that part of the reason I was reluctant to change my name back was because it was so important to my ex-husband that I did. At the time, small victories like that made me feel like I was in control when life as I'd known it had fallen apart.

Jess stared at me, eyes wide, and slowly finished chewing. "Are you serious?" she asked around a mouthful of food. I nodded and she swallowed then dropped her burger into the container. "Are. You. Fucking. Serious?"

"Okay, I can usually tell what you're thinking, but I have no idea right now."

"Are you serious?" she asked again then started laughing. A deep belly laugh that went on and on.

I sat back and focused on eating my fries until Jess collected herself.

"Are you finished?"

She wiped her eyes and took a deep breath. "J.P. and I have been taking bets on whether or not Cal would be the trigger that propels you forward."

"What are you talking about?"

"Barb, we've talked about this. You've been stuck since the divorce. Hell, since before the divorce if we're being honest." I opened my mouth but she cut me off before I could deny her words. "This is a good thing so please don't overthink it and freak out."

Sometimes it really sucks when someone knows you too well, but she does have a point. After my mother's death and my breakup with Cal, I'd felt so lost. When Stewart and I got together, it was easy to morph into his world. Once we married, I immersed myself until it seemed like I'd always been there.

"I'm not sure I'd use the word stuck, but it's true I feel different since Cal's been back in my life." I took a long drink of beer then rested the bottle on my lap and traced my finger through the condensation. "He reminds me of who I used to be and he makes me think that maybe she's not totally gone."

"Use whatever word you want, but you've basically just been treading water, especially since the divorce," she said. "And before it, you were doing a lot, I'm just not sure it was all stuff *you* wanted to do."

"I do have the career I always wanted."

I'm a true numbers geek at heart and always planned on having some sort of career where I could immerse myself in them all day long. Nepotism definitely played a part in me getting my current position, but married to Stewart or not, I never would have been promoted if I couldn't do the job.

"I'll give you that," she said. "And I know you love working with Molly and J.P., but you shouldn't have to tiptoe around Stewart every day."

I snapped the lid on my empty container and slid it onto the coffee table then placed my empty beer bottle next to it.

"I don't tiptoe around Stewart every day." I crossed my arms over my stomach.

Jess rolled her eyes and stood. She collected her garbage, then mine, and brought it all into the kitchen. I heard the refrigerator door open and close, then she was at my side handing me a fresh bottle of beer.

"Most people tiptoe around Stewart," she said and sat back down. "Because if he doesn't get his own way, he throws a temper tantrum." I can't argue with that, so I just nodded and took a drink. "While you were married, it became second nature to placate him and you still do." She sat forward, crossed her right leg over the left, and waved her hand dismissively. "But we're getting off topic here. You've definitely been more animated and colorful the past few weeks, which is why J.P. and I were discussing it. If Stewart sucked the life out of you, Cal seems to have given it back. Even if it's only by reminding you of who you really are."

I blinked until Jess's image was no longer blurry. I don't know why I'm getting teary-eyed. I'm happy, I really am. I have great friends, a great job, and am healthy. But I'll admit, my life hasn't turned out the way I'd expected. I've always wanted a big family and I thought that by now, I'd be married with a few kids. Instead I'm divorced and childless.

"Cal does make me feel more alive than I have in a long time," I admitted. "He was perfect back in college and seems even more so now. It makes me wonder—" I stopped speaking and shook my head, but Jess finished my thought for me.

"What your life would be like if you'd never broken up with him?" I nodded. "That's something you'll never know, but now you have a second chance to find out what things *can* be. You're both single, you haven't had any live-altering events messing with your head, and he's not going to be gallivanting all over the country playing baseball." Jess is right, and I told her so. "You're hot for Cal, and the air practically sizzles when he looks at you, so all you have to do is keep an open mind, go with the flow, and see where things with you and Mr. Hot Tamales go."

CAL

"Dinner is ready. Everybody out of the pool," my mother yelled. "Cal and Jimmy, go wash your hands." My nephew and I continued to throw the ball back and forth. I figure we have a few more minutes to play catch while the pool crew gets dried off. Apparently my mother didn't feel the same way. "Calvin and James, now!"

I caught the ball and walked toward Jimmy as I soft-tossed it back to him.

"Uh oh, she used our full names," I said. "We better go wash up."

"Can we throw some more after dinner?" he asked.

"Sure." I ruffled his hair and we walked toward the house together.

We weaved our way through the yard, avoiding the swing set, basketball court, and a myriad of toys, and snuck in the side door. Jimmy ran through the living room and kitchen, dropping his glove on the large island on his way to the bathroom.

When I got drafted, the first thing I wanted to spend part of my signing bonus on was a new house for my parents. After all, if it wasn't for their support, I wouldn't have made it as far as I did. Until I went to college, they'd rarely missed a game. Plus they carted me to practice, funded travel ball, and my dad even built a batting cage for me.

I placed my glove next to Jimmy's and smiled. My nephew's hand is finally big enough to use the glove I gave him with my name embroidered on the side. That particular glove and the others I've used through most of my professional career were given to me as a perk. But the first Wilson A2000 I ever owned was a birthday present from my parents when I was thirteen. It now holds a place of honor next to all my memorabilia.

I turned on the faucet and lathered up then looked around.

My parents weren't interested in a new house so I purchased the empty lot next door, doubling the size of their yard and convinced them to expand and renovate their house. Of course, since my dad is a contractor, he wasn't going to just let me write a check and have someone else do the work. So I spent my first official off season here with him, my brothers, and some of his crew building an addition, tearing down walls, and putting everything back together again.

The end result was definitely worth it. My mom is thrilled with her dream kitchen, my dad retreats to his man cave every chance he gets, and the new open concept is perfect for when the whole family is here. I'm not sure how much time either of them spends in the home office at this point, but it's there whenever they need it.

"Don't overdo it out there." I hadn't heard my mother come inside so I jumped at the sound of her voice.

Grabbing a paper towel off the roll, I dried my hands.

"I'm fine."

She reached in the refrigerator and pulled out a big salad and veggie tray and set them on the island.

"Just make sure you don't hurt your neck. Jimmy will play catch all day long." She grabbed a bowl of coleslaw and smiled. "Reminds me of someone else."

Of the four of us, I was the only one totally bitten by the baseball bug. And now it looks like Jimmy has been, too. My brothers all played, but weren't obsessed like me.

"The doctor said normal activity is fine," I told her. "But I promise if it starts to hurt, I'll stop." I gestured toward all the bowls littering the island. "Isn't this supposed to be your party? How did you and dad end up doing all the work?"

"The girls brought some," she said, referring to my sisters-in-law. "Besides, you know this is my idea of fun, and you know your father would never let anyone else man the grill. Especially when ribs are on the menu." She kissed my cheek and hugged me. "I'm just glad my entire family is here to celebrate."

I'd missed a lot of milestones during my playing years. And if I was still playing, I wouldn't be here this weekend to celebrate my parents' 40th anniversary. So I guess that's something positive to come out of my early retirement. That and meeting up with Barb again.

"So you haven't said much about the new job. How's it going?" my brother, Ben asked.

Despite all the sugar and caffeine they'd ingested, the kids were exhausted and my parents took them all inside a little while ago. I joined my brothers and their wives at the fire pit. I'm dying to call Barb before it gets too late, but like my mother reminded me, we're not all together that often, so I should enjoy the time with my family.

"It's okay. I'm finally getting up to speed so it's a lot easier than it was when I first started."

His twin, Alex asked, "Why'd you take that job again? If I were you, I'd hang by the pool all day."

"How's that different from what you do now?" his wife, Kelsey asked.

He reached over and tickled her, then dragged her onto his lap and kissed her with a little more tongue than I wanted to see.

She has a point. Alex is a graphic artist and works from home and often ends up sitting poolside with his laptop. Or so I've been told.

"Are you gonna be in the booth again this season?" Jamie asked.

"I don't think so," I said. "But I did get roped into attending the end of the year party."

"Why do you say it like that?" my sister-in-law, Nicola, asked. Nic and Jamie started dating sophomore year in high school and have been inseparable ever since.

I shook my head. "It just feels weird going to things like that now that I'm not playing anymore."

"Your fans still love you and want to meet you," she said.

"You sound like Hannah." I chuckled. "And like I said, she already got me to agree to go."

My phone vibrated and I grabbed it before it fell off the armrest. I smiled when I saw a return text from Barbara. I'd sent her a message a few hours ago letting her know I'd probably be tied up with the family until it was too late to call.

Sorry I'm just seeing this. Jess was over for a movie night and I didn't hear the text come in. I'll be up for a couple more hours so feel free to call.

I let her know that I would and directed my attention back to the conversation, which had thankfully shifted focus. We'd all had more than a few drinks throughout the day, so now that the kids are out of earshot, the smack talk has started.

From what I can figure out, my comment about Hannah spurred Ben to bust Alex about the fact that his wife, Kelsey, had acted like a fangirl the first time she met me. She also used to have a huge crush on Jack and was a bit tongue-tied the first few times she was in his presence. Through the years she's managed to act normal around us and any other Waves she meets, but my brothers still like to bust Alex about it.

Alex then reminded Ben of the time he peed his sleeping bag the one time we went camping. Then Ben told the tale of when Jamie spilled a whole glass of grape juice on my mom's new couch and blamed him. Of course, my mother believed Jamie because he's the oldest. He still hasn't confessed to this day, which is part of the controversy now.

I was just sitting there taking it all in when Jamie turned on me.

"And then the time perfect baby Cal threw a curveball right through the kitchen window and I got in trouble for it."

"It wouldn't have broken the window if you caught it."

"I would have caught it if you threw it to me instead of four feet to my left."

And on it went until the ladies had enough.

"You ready to go home?" Nic asked Jamie. They only live a few blocks away so they're walking.

He stood and stretched, then held out his hand to help her out of the Adirondack chair, pulling her against him in the process. "All these years later, she still can't keep her hands off me," he said.

She smacked his chest and moved away. "Behave."

"You know you love it." He wrapped his fingers around hers and pulled her in for a kiss then they said their goodbyes and were off.

"Tell mom we decided to share an Uber home," Ben said.

"Will do."

I watched my brothers and their wives walk around to the front of the house. They'd originally planned to sleep here since they'd been drinking all day, but I imagine having their kids staying here makes their own houses more conducive to sexy time.

Grabbing my phone, I found Barb's name in my contacts and hit the call button. She answered on the second ring.

"I didn't think I'd hear from you for at least another hour," she said.

"The kids and my parents crashed a while ago and the rest of the gang just left."

"Was it a good day?"

"It was. My mom was thrilled that everyone was here to celebrate. She cooked way too much and we ate it all. Right now, I'm sitting by the fire pit trying to figure out how I'm gonna pry myself out of this chair." Her laugh echoed through the phone. "How about you? Did you and Jess stay out of trouble?"

"Since I'm practically welded to the couch, you don't have to worry about me. We ate burgers and talked, then watched *Sixteen Candles*."

"Kicking it old school, huh?"

"It is a classic," she said.

I leaned my head against the back of the chair and looked up at the starry sky. "I wish you were here with me." I hadn't meant to say the words out loud, but once I did, I couldn't exactly pull them back. She didn't say anything and I let out a low groan. "Barb?"

"Yeah?"

"Did I just totally freak you out by saying that?"

"No." If I hadn't been listening so intently, I wouldn't have heard the word. Then she cleared her throat and spoke louder. "No, you didn't."

The knot in my stomach loosened and I dragged my fingers through my hair. From the first moment I saw her in that conference room five weeks ago, I knew I wanted to pick up right where we left off. I think I've been making my intentions pretty clear without being too overbearing. After all, the poor woman is trapped at home and can't hide from me.

I hadn't expected to have this conversation over the phone, if at all. I'd hoped things would just naturally progress as we spent more time together, especially once she's back on her feet.

Maybe it's because I've spent the past couple days with my brothers and their families, not to mention how much in love my parents are even after all these years. Or maybe it's just because I've kept a pretty steady buzz going all day, but right now, I need to know that we're on the same page.

"I miss you," I said. "I know it's insane because I just saw you two days ago, but still, I miss you like crazy."

I heard her take a deep breath and let it out slowly. "I miss you, too."

My heart pounded at her words and I let out a low chuckle.

"It's good to know I'm not alone in this."

I heard the smile in her voice when she said, "No, you're definitely not."

"How about if we explore it more Monday night? I'll bring pizza."

"Sounds great."

I figured I'd end the call on that positive note. "I'll see you then. Sleep tight."

Switching off my cell phone, I banged my fist against the armrest. "Yes!"

"Someone sounds happy." I jumped at the sound of my mother's voice behind me. "Sorry, I didn't mean to scare you. I didn't see you out here and came out to pour water on the fire." She sat down and placed a bucket next to her chair. "When you got here yesterday, I knew something was different."

I should have known. My mother's radar never fails.

"How?"

"You seem calmer, happier. I thought maybe it was because you settled into your new job, but I guess it's more than that." She paused for what I'm assuming was dramatic effect then said, "So who's the girl?"

I'm turning thirty-five this year, but right now I feel like I'm discussing my first middle school crush.

"Barbara Murphy."

"Oh Cal," She reached over and squeezed my hand. "Really?"

I nodded. "My very first big meeting at the bank was with the executives from Molly Mack Chocolate and she was the one giving the presentation. She's the CFO of the company."

I gave her the condensed version of what Barbara has been doing the past fifteen years. Then finished up by telling her about her fall and broken ankle, and how our dates have been limited to dinners at her house so far.

"Why didn't you mention this any of the times we spoke?"

"I'm trying not to jinx it."

"Oh honey, you two were meant for each other. I knew that the first time I met her," she said. "I should have pushed harder for her to come live with us. Maybe things would have turned out differently."

"It was great of you to offer at all," I said. "But if anything I should have done things differently."

"Like what? You'd just been handed your dream. It would have been foolish to turn it down."

"I've always wondered what would have happened if I turned down the offer and finished college. I could have helped Barb through her mother's death and if I was drafted my junior year, I'm sure I would have gotten some kind of offer after I graduated."

"You had no idea her mother was going to die when you got drafted," she pointed out. "And there's no way of knowing what would have happened if you'd waited a year."

"I know, it just sucks."

"That it does. You basically had to choose between your two loves," she said. "But you had an amazing career and now you have another chance with Barbara. Don't think about all the what-ifs and focus on the present and building a happy future."

Chapter 12

Cal

I pulled into Molly's driveway and chuckled, remembering how I'd missed the turn the first time I came here. Now the drive is like second nature. Circling around back, I pulled in next to Barb's place and cut the engine.

The weather today is perfect for driving with the top-down, so I'm cruising in the R8. I stepped out of the car and closed the door, then spotted J.P. on Barb's porch.

"Nice car," he said.

"Thanks. It was a bit of an impulse buy, but definitely worth it."

He stepped off the porch and circled the car, letting out a low whistle.

I'd felt like a cliche buying a six-figure car after my divorce, but Marsha had made the whole process so miserable, I wanted to do something to celebrate. And, I'd sent a matching check to my favorite charity so I guess it was a win-win.

Leaning down, I grabbed the boxes off the passenger seat. J.P. was still drooling over the car when I stood and took a step toward the house.

"Want to take her for a spin?" I asked, holding out the fob.

"Thanks for the offer, but I'm actually on my way out." He pointed toward Molly's house. "I'm parked over at my mom's."

"The offer stands," I said, tucking the fob into my front pocket.

"Don't think I won't take you up on that." He smiled, then turned and walked away.

I walked to Barb's front door, knocked twice, and let myself inside.

"Pizza's here," I said as I walked into the living room.

Barb looked over her shoulder, greeting me with a big smile. "Mmm, that smells delicious."

I placed my bounty on the coffee table and knelt next to the couch. Placing my hands on either side of her face, I leaned forward and placed my mouth over hers. Her soft lips felt like heaven and I feasted on her mouth, sipping and nipping and tasting, until I had to pull back so we both could breathe.

Kissing my way across her cheek, I nudged her hair back with my nose and nibbled on her earlobe. "I missed you," I said, directly into her ear before placing another quick peck on her lips.

I slowly pulled back and stood. With the way I'm feeling at the moment, it would be way too easy for things to get out of control, and I don't want that. I mean, I *want* that, and once Barb gets the all-clear for her ankle, hopefully I'll have it, but I don't want to hurt her or have to worry about a clunky brace getting in the way.

Spreading the boxes across the coffee table, I said, "We have garlic parm wings, a half meat lovers half cheese pizza, and cannoli for dessert." I picked up the small box holding the last item and said, "I'll put these in the refrigerator, unless you want to eat dessert first."

When she didn't answer, I looked up and found her eyes lazily touring my body, pausing at the obvious bulge in my dress pants.

"Barb?"

"Hmm?"

I shook the box in my hand and repeated, "I'll put these cannoli in the refrigerator unless you want to eat dessert first."

She looked at the box then slowly raised her gaze to mine and blinked, seeming to break from her daze. Smiling she said, "Your sweet tooth will have to wait. All that garlicky goodness is calling my name."

"Can't say I didn't try," I said. "What would you like to drink?"

"Water is good."

I walked into the kitchen and placed the cannoli in the refrigerator, grabbing a can of ginger ale, before closing the door. Leaning against the counter, I rolled the can against the front of my pants, hoping either the cold or the pressure would ease my aching dick. The effect kissing her had was bad enough but the look on Barb's face had nearly put me over the edge.

Taking in a deep breath, I let it out slowly, thankful to feel the pressure behind my zipper ease. I pulled two glasses from the cupboard and filled them with ice and filled one with water. Popping the tab on my soda, I emptied the can into the other. Grabbing both, I walked back into the living room and placed her water on the edge of the table next to her.

"They gave me paper plates and napkins. Does that work for you?"

"Sure."

Prying the plates apart, I asked, "Meat lovers or cheese to start?"

"Meat lovers."

The pizza was the perfect temperature for serving and I placed a slice on the plate then added four wings, some celery, and a small cup of blue cheese. I handed it to her and then filled another plate for myself. Closing the pizza box, I scooted it to the side.

"I think I'm gonna sit right here," I said and settled down cross-legged next to the coffee table.

"We could eat at the table if you want."

"This is perfect." I picked up my pizza and finished it in a few big bites. I worked through lunch so I'm starving. Reaching over, I opened the box and pulled out a cheese slice. "Need another one?"

"I haven't even started mine yet."

I glanced at her plate and was happy to see that she'd at least eaten three of her four wings and all the celery.

"But I see all your celery is gone."

"Of course, it's the best part of chicken wings."

"So I've been told."

By her, everytime we went for wing night at our favorite off-campus pub.

I refocused on my plate, needing to dampen the connection zinging between us so I don't say *fuck it* and jump her right now.

"Mmm, this is so good," she said, bringing my attention back to her a short while later. "Where's it from?"

"Antonio's. It's about a block away from my office."

"Molly, J.P. and I went there for lunch the day of the bank meeting," she said. "J.P. mentioned getting pizza, but I didn't want to eat anything that heavy so I just had a salad." She took another bite, chewed, and swallowed. "Speaking of the bank, I'm still not used to seeing you dressed like that."

I hadn't wanted to take the time to stop home to change so I'm wearing slate grey dress pants and a white button-down shirt. I'd ditched the tie and jacket right after work.

"It's still a little strange to me too. I used to wear suits on travel days and to formal team events, but that wasn't all day, every day." I grabbed a napkin and wiped the pizza grease off my fingers before starting on my wings. "Which look do you like better?"

"Your usual casual look," she said without hesitation, then added, "Don't get me wrong, I like what you're wearing, but it seems like you're playing dress up. Your personality is more laid-back."

How is it that a woman I hadn't seen in fifteen years knows me better than the woman I was married to? Marsha was always dressed like she was going to be photographed for a fashion magazine and as time went on, wanted me to do the same. I'm not opposed to putting my best foot forward, but unless I'm attending a really formal event, khakis and a polo are usually sufficient.

Marsha was so different from every woman I'd ever been involved with and I was instantly fascinated. I had loved her but can see in hindsight that we just didn't fit. She was a spoiled only child who was never totally comfortable with my family or my friends. And, despite the fact that she swore she wanted a big family, she kept putting it off for one reason or another. Chances are, if she hadn't ended things, I would have lived with her for the rest of my life in blissful ignorance, not realizing how much she kept trying to change everything about me.

I shook my head, pushing those thoughts away.

"Where did you go just now?" Barbara asked.

I crumbled the napkin and tossed it on the table.

"Nowhere important," I said. "Do you want another slice? More wings?"

She handed me her plate. "Cheese this time. No wings, but if there's more celery, I'll take some."

I felt her watching me as I filled her plate. Thinking about Marsha still takes me down a rabbit hole of emotions that I'd rather not visit. Mostly I'm angry about how abruptly she ended things, then dragged out the divorce. That thought gives me even more respect for Barb. She deals with her ex-husband every day and from what it sounds like, her divorce was worse than mine.

After handing her plate back, I picked up a chicken wing and continued eating. Maybe we'll discuss the details of our marriages eventually, but not tonight.

"So, what time is your doctor's appointment Wednesday?" I asked and took a bite of my wing.

BARBARA

I'm not sure what popped into Cal's head just now, but whatever it is, he doesn't want to talk about it. I can respect that. Sometimes I think about things I don't want to share, so I didn't push.

"Three o'clock," I said. "I really wish it was earlier. I'll go crazy waiting here all day."

"Is Jess still able to take you?"

"Yes."

"If anything happens and she can't, let me know. I can be available."

He took a long drink of ginger ale and I watched his Adam's apple bob up and down, fighting the urge to throw myself at him. Good Lord, after being dormant for years, my libido is fully awake and ready to party. I find everything about this man sexy. Yes, even the way he drinks his beloved ginger ale.

"Okay, I will. Thank you."

"So how are you feeling?" He gestured toward my ankle with his pizza crust. "You think the doctor is going to let you out of jail?"

"God, I hope so," I said. "It doesn't hurt anymore, so hopefully that's something. And I can honestly say that I've followed doctor's orders to the letter, so if I didn't heal, it's not because of something I did." I leaned forward and put my empty plate on the coffee table. "My butt is probably permanently imprinted on this cushion."

Cal stacked his plate on top of mine and stood in one fluid motion. He closed the pizza box and stacked the foil pan from the wings, our empty plates, and dirty napkins on top.

Looking down at me, he bobbed his eyebrows and said in a singsong voice, "It's cannoli time."

On his best day, the man has more of a sweet tooth than a woman with a bad case of PMS munchies. He was back at my side in record time holding the bakery box full of mini cannoli open to me. I picked one and he handed me a napkin before setting the box down on the coffee table.

I was surprised when he didn't take one himself, then understood when he stood at the other end of the couch. He wanted to sit there like he had last time he was here. I don't have a problem with that.

Smiling, I shifted back and he gently lifted my legs and slid underneath. But before he settled in, he grabbed a napkin and three cannoli.

"So what's the first thing you want to do when you're on your feet again?" he asked, then ate the first cannoli in two bites.

"Take a long, hot bath, and I may follow it up with a long, hot shower."

Cal took a bite of the second cannoli and looked at me as he slowly chewed, his normal chocolate-brown eyes dark. With the sparks that have been flying between us lately, I probably shouldn't have mentioned taking a shower or bath, but I didn't say it to be sexy or get him to picture me naked. It's the truth.

I haven't had a decent soak or shower since the accident. Even though I wrap my brace in a big plastic bag and tape the top closed, I still stick my leg out of the tub and take the fastest showers known to man. Besides the fact I'm worried about the bag leaking, my leg sweats inside it and the brace gets all swampy.

I rolled my eyes. "Sorry about that. You were probably expecting me to say something like go for a walk or take a yoga class, or maybe stand up for hours on end." I met his gaze, which was more amused than hot at this point and said, "I didn't mean..." I trailed off, not sure of what to say.

Cal finished his third cannoli then said, "I know you didn't mean anything by what you said." He flashed a sexy smirk, wiggled his eyebrows, and added, "But I still enjoyed the visual it offered."

"Calvin!" I pushed him with my good leg. He grabbed my foot and propped it back on his thigh and rubbed this thumb along the arch.

"After you take a long bath followed by an even longer shower, what would you like to do?"

"Just all the normal things everyone takes for granted. Cook for myself, clean the house, wash my own clothes. And it'll be nice to get back to work and actually use my brain again."

"I'm just wondering, if you get the all-clear on Wednessday, would you be interested in going out on a real date with me Friday night?"

"A real date?" He nodded and continued rubbing my foot, and I had to fight the urge to moan. "Like dinner and a movie?"

"As long as you say yes, we can do whatever you like."

"Then I say yes."

He smiled, flashing his elusive dimples. "Does six-thirty work for you?"

"Absolutely."

"Great. I'll pick you up at six-thirty. "Anything special you'd like to do?"

"Nope." I shook my head. "Surprise me."

"Will do." Shifting his back against the arm of the couch, he wrapped both hands around my foot and rotated his thumbs against the arch. "Now, assuming everything goes well Friday night, I was wondering if you're free Sunday."

"I am."

"The Waves have an off day and my friend Dan invited me over. My best friends will be there and I'd like you to meet them."

My eyes rounded and I swallowed. "Are you sure?"

"I'm positive," he said without hesitation. "Besides introducing you to the pool house I used to call home." Shifting toward me, he took my hand in his, wove our fingers together, and squeezed. "They're important to me and so are you, so I think you should meet."

How can I say no to that?

Chapter 13

Barb

When I checked in, I was told the doctor had an emergency this morning and is running behind. I thought I'd be out in the waiting room longer, but twenty minutes after I arrived, I was called back. The nurse directed me into a freezing cold room and introduced me to the radiologist who removed my brace and took X-rays of both my ankles. When we were done, I hobbled on my crutches, following the nurse through the narrow hallway, until we reached the exam room where Jess waited for me.

The nurse took my crutches and helped me onto the table, then told me that Dr. Foley would be in shortly and left, closing the door behind her. I looked down at my bare right leg for the first time in six weeks. My skin is dry and flaky and the hair on my leg hasn't been this long since I started shaving more than two decades ago.

"It's gonna be fine, Barb." Jess leaned against the sink, her arms crossed over her chest. "Dr. Foley will come in here and tell you everything is perfectly healed. You'll see."

"I hope so," I said. "But on another note, do you see this leg? I'm gonna need a weed wacker to remove all the hair."

Jess took the two steps that brought her to my side and whistled.

She ran her hand up and down my shin. "That's pretty impressive. You'll have to start hacking away at it when you get home so you're all smooth for your date Friday night." Her eyes shifted from my toes to my fingers, then stared pointedly at my crotch before meeting my gaze. "I'm going to text Sheri and see if she can fit you in when we leave here. If all the stars align, you'll be able to get a trim, a mani/pedi, and a wax. Of all those, I'll make waxing a priority, because I'm assuming things are not date-ready down there."

She pulled her cell phone out of her back pocket and texted her friend who owns a salon and spa in the same building as Jess's yoga studio. A return text came in almost immediately, but before she could tell me what it said, I heard two quick knocks on the door and Dr. Foley entered carrying an iPad.

"Barbara," he said, closing the door behind him. He placed the tablet on the counter and walked to the sink. "How are you?"

"I think you can answer that better than me," I said around a nervous chuckle.

Jess had moved out of his way and now stood just behind me. She put her hand on my shoulder and squeezed, offering silent support. Dr. Foley washed his hands and turned to face me while he dried them.

"I'll show you in a minute." He crumbled up the paper towel, stepped on the pedal to open the trash can, and threw it away. "I want to take a look first."

Cupping my heel with one hand, he wrapped the other around the ball of my foot and lifted it off the table. He moved it slowly back and forth and then from side to side. I swallowed my mortification when he slid his hand down my foot and up my ankle to my shin. Then I mentally shrugged. I'm sure mine isn't the first hairy leg he's ever touched.

"Does any of this hurt?"

He continued to manipulate and squeeze my ankle, his movements getting slightly more aggressive as he went on.

"It doesn't hurt, it just feels stiff."

Gently placing my foot back on the table, he stepped back and washed his hands again. Picking up the iPad, he leaned against the counter and used the stylus to write. Then he tapped the screen a few times, and seeming satisfied with whatever he'd brought up, he walked to the side of the table and held it out so I could see.

"This is your X-ray when I first saw you six weeks ago." He used his thumb and forefinger to zoom the screen. "You fractured your ankle here and here," he said, pointing to the spots in question.

My stomach twisted as I looked at the evidence of my broken bones. I practiced my yoga breathing to combat the nausea.

"If you remember, your fall caused a shaft fracture of the tibia and fibula, more commonly referred to as a tib-fib fracture. I know wearing that brace for over a month was no fun, but it was our best shot at avoiding surgery which would require an even longer recovery period."

Best shot? Does that mean our efforts were successful or not? Before I could ask that question, he answered it.

Shifting the screen in his direction, he flipped through a couple images then turned it so I could see again.

"These are today's X-rays." He looked at me and smiled. "You must have been very good because your bones have healed perfectly."

I felt a little lightheaded as he spoke the words I've been waiting to hear and I realized that I was holding my breath. I let out a relieved sigh and smiled. Jess wrapped her arm around my shoulders and gave me a quick side hug.

"Really?"

"Really. I want you to wear an air cast for another few weeks, and you're in for six to eight months of physical therapy to build up your strength and flexibility." Using the stylus, he tapped at the screen as he spoke. "I want to see you for a recheck in a month. You can set up an appointment on your way out. You can also pick up your PT slip when you check out. There are excellent therapists in the group downstairs, but you can go wherever you'd like for that. Any questions?"

"Can I do yoga?"

After sitting on the couch for a month and a half, I'm dying to stretch out. The foam roller Cal gave me has helped my back, but I really need to limber up again.

"Take it easy for the next week or two. Remember, you haven't had any weight on that leg in six weeks. It's going to take some time," he said. "Your physical therapist can help you determine when you're ready to get back to your normal activities."

"Anything else I need to know or be worried about?"

"Just wear the air cast and take it slow. If something hurts, don't do it."

"What about a pedicure?" Jess asked, with a smile in her voice.

"A pedicure is just what the doctor ordered," he said and shook my hand. "Sheila will be back in with your aircast and you'll be good to go. I'll see you in a month."

CAL

I sat back and rubbed my eyes. If I have to analyze one more spreadsheet, they may fall out of my head. It's been a long-ass day and I'm both mentally and physically exhausted...probably more the former than the latter.

Leaning forward, I rested my elbows on the desk and dragged my fingers through my hair then rubbed the back of my neck. When I took this job, I didn't realize how much work would be involved. I mean, I didn't expect to do nothing, but whenever I finish one project, there are four more to take its place. And I just started a few months ago. I can't help but wonder if it will get better or worse as time goes on.

Welcome to rat race, I guess.

Grabbing my mouse, I'd just clicked the next file on my to-do list when my cell phone rang. Looking at the caller ID, I felt the first real smile of the day spread across my face.

"Hey you," I said. "I hope you're calling with good news."

"I am," Barb said.

"Yes! I'm so happy for you."

"I have to wear an air cast for a few weeks and do physical therapy for at least six months, but the brace is off, thank God."

"So what are you girls doing to celebrate?"

"Jess is taking me for a mani/pedi then we're going to grab dinner."

"Sounds like fun."

I heard Jess yelling something in the background, but couldn't make out her words. Barbara must have put her hand over the phone because her voice sounded muffled.

"Everything okay?"

"Fine," she said as Jess's laugh echoed through the phone.

"Then enjoy your mani/pedi. I'll see you Friday."

"I'm looking forward to it."

"Me too."

CLIMBING OUT OF THE POOL, I DRIED OFF ENOUGH SO I WOULDN'T DRIP all over the house. The swim had helped burn off excess energy and loosen my muscles. After being glued to my desk most of the day, my neck had felt like concrete, causing things to tighten up everywhere else.

I walked through the patio doors and made my way to my bedroom, stripping off my board shorts as I entered the en suite bath. Turning the shower knob all the way to the left, I waited for the hot water to steam up the bathroom before stepping in.

Some of the best money I spent when I bought this house was on remodeling the master bath. Multiple jets pulsed down on my neck and shoulders, loosening them even more, and helping to ease the headache that had lingered all day.

I turned the water off, grabbed a towel, and wrapped it around my waist. I'm starving, but feel too tired to eat. All I'd have to do is go heat up the leftover Chinese in the refrigerator, but even that seems like it will take too much effort.

Instead I dried off, threw on some boxer briefs, and tossed the towel toward the bathroom where it landed with a satisfying splat. Climbing between the sheets, I tucked a second pillow behind my head and reached for the remote. My phone buzzed just as I clicked on the end of the Waves game.

Barbara: I'm sure you won't be able to sleep without knowing. I went with Kiss Me on My Tulips polish. It was between that and No Room for the Blues, but the pink won out.

Barb's text was accompanied by a picture of her freshly manicured fingers and toes.

Instead of texting back, I called her on FaceTime.

"Those toes are looking very nice," I said when, within three rings, her beautiful face filled my screen. "And I really like the name of the color."

"I think the name may be what convinced me to choose it."

She looked down and tucked her hair behind her ear, a small smile on her face. I couldn't help my own smile at the familiar gesture. It's a sure sign that she's either embarrassed or nervous. She never would have even made the nail polish comment a few weeks ago, so we're definitely moving forward.

"Did you cut your hair, too?" I asked before the silence got too uncomfortable.

"Just a trim."

"It looks really nice," I said. "So where'd you end up going to eat?"

"Jilly's. It's seafood night, so I ate way too much," she said. "How about you?"

I told her about my less-than-impressive night and she commiserated with my seemingly never-ending workload.

"I'm too tired to eat, so I'm just gonna watch the end of the Waves game and get to sleep early. Chances are, tomorrow will be just as exhausting. I have a bunch of work to get done plus I'm having lunch with Mr. Butler and some of his friends that's guaranteed to last at least two hours."

"Everybody wants to meet the new guy."

"I guess." I shrugged. "But chances are, it's going to be more like a

Waves meet-and-greet than a bank thing." She opened her mouth, then closed it again and stared at me. "What?"

She blinked and shook her head. "I just forget that you're kind of a big deal."

I laughed out loud at her words. She's so adorable, not to mention real.

"I'm serious," she said. "I just think of you as my Cal, but the rest of the population collects your baseball cards and wants your autograph."

"Just *your* Cal, huh? I like that." I watched her face turn red, but before she could overthink what she said or take the words back, I continued. "But be prepared to be hounded by paparazzi Friday night."

Her laugh echoed through the phone.

"I'll be sure to wear big sunglasses and practice putting my hand out to block the cameras." My answering chuckle turned into a yawn. "I'll let you get to sleep."

As much as I want to keep talking, my exhaustion is really catching up with me and I don't want to keep yawning on her.

"I'll see you Friday," I said. "And Barb, I'm really looking forward to it."

"Me too."

Chapter 14

Barb

I checked myself in the full-length mirror for the hundredth time. I'm not exactly sure what we're doing and the turquoise maxi dress is chic enough to pass in most restaurants, yet has a relaxed vibe in case he's planned something casual. And the best thing is that the wide straps allow me to wear a bra. With my DDs, letting the girls hang loose is not an option.

The air cast limited my choice of footwear, but I found a pair of flats that are both functional and fashionable. Thankfully my hem is long enough that only the tips of the shoes show.

I even splurged on a matching bra and panty set just a shade lighter than the dress. So I'm waxed and wearing fancy underwear just in case things go that far.

Looking back up at my face, I saw the blush that last thought had caused. While sex is all I can think of lately, and it's been way too long, the idea that it may actually happen tonight fills my stomach with butterflies. I'm not sure if they're from nerves or excitement and before I could obsess too much about that, I heard a car door slam. After checking my makeup one last time, I grabbed my purse and heard Cal's knock just as I left the bedroom.

I pulled open the door to find him looking sexy as hell in crisp khaki pants and a navy button-down shirt.

"Hi," I said.

"Hi." The bouquet of yellow and white daisies he held made a rattling noise when he leaned down and gave me a quick kiss. He pulled back and said, "These are for you."

I took the flowers from him and smiled.

"Come on in while I put them in water."

He followed me inside and took a seat at the breakfast bar while I retrieved a vase from a top cabinet.

"It's nice to see you vertical again," he said. "How's it feeling?"

"Still a little stiff." I turned on the water and placed the vase underneath. "But thankfully it doesn't hurt anymore."

I unwrapped the flowers and saw the source of the rattling. Cal had tucked a box of Hot Tamales into the bouquet. I looked up at him and smiled.

"Thank you."

He rested his elbows against the counter and leaned forward, watching me place the daisies in the vase.

"I had something totally different in mind when I walked into the florist today, but when I got there, I couldn't stop looking at those daisies. They looked so cheerful and just kept calling to me. So I told the woman at the counter that I had a date tonight with a very special lady and asked her thoughts on buying that bouquet for you."

I finished arranging the flowers in question and stepped back to admire my work.

"Well obviously she approved."

"Kind of. She told me they have many meanings, but that in Norse mythology, the daisy is Freya's sacred flower." He looked at me and raised his brow. "Apparently Freya is the goddess of blessings, love, lust, and fertility." Flashing a playful smirk, he added, "That seemed kind of heavy for our first official outing and while I didn't think you'd be fluent in flowers, I decided I'd go with one of the other arrangements I'd been admiring just in case. But then she added that aside from symbolizing those four things, daisies are also a sign of a new beginning." His smile widened, putting his dimples on full display. "It was a no-brainer after I heard that."

My heart pounded as I collected the vase and walked over to put it in the center of the table.

"They do look cheerful," I said and turned around, finding Cal right behind me. "Thank you again. For the daisies and the Hot Tamales. They're both perfect."

Resting my hand on his shoulder, I leaned in and gave him a quick kiss. As I stepped back, Cal wrapped his hand around my waist and pulled me in for something a little longer, a lot deeper, and with way more tongue. Not that I'm complaining.

He slowly ended the kiss and rested his forehead against mine.

"Did I mention how beautiful you look?" I peeked up at him through my lashes and shook my head. "Well you do and I can't wait to take you out and show you off."

CAL WAITED UNTIL I CLICKED MY SEATBELT IN PLACE BEFORE EASING down the driveway. He turned right onto the main road and we were off. *We Will Rock You* by Queen had been on the radio when he started the car, and as we drove along it transitioned into *We Are the Champions.*

I settled into the low-slung seat, remembering the last time I'd ridden anywhere with Cal. We were in the 4Runner he'd bought with his signing bonus. The next day, he'd left to join his team. Shortly after that, my mother died and life as I knew it was over.

"You okay?" he asked.

"Yeah, why?"

"Your breathing changed."

"My breathing?"

"Yeah, you seemed all relaxed and then you took in a sharp breath and started breathing a little faster."

I was married to Stewart for a decade and he was never so tuned into me.

"I was just thinking about the last time I was in a car with you. It was that grey 4Runner you bought after you got drafted," I said. "That was a lot different from this."

"Yeah, this is definitely different." He let out a short chuckle. "I got the 4Runner because it was comfortable for long drives and could hold all my gear. This was more of a post-divorce, pissed-at-the-world purchase." Flashing me a quick smile, he added, "But it is fun to drive."

"I bought a car after my divorce, too."

"That little Volkswagen?"

"Yeah. I wanted an Eos for a while, but when I was married, Stewart insisted I drive a BMW. So when we divorced, I went out and bought one and I love it."

Cal nodded at my words but didn't say anything else. I've been looking forward to tonight and don't want to ruin it with talk of our marriages, divorces, or our break up. So I relaxed and enjoyed the low hum of the radio.

We drove a little further before he broke the silence.

"You know, we've been driving for twenty minutes, and you still haven't asked where we're going."

I shifted slightly toward him and crossed my right leg over the left.

"That's because I don't care where we're going."

"No?"

He gave me a quick glance and turned his attention back to the road. As usual, traffic is heavy for a Friday night and, other than a few quick peeks in my direction, he's kept his eyes trained straight ahead.

Looking down, I straightened a crease in the material of my dress and said, "Nope. As long as I'm with you I know I'll have a great time, whatever we do."

I'd expected a quick response and when it didn't come, I looked over and watched his Adam's apple bob up and down as he swallowed. Reaching over, he took my hand and raised it to his lips, then kissed my knuckles. Lacing his fingers with mine, he rested our joined hands on the center console.

After clearing his throat, he said, "You were always so under-standing when I didn't have money to take you out. And you never made me feel like crap when we ended up eating boxed mac and cheese in front of the TV instead of going out for dinner and a movie."

"Cal, I never felt like our relationship was lacking in any way," I said. "Even looking back, I still think it was perfect." The light ahead turned red and he turned his head to look at me. "I'm not just saying that to make you feel better, it's true."

He leaned forward and gave me a quick kiss.

"You're so amazing."

The light changed to green and we continued on our way. And since he mentioned it, I asked, "So where *are* we going?"

"We have a date with Dean Martin."

CAL

Two adorable lines formed between her brows as she looked at me like I'm crazy, but then she smiled.

"Sounds like fun."

Having been influenced by her mother, Barbara is a big fan of Dean. In fact, she enjoys all the old crooners. I'd originally planned dinner at a nice restaurant, but when I heard about this Rat Pack dinner show we're going to, I knew it would be perfect. And it's being hosted by the local cultural center to raise funds for renovations to the venue, a former Masonic Temple. So not only do I get to spend an enjoyable evening with Barbara, I'm also supporting the arts.

We drove a few more miles in comfortable silence before I turned into the parking lot and found a spot. While spotlights illuminate the building, there aren't any signs announcing the event, so Barb still doesn't know what we're doing.

I looked over at her. "Ready?"

"Absolutely."

Exiting the car, I jogged around to the passenger side, opened the door, and held out my hand to help her out. We walked the short distance toward the building and, with her foot on the first step, Barbara stopped and looked up the stairs.

"Are you okay to walk up?"

She nodded and kept looking ahead. "I'm just looking at this building. It's amazing." Glancing at me out of the corner of her eye, she added, "And you're not carrying me."

I wrapped my arm around her waist and kissed the top of her head. "I was thinking more along the lines of finding another entrance, but I like your idea better."

We slowly walked up the stone steps toward the main entrance which boasts four imposing columns. When we reached the top, I opened the heavy wooden door and stepped aside so Barbara could enter ahead of me. The doors on the other side of the vestibule stood propped open and we were greeted as we walked through.

"Are you here for the Rat Pack or the Johnson-Findlay wedding?" the woman with a cloud of silver hair asked.

"The Rat Pack," I said.

She pointed to the left. "Gothic Hall is in that direction on the right. An usher will show you to your seats as you enter."

"Thank you," I said.

Barb smiled up at me as we walked through the large foyer. "The Rat Pack?"

"I told you we had a date with Dean Martin. I just didn't mention a couple of his friends were coming along."

She looked around at the architecture, pointing out small details.

"This building is amazing, isn't it?" She nodded. "From what I understand, they occasionally host building tours. Maybe we can sign up for the next one?"

"I'd like that."

We walked through the doors of Gothic Hall and were greeted by two young men dressed identical in black pants, white button-down shirts, and black bow ties.

"Tickets," the one with blond hair said. I reached into my back pocket and handed him our tickets. He looked down at them then said, "This way."

We walked through the large room, weaving our way through tables that ranged in size to accommodate different-sized groups. I had paid extra for an intimate table for two right in front of the stage. I pulled out a chair for Barbara and when she was settled, I sat directly across from her. Once the show starts, I'll move next to her so my back isn't to the stage, but this will be good for dinner.

"Your waiter will be over to take your drink order." The usher looked up at us for the first time. His eyes rounded. "Cal," he said before dramatically closing his mouth. "I mean, Mr. Chase. Oh wow. It's so great to meet you."

I shook his hand and smiled. "It's Cal, and it's great to meet you, too."

"You're my favorite player. I was so bummed when you got hurt." He looked at my neck, squinting as though he had X-ray vision. "But you're okay now?"

"Good enough to live, just not to play."

"That sucks."

It was obvious he wanted to hang out and chat, but besides the fact that I'm on a date, he's supposed to be working. Time to wrap this up.

"What's your name?"

"Alex. Alex Parker."

"Thank you for saying hello, Alex. It's always nice to meet a fan."

"Could I get a picture with you? None of my friends will believe this."

He pulled out his phone from his back pocket.

"Sure."

He bent so our heads were in line and held up his phone. Our faces appeared on the screen and froze in place as he touched the white circle with his thumb.

"Thank you so much." He looked around the room then added, "I'll send your waiter over right away."

"I appreciate it."

I turned my attention to Barb and found her watching me with a small smile on her face.

"What?"

"You are so sweet." She leaned forward and gave me a kiss on the cheek. Pulling back she said around a smug smirk, "And like I said, you're kind of a big deal."

Before I could comment, our waiter approached. The guy is probably around my dad's age and introduced himself as Andrew.

"Would you like something from the bar?" he asked Barb.

"What kind of beer do you have?" He offered a pretty decent list. "I'll have a Summer Shandy and a glass of water."

"And for you, sir?"

"I'll have the same."

As he walked away, I glanced around the room and wasn't surprised to find it mostly full. Dinner service starts in fifteen minutes and when I bought my tickets last week, it was nearly sold out.

"This room is so beautiful," Barb said. "And it's huge, but still feels cozy."

The lights had been dimmed in the walnut-paneled room giving it a warm glow. And even though the arched ceiling is at least twenty feet above us, the candles that adorn every table seem to reflect off the gold stars embellishing the blue paint, making them appear to twinkle.

Andrew returned with our drinks and said, "The appetizers will be out shortly. Is there anything else you need at the moment?"

We told him there wasn't and he left to check on his other patrons. I scooted my chair a little closer to Barb. Not only do I like being near her, it also puts me more in profile to the room behind us, so there's less chance I'll be recognized. Not that I think I'm "kind of a big deal" but people who follow baseball can usually pick me out in a crowd. Especially Waves fans.

As if she read my thoughts, Barbara asked, "So can you go anywhere without being recognized?"

"At any Waves event people always know who I am, but all other times, it's hit or miss."

"You seem to handle it well."

"Mr. Hanover, the owner of the Waves, is very community focused, which pretty much means that anyone on the team is, too. Players are expected to regularly interact with fans as well as visit hospitals, nursing homes, and things like that. So, I've had a lot of practice."

"Don't sell yourself short, Mr. Chase. You're a very kind, genuine person and that comes through." She tipped her glass in my direction to punctuate her words, then took a drink.

Before I could figure out what to say to that, Andrew approached with our appetizers. He set a serving of shrimp cocktail in front of each of us, and was off again. I took the break in conversation as a chance to change the subject.

"So what are your plans now that you're back on your feet?"

"My first plan is to avoid falling again," she said around a laugh. "I head back to the office on Monday, so my days will be back to semi-normal."

"Are you looking forward to getting back to work?"

She nodded and picked up a piece of shrimp then dipped it into the cocktail sauce. "I do enjoy my job and sitting around doing nothing all day gets old after a while. Being off work wouldn't have been too bad if I could have done things, but that wasn't possible." Taking a bite of the shrimp, she chewed, swallowed, then added, "I'm very lucky to have people like you in my life who kept me company, made sure I had food, and anything else I needed. Thank you so much for all you did for me these past few weeks, Cal. I'm sure you had better things to do than babysit me."

As corny as it sounds, I knew I wanted to spend the rest of my life with Barbara the day I met her back in college. Eventually I worked up the nerve to ask her out and we became inseparable. Now that I've found her again, I feel the same as I did all those years ago.

"Spending time with you isn't exactly a hardship. Now that you're back on your feet, I hope we'll be able to do more together. "

Even in the dim light, I saw the blush spread across her cheeks. But instead of shying away, she looked me in the eye and offered a small smile.

"I'd like that."

THREE HOURS LATER, AFTER A GOOD MEAL AND EVEN BETTER SHOW, WE took a slow walk back to the car. We'd taken our time leaving to avoid the rush of the crowd, but I still held on to Barbara to make sure she didn't get jostled.

"That show was amazing. The performers were so realistic," she said. "I felt like it was 1960 and we were in Vegas."

Without missing a step, I squeezed her closer and kissed her cheek.

"I'm glad you enjoyed it."

The show was really good, but my favorite part was watching Barbara's reactions. When she wasn't laughing or singing along, she had a huge smile on her face.

We reached the car and I opened her door and held her hand as she settled into the passenger seat. A man jogged over from the next row as I walked around the back of the car. Thankfully he just wanted to say hello and shake my hand. No autograph. No picture. No long-winded conversation.

Barbara greeted me with a big smile as I got behind the wheel.

"What?"

"Nothing." She shook her head and laughed. As I started the car, I heard her mumble, "Kind of a big deal."

Leaning over the console, I tickled her waist, making her laugh even harder. I stopped, but kept my hand on her waist, stroking my thumb along the silky material of her dress. She looked up at me and let out a short sigh as her laughter faded.

We just sat there frozen, staring into each other's eyes until I couldn't stop myself from kissing her. Skimming my hand along her waist, up her arm, and over her shoulder, I slid it along her jaw, tilted her head slightly, and put my mouth on hers. It didn't start off soft or hesitant. From the moment our lips met, I devoured her, pouring all my feelings into the kiss.

Barbara wrapped her arms around my neck and twisted her fingers into my hair. Our mouths opened and closed, our tongues thrusting and exploring and I pulled her closer, practically dragging her into my lap. Adding a degree of suction to the kiss, I was about to move my hand to touch the nipple poking against my chest when I heard voices. Reluctantly I slowed the pace of the kiss and eased my hold on her so she fell back into her own seat.

Taking in a deep breath, I let it out on a chuckle.

"Sorry about that," I said. "I didn't mean to attack you in the car outside the venue."

She licked her lips and smiled. "You don't ever have to apologize for a kiss like that."

I shifted in my seat and clicked my seatbelt into place before I was tempted to kiss her again. Starting the car, I cracked the windows open to clear the fog our antics had caused.

"Can we put the top down?" Barbara asked.

"Sure," I said. "As long as you don't mind."

"I would have suggested it on the way here, but wanted my hair to look semi-decent for tonight." She pulled her hair into a ponytail and held it in place until she retrieved an elastic from her purse to secure it. "There's nothing like riding around with the top down, especially on a beautiful night like this."

I pushed the button to drop the top and open the windows.

Barbara leaned her head back and looked up at the starry sky. I just looked at her.

"It's still early, did you want to stop and get a drink somewhere?"

She didn't answer immediately and I wondered if she heard me. I was about to repeat the question when she turned her head to look at me.

"You've spent a lot of time at my place but I haven't seen yours yet."

"You want to go to my house?" She nodded. "I think I can manage that."

My house is actually closer than hers, which is both good and bad. It means I'll get her alone faster, but it also gives me less time to calm the erection that's trying to push its way through the material of my pants.

Chapter 15

Barbara

Cal turned at a yellow mailbox and the tires crunched on the stone driveway as we drove toward the house. One of the two garage doors opened and we pulled inside. I looked around and unbuckled my seatbelt. A workbench took up the entire far wall with a pegboard behind it holding a variety of hand tools. A bicycle hung on one wall and a kayak and surfboard rested up in the rafters.

I hadn't taken in all my surroundings when my door opened and Cal held his hand out. I took it and stepped out of the car and he closed the door behind me then held onto my hand as he led me across the garage toward a door.

We passed a grey SUV in the other stall and I did a double-take. With our hands still joined, our arms stretched out between us when I stopped walking. He turned and looked at me as our hands slipped apart.

"Something wrong?"

"Is this—" Without finishing the question, I took a few steps to the left and glanced down the passenger side. Pointing at the vehicle, I continued, "Is this the same 4Runner?" He walked toward me and nodded. I looked from him to the SUV and back again. "I can't believe you still have this."

"It's the first thing I bought when I got signed." He shrugged "Every time I went to get rid of it, I just couldn't. So I'd buy something else with the intention of parking the 4Runner to give it a well-deserved rest. But that never really happened. I drive it the majority of the time."

"It must have a million miles by now."

"Not quite. Just short of a half-million."

"Wow." I walked around the vehicle, still amazed he didn't get rid of it years ago. Aside from a couple small dings and a few scratches, it's in great shape. He obviously takes good care of it.

After indulging my curiosity and letting me look my fill at the 4Runner, Cal took my hand again and ushered me through the door. We walked up a short flight of stairs and into a large living area.

"This is the rec room or man cave," he said. "Whatever you want to call it."

A brown leather sectional and two recliners surrounded a huge TV that hung on the side wall. A pool table separated that from the small kitchenette in the corner. A gym area was set up on the other side of the room toward the windows at the front and a pinball machine and two full-size arcade games stood across from that.

"Laundry room is through here and those are guest rooms." We peeked in one door then the other two before he led me up another flight of stairs. At the top, we walked into a large, open-concept living room and kitchen area. "There's another guest room there, that's my home office, and the master bedroom is over there." He pointed to the two doors on the left and a single door was on the right side of the room.

"Cal, this house is amazing."

The white walls and soft lighting gave the room a homey feel. Adding to that were all the family photos scattered throughout. I walked over to a side table and admired the pictures in mismatched frames. He just watched me for a few heartbeats then came up behind me and offered names to the children in the pictures. On the mantle over the stone fireplace, he had some candid shots of him and his brothers and parents, as well as posed photos from his brothers' weddings.

"Why don't I grab us something to drink and I'll show you the best part?" he asked more than said.

"Sounds good."

He walked to the kitchen and opened the refrigerator. "I have beer, wine, sweet tea, or water."

"I'll have water."

I only had one beer with dinner and another won't get me drunk, but if we're going to get physical, I want to be totally clear-headed.

He walked around the island carrying two glasses and handed one to me. "Come on." Smiling, he led me to the wall of windows, which turned out to be large patio doors that opened onto a deck overlooking the ocean. A set of stairs off to the left led down to another deck and an inground pool.

Leaning my elbows against the railing, I watched the moonlight ripple off the ocean's surface and listened to the hypnotizing sound of the waves crashing against the shore. Cal set his glass on the railing and stepped behind me, his arms encircling my waist. I put my glass down next to his, then leaned back against him, resting my head on his shoulder.

I'm not sure how long we stood like that, listening to the sounds of the night. A gust of wind kicked up making my dress swirl around my legs. I shivered as the soft material settled back into place.

"Getting cold?" Cal asked, his warm breath against my ear making me shiver again.

I shook my head. "I just got a chill from that wind."

He rubbed his hands up and down my arms, his warmth chasing away the goosebumps.

"Better?" he asked.

"Much."

He wrapped his arms over mine and pulled me closer against him, engulfing me in his warmth. Things with Cal had always been so comfortable and easy. I never felt like I had to fill the silence with needless chatter or act a certain way to make him happy. And all these years later, it's just the same.

Turning within the circle of his arms, I wrapped my hands around his waist and looked up into his eyes.

"When you walked into that boardroom six weeks ago, I wanted to run away," I said. "So much so that I broke my ankle in the process," I added around a nervous chuckle. "But I'm glad you did. I'm so happy to have you back in my life."

He leaned closer and ever so slowly, raised his left hand and caressed my jaw.

"And I'm very happy to be here," he said.

I let out a breath I wasn't aware I'd been holding and leaned into his touch, dropping my gaze to his mouth.

"Barb."

The whispered word brought my eyes back to his. His normal milk chocolate depths

looked almost black and reflected all my emotions back at me. It's nice to know I'm not in this alone.

He lowered his head a fraction, but stopped and searched my gaze once again as he tunneled his long fingers through my hair. Exerting a hint of pressure, he tipped my head slightly back and to the right. My eyes grew heavy and I gave up the fight and closed them completely a second before I felt Cal's lips against mine. They brushed once, twice, then a third time before settling into a full-fledged kiss that, while on the chaste side, felt amazingly erotic.

He applied just the right amount of pressure and a delightful degree of suction. His right hand moved under my arm and around my waist, before settling at the small of my back, pulling me closer to him. My breasts flattened against his chest, my erect nipples dying for his touch. I moved, brushing them back and forth, trying to ease the ache.

Cal's hand moved from the small of my back and inched its way up my ribs. I pulled back, making room between our bodies. He accepted my invitation and cupped my breast, gently at first, almost hesitantly. His thumb grazed my nipple, and I couldn't contain the moan or the shiver that ran through my body. My heart pounded and I lost myself in the sensations.

He slowly pulled back and I found myself staring into brown eyes full of passion and promise. I shivered again at both that thought and the ministrations of his hand.

"You used to have the most sensitive nipples." He rolled the hardened nub between his thumb and forefinger sending a jolt to my long-neglected lady parts. I squeezed my thighs together to ease the ache. His low chuckle sounded like a sexy promise. "Seems like they still are."

Lowering his head, he sipped and nipped at my bottom lip before opening his mouth over mine again. This kiss felt hungrier and a bit more out of control. I curled my fingers into his scalp and matched the rhythm of his mouth.

Cal moved his hands down and cupped my ass, squeezing possessively, pulling me onto my tiptoes and flush against him. His erection pressed into my abdomen and I shifted myself higher to get closer. He thrust against me twice, then groaned and pulled his mouth from mine and took in a deep breath.

My heels clicked against the deck as he removed his hands from my bottom. A mere inch separated us, but I still missed his heat. He placed his hands on either side of my face, his thumbs softly stroking my cheeks.

"Let's head inside," he said.

I nodded and he took my hand and kissed it before leading me through the patio doors and into the house. Instead of taking me to the bedroom like I thought he'd do, he walked to the couch and gestured for me to sit.

He sat beside me and rested his elbows on his knees then stared straight ahead.

"This is why I didn't want to put my hands on you before your ankle was fully healed. I knew things would get out of control, and I didn't want to hurt you. But now that you're okay and we're at this point, I want to discuss a few things before anything else happens." He finally looked at me. "Barb, I want you. And I don't just mean that

I want to fuck you. I. Want. You," he said slowly, enunciating every word.

My heart pounded as he stood and dragged his fingers through his hair as he paced in front of me.

"In a perfect world, we never would have broken up all those years ago. I guess everything happens for a reason. Maybe we just weren't ready for each other or..." He stopped and faced me again then shrugged. "I don't know. I don't know why we didn't stay together back then." He sat next to me again and took my hand in his. "I'm not into casual relationships or one night stands. I never have been." He opened his mouth to say something else, then closed it and flashed an adorable smile. "I'm sorry I'm babbling here. All I want to say is now that you're back in my life, I want you to stay here. But I need to know that's what you want too. Because I'm all in here. And if we do this, if we end up in that bedroom, as far as I'm concerned, you're mine. I just need to know that you're in as deep as I am."

I blinked until his image wasn't blurry anymore. How is it that I'm so lucky that this man, this perfect man, has entered my life twice? I was young and stupid and lost him once. I'm not going to make that mistake again.

Scooting closer to him, I placed my hand on his cheek, smiled, and said, "Which way is the bedroom again?"

CAL

Once Barbara asked that question, I didn't waste time leading her to my room. She looked around, checking out the space as much as she could in the dim light. In the morning, I'll let her look her fill and tell her about how I'd combined two smaller rooms to make a big master suite. But right now, I just want to touch her and taste her. I can't wait another second. I've waited forever already.

I stepped closer to her until we stood toe to toe. Twisting her pretty hands together, she stared at my chest, looking unexpectedly shy. Placing my hands on her shoulders, I squeezed then rubbed my thumbs against her collarbone.

"Hey, you okay?"

She looked up at me, her blue eyes wide.

"I want to do this. Trust me, more than anything I want to do this with you. I'm just a little nervous," she said, then licked her lips and added, "It's been a long time."

Skimming my hands down her arms, I took her hands in mine and kissed one then the other.

"It's been a long time for me, too," I said around a small smile. "But I hear it's like riding a bike." She rolled her eyes and chuckled. "But seriously, we'll take it slow and if you want to stop, just say the word and we'll stop. Okay?"

"Okay."

"Come here."

I tugged her hand and placed it on my waist. She wrapped it around until it rested against the small of my back. Sliding my hand across her jaw, I curled my fingers through silky hair and cupped the back of her head.

Keeping my eyes on hers, I lowered my head until our mouths touched. Her lips are slightly swollen from our make-out session on the deck and I enjoyed the feel of their plump softness and slowly pressed our mouths together. She wrapped her other arm around my waist and pulled me closer, rubbing her delectable body against mine. I bit down on her lower lip and tugged, drawing her gaze up to mine.

Resting my forehead against hers, I took in a deep breath then let it out on a low chuckle.

"You're killing me."

I kissed her temple then moved down her cheek to her ear and sucked at the lobe before nibbling just behind it. That had always been one of Barbara's sweet spots and it seems that's still the case. She moaned low in her throat and dragged her hands up my back, then twisted her fingers into my hair.

I nipped and licked, enjoying her taste, scent, and sexy sounds. I worked my way down her neck and across her collarbone and sucked at the pulse beating against the base of her throat.

Her knees bumped against my shins and she gripped my hair tighter, pulling my head back. I looked into her beautiful blue eyes, shining with desire. Any nervousness she felt seemed to be gone.

Squeezing my arms around her waist, I pulled her off her feet until she rested flush against me. I opened my mouth over hers, our teeth clashing as she met my tongue thrust for thrust. Holding her in place with one arm, I cupped her ass with my other hand and pulled her hips forward against my raging erection.

Breaking the kiss, she dragged in a deep breath, saying my name on a long groan as she let it out.

I took two steps forward and set her down at the side of the bed. Keeping my gaze locked on hers, I reached behind her and slowly lowered the zipper of her dress. She swallowed as I moved my hands forward, taking her dress with them. When I let go, the material pooled around her feet, leaving her standing in nothing but a bra and panty set the same color as the dress.

"You're perfect." The words slipped out, but the fact that I didn't mean to say them out loud doesn't make them any less true.

Taking her mouth in another deep kiss, I unhooked her bra and slowly edged the straps along her arms, savoring the feel of her soft skin. We parted just long enough for me to remove it and toss it to the floor. Her bare breasts brushed against my shirt as I kissed her again, her hard nipples poking against the material. I couldn't wait to feel them against my bare chest.

As if she read my mind, Barb shifted her hands between our bodies and unbuttoned my shirt then dragged it off my shoulders. I groaned deep in my chest as I felt her plump breasts against me, skin on skin, for the first time in fifteen years.

Ending the kiss, I looked down into her dazed blue eyes and backed away just far enough to fit my hands between us. Placing them against her breasts, I looked down and watched, mesmerized, as I squeezed and molded them to my palm before moving my thumbs in circles around her nipples. Barbara closed her eyes and groaned, arching toward me, begging for more.

I bent my head, placing my mouth directly over her nipple, licking and sucking it into an even tighter peak before moving to the other and giving it the same treatment. Barb fought to get closer, hiking her leg over my thigh, her hips beating a steady rhythm against my rock-hard dick. I wasn't lying when I told her it's been a while for me and I knew if I didn't stop her from doing that, I'd seriously embarrass myself.

Letting her nipple go with a soft pop, I stood straight and admired my handiwork before urging her to sit on the bed. She watched as I removed my shirt and tossed it on top of her discarded dress. I unbuttoned my pants, slowly lowered the zipper, and let them fall to the floor then stepped out and kicked them onto the pile. My boxer briefs did nothing to hide my erection and Barb's eyes widened when she caught sight of it. She licked her lips and leaned forward slightly, but I couldn't let her touch me or God forbid put her mouth on me. This would be over before it began.

Kneeling in front of her, I placed my hands on her waist, urging her to lie back. Once she rested against the soft grey comforter, I slipped my index fingers into the waistband of her panties and slowly dragged them down her long legs, dropping them on the growing pile.

I stood and wrapped my hands around her waist, pushing her back further on the bed so her legs no longer hung over the side. Resting my knee between her thighs, I urged them further apart and kissed my way up her leg and nipped her soft, sweet skin from one hipbone to the other. She let out a low groan as I licked my way back toward her navel then continued down toward the perfectly trimmed brown hair acting as a landing strip to heaven.

Next time I'll tease her and draw things out, but I think right now, we both need this to be fast. And I know that when I get inside her, I won't last long so I want to make her come at least once before that happens.

Lowering my head, I breathed in her sweet scent before dragging the flat of my tongue up the seam of her pussy, flicking my tongue against her clit before doing it again then again. Barb bent her leg, placing her left foot against the bed and shifted the one with the aircast to the side, opening her up to me even more.

Sliding one finger inside her, I groaned then added another. Barb squirmed beneath me as she made the sexiest sounds I've ever heard.

"You're so fucking wet," I murmured, pulling back slightly as I pumped in and out, just enjoying the feel of her.

"Cal."

She panted my name over and over and dug her fingers into my scalp holding me in place. Her internal muscles kept tightening against my fingers so I knew she was close. Time to tip her over the edge. Curling my fingers forward inside her, I stroked then fastened my lips over her clit and sucked hard.

Barb let out a loud squeal a second before her pussy clamped down on my fingers. I stroked and licked her until the flutters stopped and she released her death grip on my hair. Slowly removing my fingers, I looked up the expanse of her body taking pride in her small sated smile. I crawled up between her thighs, and placed a small kiss on her lips. She opened her eyes and blinked me into focus.

"Hey," I said.

"Hey." Her smile widened.

"You feeling okay?"

She let out a sexy chuckle. "Oh yeah."

I nipped at her collarbone. "I meant your ankle."

"That's okay, too."

She shifted her leg and the velcro from the aircast brushed against my calf. The slight change in position must have made her more aware of the erection peeking out of the waistband of my boxer briefs because she thrust up against me.

"Are you gonna keep him all to yourself?"

I chuckled at her question. *This* is my Barb. Sweet, sexy, funny, and mischievous. The shy, self-doubting woman I met at that bank meeting is nowhere in sight.

"I'm not confident he'll behave himself."

"You won't know unless you give him a chance."

Shifting backward off the bed, I stood and retrieved a condom from my nightstand drawer. Throwing the foil packet beside her head, I removed my boxer briefs, allowing my dick to spring free. Kneeling between her thighs, Barb watched me, eyes wide, as it bobbed forward.

"Barb?" She nibbled on her bottom lip and met my gaze. "Having second thoughts?"

"No," she said, her voice hoarse. Clearing her throat, she repeated the word, stronger this time. "You're just—" She stopped, her gaze shifting from my erection then back up to look me in the eye. I raised my brow, urging her to continue. "I just forgot that you're really big."

I've spent a lot of time in locker rooms with naked guys and I know I'm a little better than average, but wouldn't call myself *really big*. But if Barb wants to, I certainly won't stop her.

Reaching down, she wrapped her fist around me and slowly stroked. I ground my teeth together and let her play as long as I could stand it. Which wasn't nearly long enough. Even with a condom, I know that once I get inside her tight, wet pussy, it's going to be over faster than I'd like. But I want to make this good for her. I may have to mentally recite baseball stats like I used to do back in college.

I peeled her fingers off me and kissed her palm then released her hand and grabbed the foil packet. Ripping it open, I pulled out the condom and rolled it down my length.

"Ready?"

"God yes."

My chuckle ended on a low moan as I positioned myself between her thighs and pushed forward slowly, not stopping until I filled her completely. I held myself still, resting my weight on my elbows. Her inner muscles rippled as she adjusted to me being there. I forced back the orgasm begging to be released and searched my memory bank for stats.

Meeting her gaze, I stared into her blue eyes and saw the same want, need, and memories she could probably see in mine. I nibbled at her bottom lip then lightly bit it and pulled. As I let go and opened my mouth over hers, I started to move, slowly out then in. Her tight, wet heat welcomed me with each thrust and gripped me tight every time I retreated, as if trying to hold me in place.

I kept the pace slow as long as I could. In and out. In and out. In and out. But it was impossible to keep it that way. It's been too long and she feels too fucking good. Speeding up, I thrust deeper, harder, grinding myself against her clit with every plunge.

Barbara muttered my name along with little nonsense words, urging me to move faster. She wrapped her leg around my waist, pulling me closer as her fingers squeezed my biceps and held on.

I'd just finished reciting the statistics of Baltimore's 1983 AL Pennant team when I drew a blank. No more numbers came to mind...hell no more baseball teams came to mind...and I knew I couldn't hold on much longer.

"Barb..." I panted, not losing my rhythm. "Barb, I can't...I'm gonna...*fuck*."

I held on just a few seconds longer, just enough time to feel Barb explode around me. Her soft sounds seemed to echo in the room as I growled her name and came with a final hard thrust.

Chapter 16

Barbara

When Cal tried to pull back, I wrapped my arms around his shoulders, holding him close.

"I'm crushing you," he said around a chuckle.

"Don't move just yet. This feels too good."

He settled his weight back against me, his cheek resting on my shoulder. I felt his warm breath on my neck, the puffs of air more spaced out as his heartbeat slowed. I dragged my fingertips up and down the back of his head, enjoying the silky feel of his hair.

"Why do you cut your hair so short?" I asked.

"It's just easier. I don't have to get it cut as often or worry about putting stuff in it to keep it under control." He kissed the side of my neck and added, "Plus my hat fit better with it short."

"I used to love running my fingers through your curls."

"Hmm, I remember." I continued stroking his hair, the short strands tickling against my palm. "You could probably convince me to let it grow if you promise to do that regularly."

"I promise."

I kissed the top of his head and snuck a peek at Cal's face. His soft, contented smile melted my heart. Closing my eyes, I continued to trail my fingers through his hair and enjoy the moment.

We stayed like that for I don't know how long and I didn't want to move, but my legs started to tingle. I shifted slightly, trying to restore their circulation.

"I must be hurting you." Cal kissed my shoulder and rose up onto his elbows.

"You're not, but my legs are falling asleep."

"Let me go take care of this and then we can get a little more comfortable."

He reached down and held the condom in place as he pulled out of me. I missed his warmth when he shifted away, but enjoyed the view as he walked to the bathroom. Someone should sculpt his ass and put it in a museum. I tried not to stare as he walked back toward me, but wasn't very successful. I would have felt bad about ogling him, but his eyes devoured me, too.

I shifted to my knees in the middle of the bed as he approached. It's been a long time since I've been naked in front of anyone and felt a little self-conscious as his gaze took a slow tour of my body. Staring down at the comforter, I tucked my hair behind my ear.

Cal rested his knee on the bed and circled his hands around my waist, pulling me toward him.

"You are so beautiful." He placed gentle kisses on my forehead and the tip of my nose then my mouth. "And I'm so happy you're here. I've missed you."

I blinked up at him and saw the sincerity in his eyes. Even back in college, I never had to wonder what Cal was thinking or feeling. He never played games or tried to play it cool...he'd tell me or show me. At the time, I didn't realize that was a rare trait. But after hearing dating horror stories from friends and my experience with Stewart, I know that it is, and I appreciate it even more now.

During my marriage, I slowly retreated into myself. At first everything was fine, but as the years went on, Stewart had a way of picking at everything I said or tucking little tidbits away to use against me later. The sad part is, I didn't even realize it was happening. But, things are always clearer in hindsight.

I mentally shook myself. This is Cal, not Stewart. And he deserves the same open honesty he gives.

"I've missed you, too." He gave me a full smile. I reached up and brushed my thumb across his cheek. "I love these dimples."

Cal kissed me again then shifted back and stood at the side of the bed.

"What side do you sleep on?" he asked.

It took a second for his question to process. I'm not sure what I thought he'd say, but that definitely wasn't it.

"Um, I really don't have a side." His brow rose in question. "About a year after my divorce, I was still sleeping on the right side of the bed. One night, I was watching a talk show and some counselor was talking about how to move forward when your marriage breaks up. She suggested changing your habits, including which side of the bed you sleep on, and even recommended 'claiming' the whole thing and sleeping in the middle. Because why not? So that's what I did."

"Seriously?" he asked.

I tucked a strand of hair behind my ear then shrugged. "I know it sounds bizarre, but it helped."

"It doesn't sound bizarre at all," he said. "In fact, I saw that show...or at least that counselor...and did the same thing. And you're right, it did help."

He reached down and flipped the comforter back then picked me up and placed me down in the middle of the bed just below the pillows. Crawling in next to me, he wrapped his arm around my shoulder and we slowly slid into place under the covers. I rested my head against his chest, wrapping my arm around his waist.

In my thirty-four years, I've only been with three men. My high school boyfriend, Joe, Cal, and Stewart. Joe and I had a few fumbling encounters in his old Chevy Blazer and afterward, he'd take me home. When Stewart and I started getting physical, the sex itself was fine but afterward I felt self-conscious. I was never sure what to do or how to act, and while I can't blame that totally on him, it should have raised a red flag. Especially after what I had experienced with Cal. I always felt comfortable with him and there was never anything awkward about the before, during, or after of our sex life.

I snuggled closer to Cal, resting my cheek between his shoulder and neck. The spot had always felt custom-made for me and still does, even though he's bigger and more muscular now.

"Do you have any plans for tomorrow?"

"No." Time for more honesty. "I figured that tonight and meeting your friends Sunday would be enough excitement after being cooped up for weeks." I both heard and felt the vibration of his chuckle. "Did you have something in mind?"

"I thought maybe we could hang out here, maybe swim, be lazy on the beach."

"I'd love that." I tilted my head back to look at him and added, "But I don't have any clothes or a swimsuit."

His wicked grin got my heart pounding again.

"Maybe we'll just stay inside then."

CAL

We lay still side-by-side and Barb's breathing became slower and quieter. After making love for the third time, this is how we ended up, facing each other, our legs entwined. Without disturbing her, I reached behind me and pulled a tissue from the box on the night-stand and disposed of the condom.

I'll have to make it a point to have a conversation about contraception with her sooner rather than later. Barb said she hasn't been with anyone in a long time and neither have I. With any potential health risk eliminated, I'm hoping she's taking some form of birth control so we can forego the condoms sometime soon.

Barb wrapped her arm further around my waist.

"Mmm."

There was an abundance of satisfaction in that little sound and I couldn't help the smug grin that crossed my face. Snuggling my head further into the pillow, I studied her every feature. She looked peaceful in a way she hadn't in the past six weeks. And while I'm sure the orgasms have something to do with that, I hope they're not the only reason.

When Barb broke up with me, I tried to get her to change her mind, but finally gave up when it was obvious she wasn't going to. She wanted me but not the baseball lifestyle, and looking back, I understand that now better than I did back then. Everyone handles grief differently, and she dealt with hers by nesting in place.

Once I knew I didn't have a chance of getting her back, I moved on and didn't look back. I put all my energy into working out and honing my skills. So in a way, I owe my career and every award I ever won to her. Without that single-minded focus, I may not have ended up where I did.

Baseball was never just a game to me, it's my passion and I loved playing more than anything else. The fact that I can't play anymore has left a gaping hole. I miss it. Every second of every day.

I played those last thoughts in my head as I watched her sleep. My mother always says that everything happens for a reason and for the first time, I'm thinking she might be right. Because no matter how much I loved Barb, I probably wouldn't have been able to be what she needed and be successful professionally. Hell, I hadn't been able to do it years later with Marsha.

Reaching up, I caressed her cheek and watched her lips curve into a small smile. Her eyes slowly opened and she blinked a few times before finally focusing on me. She frowned at first then her smile widened.

"I was afraid I was dreaming and you weren't real," she said, her voice hoarse.

"Nope, I'm real."

"Good."

She snuggled closer and kissed my chest before resting her head against my shoulder.

And for the first time since I was forced to retire, I felt like I could truly be happy again.

Chapter 17

Barbara

The mouth-watering scents of bacon and coffee pulled me from a sound sleep. Rolling onto my back, I stretched, wincing as my overworked muscles protested the movement. Then again, I guess they're more underused than overworked. Hopefully once I get to exercise them regularly again, they won't be as sore.

I sat up and shifted my legs over the side of the bed and looked around for my discarded dress. Our clothes had ended up in a pile on the floor last night but they were now nowhere in sight. Before I could search the room to find something to wear, I really needed to pee.

I made my way to the bathroom and was happy to find a robe hanging on the back of the door. It would have to do. Remembering his comment last night, I chuckled.

Maybe we'll just stay inside then.

I'd have no problem hanging out naked with him all day.

After I washed my hands and face, I squirted toothpaste onto my index finger and cleaned my teeth the best I could. The thought of sharing a toothbrush freaks me out and I don't want to go rummaging through his cabinets to see if he has a spare. Rinsing out my mouth, I was happy it at least felt clean. I finger-combed my hair then stared at my reflection in the mirror.

Besides some beard burn on my stomach and breasts, I don't look any different even though I feel like I should. It's like when I lost my virginity, I thought everyone would be able to look at me and just know. I feel so different inside, it seems logical that it would somehow show.

I looked back at my face and shrugged. It doesn't matter if it shows or not, I feel different. I feel happy.

Slipping into Cal's robe, I raised the collar up to my nose and inhaled. His clean scent assaulted my senses and I thought about curling up in bed and just breathing him in. But why do that when the man himself is somewhere outside the room waiting for me?

I walked out of the bedroom and found Cal in the kitchen. His loose shorts hung low on his hips and I just stared, watching his back muscles ripple as he flipped something on the stove. I must have made a noise because he lifted his head and looked back at me.

"Good morning," he said around a big smile.

I looked from his dimples down his chest to those sexy cuts in his hips then back up to his eyes.

"Good morning," I said. "Can I help with anything?"

"Nope, I'm almost done here." He turned back toward the stove. "I wasn't sure how you take your coffee or I would have had it ready for you."

I took a seat at the breakfast bar and watched him work. The man is gorgeous, sexy as hell, and cooks. Plus he's a nice guy, not to mention amazing in bed. Talk about a mythical creature. He's my own personal unicorn.

He glanced back at me and said, "So?"

"So what?"

"How do you take your coffee so I know for future reference?"

"Oh uh, usually just cream and a half a spoon of sugar."

"Only a half a spoon?"

I chuckled. "And how much sugar do you take, Mr. Sweet Tooth?"

"Depends on the coffee, but I do like it hot and sweet." He

waggled his eyebrows at me. "That's probably why I like you so much."

He opened the stove and pulled out a sheet pan of bacon.

"Why don't you go get settled at the table on the deck? I'll be out with breakfast in a minute."

Yep, definitely a unicorn.

I FINISHED EVERYTHING ON MY PLATE AND HAD TO FIGHT THE URGE TO lick it clean.

"That is the best French toast I ever ate," I said. "And the bacon was perfect."

"I've found that cooking bacon in the oven has a better outcome than on the stove." Cal held up a piece to punctuate his words, then shoved it into his mouth and chewed. "Besides the fact I don't get burned to hell with popping grease."

We sat at a table in the corner of the deck, a large yellow umbrella shading us from the sun. A few people walked along the beach, but it was otherwise deserted. I asked Cal if it's always this quiet.

"There are more people in the summer and on holidays, but it's not crowded like you're probably thinking. This is a private beach, so it never gets really crazy."

"It's so nice here and your house is amazing. How long have you lived here?"

"About two years. I bought it after my divorce."

He pushed his plate away and picked up his mug of coffee, finishing it in one long gulp. It's obvious he's not comfortable discussing his divorce, but we have to do it sometime. Which is exactly what I said.

He shrugged. "I just don't want to spoil any of our time together talking about old news."

"I understand that, but I don't think that will happen. If anything, it will help us get to know each other again. We were apart for a long time. Obviously things happened during those years...marriages, divorces, all-star careers." Those last words earned me a smile. "I'd like to know how you got to be such a big deal."

Plus I'll admit I'm curious about his ex-wife. I'm sure I could Google whatever I want to know about him and his divorce. The Waves are all over the news here all the time. I just studiously avoided it for years. But besides the fact I don't totally trust the media to tell the whole truth, it seems like an invasion of his privacy and I'd rather hear the facts from him.

"Well, as far as my career goes, you know I got drafted by San Diego after my junior year and moved to Texas." I nodded. "I started in Rookie ball and ended up in Low A by the end of the season. I was invited to play fall ball that year and started the next season off in High A. In the middle of that second season, I was part of a multi-level trade deal with Arizona and ended up playing Double A in Oregon. I finished out that season and played my whole third year there." He stopped and smiled. "Had enough yet?"

"No, this is all fascinating," I said. "I feel like I should take notes."

Honestly, I always loved listening to Cal talk about baseball. He really loves the game and it shows. When we were together before, we'd spend hours talking about possibilities and wishes. Now I'm hearing what really happened. It's just a shame I wasn't there to see it all myself. Before I could mentally kick myself too much, he continued.

"My fourth season, I was fortunate enough to get traded into the Waves organization so I started off that year playing in Florida. My parents were thrilled I was finally on the East Coast."

"It must have killed them not being able to be at every game."

"It did," he agreed. "It bothered me, too. I was so used to them being there, at least most of the time. They did manage to make some games, but traveling was always tough in the summer because of my dad's business."

As someone who grew up with just my mom, I'd loved Cal's loud, close-knit family. And thankfully, they'd welcomed me with open arms from the day I met them. In fact, his mom had asked me to move in after my mom died. I shook that thought away, too.

We're moving forward here. There's no time for what-could-have-beens.

"So how'd you finally get here?"

"The Triple A third baseman needed Tommy John surgery mid-season so they called me up to Fayetteville," he said. "I had a great season and so did the team. We made it to the World Series, and even though we ended up losing, it was an amazing experience. And I must have caught someone's eye because they invited me to spring training the following year."

"So you played for the Waves your whole major league career?" He nodded. "Isn't that unusual nowadays? Don't players usually hop from team to team looking for a bigger contract?"

I stopped following all things baseball after I broke up with Cal, but Stewart followed all the sports so he could at least talk the talk with whoever he was trying to impress. So through the years I picked up on fun facts like that.

"It is more common for players to have a few teams under their belts by the time they retire, but I was happy with the Waves and we always managed to come to contract terms. So why look elsewhere? And the funny thing is that my three best friends have only played for the Waves, too."

I saw pain flash in his eyes but then he blinked and it was gone. Getting hurt and having to retire must have been excruciating for him. Plus his divorce happened around that time, too. I'm amazed he's still so sweet after being dealt that shitty hand. But that's a conversation for another time.

"Those are the friends I'll be meeting tomorrow?"

"Yep. Dan, Jack, and Dale aka Monte." I frowned and he added, "His name is Dale Montgomery, but we all call him Monte. However, Sabrina, Hannah, and Lexi always call him Dale."

"Sabrina is Dan's wife, right?" I've heard him mention her before.

He nodded. "And Lexi is his daughter. She's ten, and they have a little boy named Gavin, who's turning two soon. Hannah is Jack's fiancé, but she also works for the Waves in the public relations department."

I'll admit, I'm equal parts nervous and excited about meeting his friends. Breaking into an established group is never an easy thing and these guys are obviously tight.

My concern must have shown on my face because Cal said, "Relax, they're gonna love you."

"I hope so, because I'm not going anywhere," I said around a nervous chuckle.

"That's good to hear." He stood and stacked our plates. "Come on, I'll give you the full tour."

CAL

Barbara stood in the middle of my office, looking around at the various photos, trophies, and memorabilia. I don't want to be one of those "glory days" guys, but this stuff is all part of me and I needed to put it all somewhere. This seemed like a good compromise. It's not hiding in a storage container somewhere, but it's in a room that not many people go in. And I only have the important stuff displayed, the rest is in the closet.

"You have *three* gold gloves?" That was obviously a rhetorical question because she didn't wait for an answer before moving onto the next thing. "Is that Derek Jeter?" She practically touched her nose to the picture hanging on the wall of me and the legendary shortstop.

"I thought you didn't follow baseball."

She looked at me, rolled her eyes, and said, "Like you need to follow baseball to know who Derek Jeter is."

Can't argue with that.

"Let me know when you're done ogling Jeter so I can show you the rest of the house."

Barb looked at the picture in question for another few seconds then gave me a smug smile, turned on her heel, and walked dramatically out the room. I followed her out and pointed to the view of the ocean.

"There was one picture window there and a regular door over

there that led onto a small deck," I said, pointing to the spots I was referring to. "But the view is so amazing, I wanted to see it from the whole room. Using patio doors gave easy access to the bigger deck I built and I can leave them open to let in the ocean breeze."

"How long did it take you to do all this?"

"It took about a year to finish everything, but thankfully the major construction was done before I moved in so I didn't have to deal with it twenty-four-seven."

I took her hand and led her to my bedroom.

"This was originally two bedrooms, but I combined them to make a master suite." I pointed to the spot where the dividing wall had been. "That was one room and this was a larger room with a decent-sized closet. The bathroom had originally opened up into the living room, but I blocked that door, took half the closet to expand and made it an en suite. I also added the large windows and of course the blackout curtains so I'm not up at the crack of dawn everyday."

I picked up the remote and pushed the button to open the curtains so she could see the view.

"Cal, this house is wonderful. The views are amazing, but the house itself is so cozy and welcoming."

Circling my hands around her waist, I asked, "You really like it?"

"I really do."

"Good, because I hope you'll be spending a lot of time here."

I leaned down and kissed her, intending on it being just a small peck, but of course, it turned into more than that. Slipping my tongue past her lips, I thrust it against hers over and over, tilting her head back and opening my mouth wider to taste more of her. She's so sweet. Even sweeter than the lingering maple syrup I'd tasted when our mouths first touched.

Slipping my hands between us, I untied the belt of her robe. *My* robe. And as adorable as she looks in it, I know she looks even better out of it. I slid it off her shoulders and let it fall to the floor.

I walked her backwards to the bed then got another idea. Ending the kiss, I pulled back just enough to look her in the eye.

"Want to take a shower?"

She bit her lip and nodded. "Sure."

I reached into the nightstand and grabbed a condom then led her to the bathroom. Kicking off my shorts and boxer briefs, I opened the shower door and turned the knob to get water flowing through all the jets. Then I leaned down and removed Barb's aircast.

"After you."

I held her hand as she stepped inside then followed her and closed the door behind me. After placing the condom on the built-in shelf, I grabbed the soap, and rubbed it between my hands to create a lather.

Barbara watched me with wide blue eyes, probably having the same memory as me. We'd done this once before back in college, but it was in a regular shower with a single spray, so only one of us could be under the water at a time. I had been torn between letting her stay warm and avoiding shrinkage. So we alternated who stood under the showerhead. That's definitely not an issue in this shower.

I placed the soap back on its shelf and stood behind Barb. Reaching around, I cupped her breasts with my soapy hands and proceeded to alternately knead and shape them, then pluck her nipples between my thumb and forefinger.

Her moans echoed off the shower walls as she leaned back against me. I stroked the underside of her breast, ending each one by twisting her nipples, while licking and nibbling the parts of her neck the new position had allowed me to access. Her hips started to move in rhythm with my hands, rubbing her glorious ass against my erection.

Pulling out of my grasp, Barb turned in my arms and dropped to her knees. A ragged moan escaped me as she wrapped her lips around my dick and alternately sucked and rolled her tongue around the head like it was her favorite lollipop. She wrapped her hand around the base of my shaft and leaned forward, pulling me into her warm mouth inch by inch.

I dug my fingers into her hair and watched her lick, suck, and stroke me until I couldn't take it anymore.

"Barb." My voice came out as a low croak, so I said her name again. Instead of stopping, she looked up at me with those big blue eyes. "Barb, if you don't stop, I'm gonna come."

I swear she squinted and I *know* she reached up and cupped my balls, and slowly rolled them in her hand then lightly tugged. Tightening my fingers in her hair, I braced myself. She seemed like she was on a mission and I was losing the will to stop it.

Her head bobbed faster and faster as she increased the rhythm. I was barely holding on when she moved her hand from my shaft and, without her fist as a barrier, pulled me to the back of her throat. Then finally lost it and let myself go.

"Fuck! Barb!" I groaned as she swallowed and continued to gently lap at me until I released my grip on her head, backed up, and collapsed onto the built-in bench.

I took in deep gulps of air, trying to get my breathing back under normal. When I finally opened my eyes, I found Barbara watching me with a satisfied grin. Still on her knees with the steam surrounding her, she looked like a sexy nymph.

When I was confident my legs would hold me, I stood and held out my hand to help Barbara to her feet. Pulling her flush against me, I growled, "That was fucking amazing."

Then I kissed her the way I wanted to fuck her. Deep, hot, and hungry. Like I'd never get enough. And she kissed me back. She opened immediately, her tongue meeting mine stroke for stroke.

I backed her up against the wall and dragged my mouth from hers to her neck, along the curve of her breast and to her nipple that was just begging for attention. Her needy little noises got louder as I tongued one hard nub then the other, moving back and forth in a frenzied rhythm.

Her hips thrust against mine and I was happy when I felt my dick stir to life again. I was afraid she'd sucked him into a coma.

She dragged her hands down my back and squeezed my ass. I pulled back before she got any ideas of grabbing my front, too. Even though I'd just had a mind-blowing orgasm, I feel another one coming on fast. Time to take care of my girl.

Reaching down, I slid my finger through her wet folds and let out a low groan.

"You feel so fucking good."

She's so hot and wet, and it's not from the water, that's for sure.

I slipped one finger inside her slick heat and pumped in and out, loving the feel of her tightening around me. When I added a second finger, she shifted down the wall and tilted her hips slightly, giving me better access. I dipped my head, and caught her nipple between my teeth and nibbled before alternately sucking and laving with my tongue. Her panting got louder, eventually matching the rhythm of my fingers moving in and out of her.

"Cal...Cal..."

She has a way of chanting my name in the sexiest voice I've ever heard when she's close.

I lifted my head and looked into her heavy-lidded eyes. They started to drift closed but opened wide when I brushed my thumb against her clit.

"Eyes on me," I said. "I want to watch you come."

I continued to finger fuck her and when I rubbed my thumb against her clit again, she shattered. My fingers were still inside her when her orgasm ended, our eyes still locked on each other. She blinked and let out a small sigh as her lips curled into a smile. I'll take that as a positive sign. But we're not done yet.

She groaned as I pulled my fingers out of her and reached for the condom, then watched as I tore it open, and rolled it down my now-throbbing erection. I ran my hands down her sides to her thighs and lifted her.

"Wrap your legs around me."

She quickly complied and wrapped her arms around my neck to hold herself in place. I pushed her against the wall and slid inside. She's so swollen and hot, I searched my mind for suitable stats, but realized I wouldn't need them when I felt tiny ripples around the tip of my dick. Hopefully it won't take much to turn them into full-blown waves.

I thrust into her soft and hard, shallow and deep, tilting her hips to adjust the angle until I found one she *really* liked. Making sure to keep that position, I moved in and out of her, increasing the pace until she squeezed her legs tighter around my waist and her inner walls clamped down over and over, pulling me over the edge with her.

"IS IT WEIRD WATCHING THESE GAMES NOW?" BARBARA ASKED.

We planned on hanging out by the pool, but when my cell calendar chimed and I told her it signaled that the Waves were playing, she wanted to watch the game instead.

"Yeah. A little." Her raised brow said she didn't believe that one bit. "Okay, a lot. The thing is, I feel fine most of the time. And like I told that usher last night, I'm good to live, just not to play." I glanced at the TV and watched Nicky Rios strike out the batter for the third out of the inning. "Do you want another drink?" I nodded toward her empty glass, figuring a commercial break is the perfect time to get a refill and maybe change the subject.

"I'll get it," she said. "You've waited on me enough these past six weeks."

She handed me the platter of nachos we'd been snacking on and stood. I watched her walk to the small kitchen and fill our glasses with sweet tea. As much as I would have loved to have her sit here naked all day, after our shower, she'd asked for her clothes. Instead I gave her one of my T-shirts and a pair of shorts to wear. Knowing she's commando is driving me crazy. But I have to behave. I know she's sore after that last time. She winced more than once while drying off.

"What's that smile for?" she asked when she returned and set our glasses on the table.

"I like the way you look in my clothes." I flashed a wicked smile. "I also like the way you look out of my clothes."

Rolling her eyes, she reached for a nacho. "I'm just happy the shorts fit. Your hips are so lean and mine are...not." She took a bite of the nacho, punctuating that last word.

"Your hips are perfect. So is the rest of you." I let my eyes take a lazy tour from the tips of her toes to the top of her head before meeting her eyes again. "I swear, if you were alive in the fifties, you would have given Marilyn Monroe a run for her money."

Barbara bit her lip and gave me a shy smile. I put my arm around her and pulled her closer, placing the nachos between us. She rested her head on my shoulder and we watched the game. Sometimes in silence, sometimes with me telling her silly stories about my ex-team-mates, and sometimes yelling at the TV as if we could change the outcome of what was happening.

"So your friends will finish this game and fly home from Texas then want to have a party tomorrow?"

"It's not really a party," I said. "Dan will throw something on the grill and we'll just hang out."

She pulled back and looked at me with wide eyes.

"I never even asked what I can bring."

"Relax, I've got you covered. We'll grab a few things from my favorite coffee shop. The brownies I brought last time were a big hit, especially with Lexi." I smiled at her. "Her sweet tooth rivals mine."

"I find that hard to believe."

"You'll see."

We snuggled up and turned our attention to the game again, watching the Waves beat Texas by two runs.

"At least the guys won't be whining about a loss tomorrow," I said, grabbing the remote, switching to a Seinfeld rerun. I hate listening to the commentators nitpicking every detail of the game, not to mention the reporters asking stupid-ass questions.

"Speaking of tomorrow. I need to go home at some point to get dressed. I think the dress I wore yesterday is too formal and I don't think your clothes will work."

"Hmm, that's debatable, but if you insist, we can stop by your place before heading to Dan's." I gave her a quick kiss. "Maybe you can shower here so all you have to do is get dressed there."

"Maybe," she said around a sexy smile.

That obviously got me thinking about the shower we'd just shared and decided there's no time like the present to have the birth control conversation.

I shifted sideways so I faced her.

"There's something I wanted to talk to you about."

"What's that?" She shifted too, mirroring my position.

"Are you on birth control?"

"Oh," Obviously she hadn't been expecting that question. "No, I'm not." She blinked. "I could get some, I guess. I..." she trailed off and shook her head.

I don't want to pressure her into anything and told her so.

"I'm the one who said we needed to talk about these things," she said with a sheepish grin. Taking in a deep breath, she let it out slowly. "I went off the pill back when I was married because Stewart and I planned on having a family. But it just never happened. Once we divorced, I wasn't seeing anyone, so I didn't see a reason to go back on it."

The questions running through my head must have shown on my face.

"We both got tested and according to a doctor and two specialists, there was nothing wrong with either of us. So we tried fertility treatments, but again, it just didn't happen." She looked down at her lap. "I was researching IVF when I found out about Frances." Meeting my gaze again, she added, "Thank God I found out before I started anything like that."

"Would he have agreed to do it?"

"Probably." She shrugged. "The affair was going on over a year before I found out and we were doing fertility treatments then. I'm not sure what would have happened if I didn't find out and ask for a divorce. He was obviously content to have his cake and eat it too."

Maybe it's none of my business but I had to ask.

"Do he and Frances have children?"

"No," she said. "And I obviously don't know their personal business, but I do know that when we got divorced, he said they planned on it."

"Why do I think you just sugarcoated what was really said?"

She laughed at that, lightening the mood a little.

"He really said that he was happy to be ridding himself of a woman so pathetic, she couldn't even do the one thing she was put on the Earth to do. And he said Frances was a real woman and he knew they wouldn't have any issues."

I clenched my jaw at her words. That motherfucker better hope I never get him alone because I swear, I'll pound him into the ground. I was still working on controlling my breathing when Barb climbed into my lap and rested her head on my chest.

"Don't waste your energy on Stewart. He's not worth it." Then in the next breath she said, "I'll make an appointment with my gynecologist and see what she suggests."

"There's no rush. I just figured I'd ask just in case. Since neither of us have been sexually active for a while, diseases aren't an issue, just pregnancy. We can use condoms, but—"

She looked up at me. "But what?"

"I'd love to feel you skin on skin again."

Her eyes darkened. "I'll call for an appointment Monday."

Chapter 18

Barbara

I looked around the well-kept interior of the 4Runner, feeling like I'd stepped into a time warp. He'd planned on driving the R8, but I asked to take this instead. Cal had bought it right after he got drafted and while we'd broken up a few short months later, we still managed to make a lot of memories in it. We'd taken road trips and spent a lot of time just driving around enjoying each other's company before he had to leave to join his team.

He turned into the driveway and pulled in front of the pool house. Cal walked around the SUV to open my door so I could get out. I grabbed the bag holding my dress and stepped down.

"Barbara. Cal."

I looked over and saw Molly walking in our direction. Glancing over her head, I spotted Stewart, Frances, and Bill Robinson sitting at a table beside the pool.

I'm never overly thrilled to see Stewart but am even less so dressed in Cal's clothes in an obvious walk of shame. Not that I'm ashamed of spending the weekend with Cal, nor is it any of Stewart's business. But he tends to use whatever's available to make people feel inferior and I try to avoid handing him ammunition.

"We're having brunch. Why don't you join us?"

Molly didn't even try to dim the smile that spread across her face or the delighted look she shifted between Cal and me. I concentrated on not letting the dread thoughts of sitting with Stewart and Frances made me feel show, but mustn't have been very successful.

"I invited Bill over and Stewart and Frances just popped in. I'm sure the addition of you two would lighten the atmosphere a bit," she said.

"Oh, thank you for the invite, but we actually have plans," I said. "We just stopped by so I can change."

She looked at my borrowed outfit and I wouldn't have been surprised if she clapped her hands and jumped up and down like a child. The look of joy on her face was that great.

"I'll go say hello to Mr. Robinson while you get dressed," Cal said.

He smiled at my are-you-sure look then nodded and gave me a quick kiss. Molly wrapped her hand around his bicep and pulled him to her side.

"I'll take good care of him, I promise," she said.

I shook my head and chuckled. "I'm sure you will."

She led him away from me and I unlocked the door to the pool house and stepped inside. I know Cal can handle whatever happens over there, but I still want to change as fast as humanly possible. Unfortunately, as I stared at the contents of my closet, I knew I wouldn't be as quick as I'd intended.

My initial thought was to wear a sundress long enough to cover the aircast, but Cal is dressed pretty casual in shorts, a T-shirt, and slides. No matter how informal a dress I choose, we still won't match. After rifling through my closet and rummaging through my drawers, I decided on navy Bermuda shorts, a blue and ivory striped shirt, and a pair of beige boat shoes.

Even though we didn't head outside until early evening, I'd gotten some sun at Cal's yesterday so I just applied mascara and lipstick. I hung upside down and brushed my hair then flipped it back and sprayed it into place. After checking myself out in the full-length mirror, I called it good.

I grabbed my purse and walked toward the front door hoping to find Cal waiting for me by the 4Runner. Unfortunately, that didn't happen and since he still stood talking with Mr. Robinson, I felt obligated to go say hello.

Cal's eyes followed my progress around the pool without missing a beat in his conversation. I chose to focus on his lusty look instead of Stewart's scowl. I honestly have no idea why my ex-husband has such a problem with me. He's the one who cheated and I hadn't taken half of what I could have in the divorce. Then again, I still don't know when he changed so much. He wasn't always the self-absorbed prick he is today. I wouldn't have married him if that was the case.

"Barbara, it's wonderful to see you again." Bill Robinson stood and took my hand and held it between his in a warm gesture, more than a shake.

"It's nice to see you, too," I said.

"I'm happy to see you up and walking around again," he said. "It's a shame you can't join us. I've been meaning to get some casual time with this guy to talk baseball, but he's always really busy at work. His boss is a real slave driver."

Everyone laughed at his self-deprecating joke. We stayed and chatted for a few more minutes, which mostly consisted of Cal charming Molly and Mr. Robinson, ignoring Frances's attempts to get him to look at her, and answering Stewart's questions. My ex-husband has always been fascinated with athletes, so despite the fact that Cal is with me, I'm sure he couldn't help himself.

"We better head out," Cal said, then placed his hand on the small of my back. "I know my friends are looking forward to meeting my girl here."

It's been years since my divorce so I shouldn't take such satisfaction when Stewart clenched his jaw at Cal's words. But I'm only human.

I LOOKED AROUND AT THE GROUNDS AND THE HOUSE IN FRONT OF ME AS

Cal grabbed the box of sweets from the back seat. This setting is beautiful and I can understand how someone in the spotlight would appreciate the privacy it affords.

"Ready?" Cal asked, holding out his free hand for me to grasp.

I took in a breath and let it out. "As I'll ever be."

"You're perfect and they're gonna love you." He gave me a quick kiss and led me away from the front door. "They're usually around back so I normally go this way."

We walked around the garage and he opened the large gate and led me into the yard. I spotted a man standing at the grill and two others sprawled on lounge chairs. Two women sat at the table with what looked like margaritas in front of them and two girls were on the other side of the yard playing catch.

"Cal!" One of the girls came running toward us, her glove still on her hand.

"Hey Lex," he said, releasing my hand to give her a one-armed hug.

She shifted her beautiful green eyes between me and the box in his hand, seeming undecided as to what she should ask about first. Cal made the decision for her by giving us a proper introduction. She gave a polite greeting, then asked, "What did you bring this time?"

He handed her the box, shifted his gaze to me, and smirked. "I told you she has a bigger sweet tooth than me."

Before either Lexi or I could comment, the rest of the group approached. After watching the game yesterday, I easily recognized Dan, Jack, and Dale and I correctly identified Sabrina and Hannah. But I waited for him to introduce me to each in turn starting with the women, which included the girl who had been playing catch with Lexi, who was Dale's sister Penny. And she wasn't a girl as I'd originally thought, but a young woman in her twenties.

Jack Reagan shook my hand and said, "It's really nice to meet you. We thought maybe he was making you up."

Hannah slapped his arm and said, "Behave."

"Yes dear," he said, then pulled her close and dipped her backward over his arm before kissing her soundly.

Apparently this was a common occurrence because no one blinked an eye. Instead, they just walked back toward the patio area.

"Mom, can I have a cookie?" Lexi asked as she set the box Cal had given her on the table.

"Just one," Sabrina said. "Are you all packed to go to grandma's house?" Lexi nodded and carefully selected a chocolate chip cookie from the box then closed the top. "They'll be here in about half an hour."

"Can you do my hair before I go?" Lexi asked.

Sabrina nodded. "Go grab a brush and a hair tie."

Lexi ran into the house, taking a big bite of cookie on the way.

"Would you like a margarita?" Sabrina asked.

"That sounds great."

She poured me a frozen drink and handed it to me.

"Have a seat," she said, then looked at Cal who hovered behind me and made a shooing motion with her hands. "You go hang with the menfolk so we can get acquainted."

Cal's chuckle vibrated against my ear a second before he kissed my cheek.

"I'll be right over there if you need me," he said.

I smiled over my shoulder at him then enjoyed the view as he walked away and settled onto a lounge chair. He, Jack, and Dale sat in a row and Dan left the grill and pulled a chair over to face them.

While I only have eyes for Cal, I'm not blind. His friends are extremely good looking and I imagine they garner a lot of attention when they go out together in public. The professional athlete thing would be like icing on the cake with these guys.

"All that prettiness almost hurts to look at, doesn't it?" Sabrina said, then gestured for me to sit.

Pulling out a chair, I sat between her and Hannah. Penny sat across from me.

"They are a lot to take in at once," I said around a chuckle before taking a sip of my drink. "Mmm, this is delicious." Placing the glass back on the table, I looked at the woman across from me and said, "Your hair is stunning."

She patted her dark copper locks. "Thank you."

"Don't tell me, you hate it," I said.

"How did you guess?"

"The look on your face. It's the same one Cal used to get when I told him how much I loved his curls."

"At least it's gotten darker over the years. When I was younger, it was a lot brighter." Penny took a sip of her drink. "I tried dying it different colors...mostly during my teenage years...but it never looked right. So this is it."

Lexi returned and Sabrina moved her away from the table and ran the brush through the girl's hair. I watched as she proceeded to quickly weave her long blonde hair into a French braid. My mom used to do the same thing for me and I smiled at the bittersweet memory.

"You're all set," Sabrina said and kissed the top of her daughter's head.

"Thanks!"

Lexi walked toward the guys and said something to Jack. He threw his head back and laughed, then schooched over and patted the space next to him for her to sit. She settled next to him and they continued to talk.

Hannah looked at Sabrina and said, "You know, I think I fell in love with him when I saw him dancing to Cotton Eye Joe with her."

"They are adorable together," Sabrina agreed.

Hannah nodded and gazed adoringly at her fiance, then shifted her blue ombre glasses back into place and looked at me. "Barbara, Penny here just found out she made the Olympic softball team."

It took me a second to follow the change of topic.

"Oh wow, that's so cool!" I said. "What position do you play?"

"Third base."

"Just like Cal."

"He was always very patient when I was an annoying tween bugging him with questions." She nodded and took another drink. "And he gave me some awesome tips that have no doubt helped me get where I am."

Sabrina ran into the house and brought out some chips and pretzels to help absorb the alcohol we were drinking. Cal had cooked me a large breakfast again, but I still found myself picking on the snacks.

We chatted more about the Olympics and how she was enjoying a brief hiatus before reporting to training camp in Florida in a few weeks. I was happy to keep hearing about Penny, but after Sabrina poured another round, she decided it was time for a change of subject.

"So, you and Cal," she said.

I looked around at all three women, who just stared back with big smiles.

"Yeah," I said around a chuckle. "Me and Cal."

"According to Dan, Cal says you're the one who got away," Sabrina said.

I wasn't sure how to respond to that, so I just said, "Well, we did date back in college."

"Was he always so sweet?" Hannah asked.

"Yeah, he was."

"Cal's divorce happened before Jack and I got together so we were really more professional acquaintances than friends. But even then, I wanted to bitch slap that woman."

Sabrina laughed. "Here, have another drink, Hannah. Maybe we'll get you to say more things like that."

After topping us all off, she placed the empty pitcher in the middle of the table. Dan reached around her and grabbed it.

"I'll check on Gavin and make another batch," he said, then leaned down and kissed his wife. "Just promise not to get too drunk. Remember we're empty nesters tonight."

She gave him a sappy smile and watched him walk away before turning her attention back to me.

"It's funny, Cal mentioned you to Dan after we got married."

"When was that?" I asked.

"Almost three years ago." I glanced over at Lexi, who was still sitting with Jack, and she added, "Lexi is Dan's daughter from a previous relationship. I adopted her after we got married."

With the way they interact, you'd never know Sabrina didn't give birth to Lexi.

"So Cal mentioned me three years ago?" I asked.

"Not by name, but he said there was a girl he dated through college and after seeing how Dan and I got back together, he wondered if you two could do the same."

I'd just absorbed her long-winded sentence into my semi-soggy brain when she spoke again.

"I'm sure he eventually planned on looking you up and then you ended up in the same bank meeting." She picked up a pretzel, took a bite, and chewed. "And if that isn't fate, I don't know what is."

CAL

Dan's mother and step-father showed up to pick up Lexi and Gavin. They're taking them for a couple nights, giving Dan and Sabrina some time alone. Since that's the case, we won't be staying very late. Which is just as well since Barbara has to get up for work in the morning. I know she's looking forward to getting back, but I'm sure it's going to be a shock to her system after being home for six weeks.

"So how are things going?" Dan asked, nodding his head in Barbara's direction.

"So far, so good," I said. "We had our first out of house date Friday and she's been with me since, so that's something."

"Not that we've interacted much, but I already like her much better than that bitch you were married to." One thing about Jack Reagan, he doesn't mince words.

There was a time when I would have taken any opportunity to bash my ex-wife with my friends, but I've moved on from that.

"Barbara is nothing like Marsha, that's for sure."

.   .   .

"I DON'T KNOW HOW YOU ENDED UP WITH THAT OTHER ONE IN THE FIRST place."

I finished the one beer I'd allow myself in a long gulp and chuckled.

"You really want to go there?" I asked him.

The whole book thing sucked. I wouldn't have busted his ass about it at the time, but now that it's over and he's happy with Hannah, the subject is fair game. As is my divorce.

He saluted me with his bottle. "Yeah, but at least I didn't marry my lunatic."

"Touché."

"Okay children, behave." Dan stood and walked to the grill. He dramatically opened the lid and said, "I believe the ribs are ready."

"Hell, it's about time," Monte said.

"You can't rush perfection."

Jack, Monte, and I walked over to the table as Dan stacked his slow-cooked ribs onto a platter. I told Sabrina I'd grab the sides when she stood up to get them. She's looking as wobbly as Barbara, Hannah, and Penny. I'm starving and don't want to take the chance she'd drop something.

Jack and Monte followed me in and we found cooked corn on the cob and macaroni and cheese warming in the oven and coleslaw and salad in the refrigerator. We collected everything and placed it outside on the bar. Once Dan brought over the ribs, everyone helped themselves and we squeezed eight people around the table that normally fits six.

We'd busted Dan's ass about the food taking so long to cook, but I have to admit, the ribs are worth the wait. They literally fell off the bone and melted in my mouth. All the side dishes were delicious too and it didn't take long for us to finish it all.

The women seeemd to sober up a bit after getting some real food in their stomachs and switching to water. They were still a bit giggly, but I was enjoying watching Barbara interact with them. I knew they'd all get along well.

"So Barbara," Sabrina said. "Dan mentioned you hurt your ankle, but what exactly happened?"

"My heel got stuck in the carpet and as I turned, I fell and got what the doctor referred to as a tib-fib fracture."

"Ouch."

"Thank God most of the meeting attendees had already left the room. Cal and my ex-mother-in-law were the only ones who witnessed the actual event." Barb glanced at me and smiled. "Which was embarrassing enough."

I lifted her hand to my lips and kissed her knuckles.

"Nothing to be embarrassed about. I'm just happy you're okay."

"That's my next question," Sabrina said. "It healed with rest?"

Barbara nodded. "Thankfully, yes. I was so afraid I was going to need surgery and being laid up for another couple months would have driven me crazy. I still need to do physical therapy and wear this aircast, but it's better than the alternative."

"Who's your physical therapist?" Sabrina asked.

"I don't have one yet. I plan on figuring that out this week."

"My wife here works wonders." Dan wrapped his arm around Sabrina's shoulders. "She got me back on my feet and in the game when no one else could."

Sabrina rolled her eyes. "That's because you wouldn't listen to anyone else."

"True." He kissed her cheek.

"I'd be happy to either work with you myself or recommend someone," she told Barb.

"Oh, that'd be great."

"Cal has my information. Give me a call and we'll set something up this week and maybe grab lunch afterwards."

"I'd like that," Barb said. "I'll give you a call Tuesday or Wednesday. I know I'm going to be swamped getting caught up tomorrow."

We hung out for another couple hours, with Barb participating in the conversation as much as anyone else. I love the fact that she's fitting in so well with my friends and didn't even blink at the usual shit talk between the guys and me. She even participated once or twice, especially when her place of employment was mentioned.

"Don't let Cal talk you into bringing him free samples all the time," Dan said.

"And if he visits you at your office, make sure to check his pockets," Monte chimed in.

I flipped them both off, which of course, just spurred them on. The comments continued, and of course Barbara wasn't surprised to find out that I always kept sweets in my locker and duffle bag.

"We tried our best to keep him away from it, but we couldn't watch him twenty-four-seven." Jack sighed. "He really needs a twelve-step program."

Barbara giggled and patted my chest. "I'll do my best to keep him on the straight and narrow."

With the subject of my sweet tooth exhausted, I figured it was as good a time as any to leave. Of course, once we made the move, the others followed so it took forever to actually go.

Hannah gave me a quick hug and said, "Mr. Hanover is looking for you to sit in the booth again."

"When?"

"Defintely during the playoffs, but if you're willing in the next couple weeks, I'm sure he'd be thrilled."

"Let me know specific dates and I'll see if I'm available."

"One of us will be in touch."

I took Barbara's hand, but since it was getting dark, I walked her through the house to go out the front door. She got settled into the passenger seat and I leaned down and kissed her before closing the door. I jogged around the back of the 4Runner and got behind the wheel. Beeping the horn at Monte and Penny, I pulled down the driveway.

Before turning onto the main road, I glanced at Barbara and said, "How was that?"

It seemed like she'd enjoyed herself, but I wanted to make sure.

"I had so much fun," she said. "Thank you for bringing me."

Happy with her response, I stepped on the gas. It'll take a half hour to get to Barbara's place, we can talk on the way.

"I couldn't wait for you to meet them. Aside from my family, they're the people I spend most of my time with. And since I plan on spending a lot of time with you going forward, I wanted you all to meet."

Out of the corner of my eye, I saw Barb shift in her seat to face me better.

"Sabrina said that you mentioned me to Dan a couple years ago."

"I did."

"Were you planning on trying to find me?"

"Probably eventually. It was right around their wedding and I was still pretty shell-shocked from my divorce so I definitely wouldn't have done it then. But Dan and Sabrina's story definitely got me thinking. They dated in college too and he'd mentioned her through the years and even looked her up. Long story short, when he got hurt, he used that to get her back into his life as his physical therapist. Then he worked his charm." I shrugged. "I wondered if we could have the same second chance."

When she didn't say anything immediately, I glanced at her quickly before turning my eyes back to the road.

"I've thought about you, too, and I wouldn't have had to look too hard to find you," she finally said then chuckled. "In fact, I had to make an effort to avoid hearing about you."

"So would you ever have looked me up?" I asked in a playful tone.

The tone she answered in was much less playful.

"After how I ended things, I didn't think I had the right."

Considering how upset she looked, I was sorry I'd asked. But if she's feeling this way, I'm glad I know. I reached over and laced our fingers together.

"I never thought that our break-up was more your fault than mine."

"How can you say that?"

"You were the one who said the words, but I definitely contributed to your decision."

"Yes you left, but first of all, that happened before my mom died. And second, baseball was your dream. Of course you had to follow it."

This is a pretty heavy conversation to be having in the car, but maybe the dark and the fact that we're not facing each other makes it easier.

"I was just talking to my mom about this. I've wondered what would have happened if I finished school and waited for another offer. I would have been there for you after your mom died and maybe an East Coast team would have drafted me so I wouldn't have been so far away."

"And what if you got hurt? Or no one drafted you?" Out of the corner of my eye, I saw her shake her head . "No, you needed to follow your dream."

We went back and forth, sharing our thoughts and feelings about what had happened back then. By the time I turned into her driveway, we managed to agree on two things...we can't go back and change things and we need to remember the good times and move forward.

I pulled outside the pool house and turned off the engine. Barb had opened her door by the time I walked around, so I held her hand as she stepped down.

She unlocked the door and opened it.

"Do you want to come in?"

I wrapped my arms around her waist and pulled her close.

"More than anything." I gave her a quick kiss. "But you have work tomorrow and need to get a good night's sleep. If I come in you know that won't happen." Her sexy smile almost had me changing my mind. Instead, I kissed her soundly and stepped away. "I'll talk to you tomorrow."

She stood in the doorway watching as I got back into the 4Runner and drove away.

Chapter 19

Barbara

My entire morning was spent going through emails and getting caught up on the financials. J.P. had popped in earlier and asked me to have lunch, probably just to make sure I took a break. Whatever the reason, I looked forward to it.

I'd just finished analyzing a spreadsheet when I heard my office door open. Assuming it was J.P. coming to fetch me, I looked up with a smile. Which quickly disappeared when I spotted Stewart standing there.

As usual, he just barged in without being invited and rested his hip against the edge of my desk.

"Nice of you to finally come to work," he said, his usual sneer in place.

I started to defend myself and say I'd wanted to come into work but Molly had insisted I stay home. But through the years, I've found that when it comes to Stewart, less is better. Jess calls it backing down. I call it avoiding aggravation.

"Did you need something?" I asked, sitting back in my chair.

"I heard you were coming back today and stopped by to make sure that actually happened."

"Well, as you can see, I'm here."

I sat forward again and clicked the space bar of my computer, bringing it back to life. Of course, he didn't take the hint.

"What are you doing with Cal Chase?"

"What?"

"You heard me. You're just setting yourself up for failure dating someone like him." He stood and struck his power pose. "And my mother said you dated him in college. Why didn't I ever hear about this before?"

I closed my eyes and took in a deep breath then slowly let it out before looking up at my ex-husband.

"Stewart, why would I have told you who I dated in college?"

"You didn't think I'd want to know you were involved with a professional baseball player before we were married?"

I logged off my computer again, grabbed my purse out of the bottom desk drawer, and stood.

"*You* didn't think I'd want to know you were dating my friend *while* we were married?"

For the first time in years, I'd not only spoken back to Stewart, but I'd shocked him speechless. Before he could think of a come-back...and trust me, he would...I walked out the door. J.P. was just leaving his office when I approached.

"I was just coming to get you," he said.

Looping my arm around his elbow, I kept walking and dragged him along. At his shocked look, I said, "I'll explain on the way."

We left the building and hopped into J.P.'s Audi. As we drove out of the parking lot, what I'd done hit me and I started to laugh. Hysterically.

Once I was all laughed out, J.P. said, "I hope you're going to let me in on the joke."

"Oh God, you're gonna love it."

"Before you tell me, where are we going?"

"How about sushi?"

"Sushi it is." he turned right at the light. "So what had you laughing just now?"

I told him what I said to Stewart and I wish I could have gotten a picture of his shocked face. Then he laughed. Not quite as hard as I had, but it was pretty impressive.

"I wish I was there to see that."

J.P. pulled into the parking lot at Misu and cut the engine. Thankfully our favorite sushi place is only a mile from the office. The sushi bar was pretty crowded so we decided to get a table instead.

After we placed our orders, I decided to see if J.P. could answer the questions running through my head.

"What happened to him, J.P.?" I asked. "He wasn't like this when we first got married."

He shook his head. "I wish I could tell you, Barb. It's like he read a biography about a tyrant business tycoon and took it as a self-help book."

"That's exactly what it's like, but the question is why. And it's not just me he's awful to, it's pretty much everyone besides your mom. And with her, he acts like a teenager pushing the limits. He knows just how far he can go before she shuts him down."

The waitress approached with our sushi and set it down in front of us. Once she left, I continued my thought.

"Even looking back, I can't pick an exact moment when he started to act this way. It was definitely a gradual thing and I see how I changed in reaction. We stopped being partners in our marriage and it became a dictatorship. My days circled around not upsetting him and trying to make myself into the perfect Stepford wife to avoid his negative comments. I realize now that it had become a mentally abusive relationship...it still is in some ways."

I picked up a piece of tuna avocado roll, dipped it in soy sauce, and placed it in my mouth. J.P. had finished off his yellowtail roll during my little speech and moved onto the spicy crab. We ate in silence for a few minutes before he spoke.

"I hear what you're saying, and the same thing happened with him and me. We were close growing up and while we weren't as tight as we got older, we were still there for each other. But now we only speak about work-related things."

Using my chopsticks, I added another dab of wasabi to my soy sauce and stirred. I know I shouldn't waste my time trying to figure out the past, but it's the basis of some other things that have been running through my mind. Having a little insight might help me make some hard choices. Unfortunately, I don't think I'll ever get any, so I'll have to decide blind.

The weeks I was stuck home gave me both the time and distance to think about my life. In some ways I've moved forward since my divorce, but in others, Jess is right, I've been in a rut. Now I feel like I'm at a point where I either have to change what I'm doing or I'll be stuck forever.

"I was going to bring this up at dinner tonight, but telling you what happened in my office with Stewart just led into it. Plus it might be better to talk about this without Jess first. You know how she reacts to all things Stewart."

J.P. finished chewing his sushi around a chuckle. "Yeah, he's definitely not her favorite person."

"That's an understatement. Plus she has very strong opinions about what I want to discuss and I'd like to hear what you think independent of her." I ate the last piece of sushi and slowly chewed. After swallowing, I added, "Because since we work together, you'll have more insight on this."

He sat back and took a long drink of sweet tea. "Sounds serious," he said as he put the glass back down

Placing my chopsticks on the plate, I pushed it away and rested my folded arms against the edge of the table.

"I'm thinking about looking for a new job."

I would have found the look on J.P.'s face comical if the subject wasn't so serious.

"Did something else happen with Stewart?" he finally asked.

"Not like you're thinking." I shook my head. "Nothing specific anyway. It's just...you know how he is. And that's a problem. Right now, I have Molly as a buffer but what's going to happen when she retires?"

"I haven't let myself think about that." He blew out a breath.

"Unfortunately, the more time she spends with Bill Robinson, the closer I think that day is getting."

I nodded. "That's what I've been thinking, too. And maybe it's because I was forced to take a step back from everything with my injury, but it became blatantly clear that I'm better off leaving on my own terms."

"I'd never let Stewart fire you," he said.

"I know that, but without your mom around to control him, he'll make my life a living hell. I can handle it, but you know it wouldn't be good for the company."

"I think if we join forces against him, we'll be okay even without mom."

"I wish that was true, but you know how he is when it comes to me. The fact that you're his brother counts for something with Stewart and even though he'll give you a hard time, he'll work with you. I'm nothing more than his ex-wife. *Once removed* as he likes to call me."

J.P. dragged his fingers through his hair, then looked down at the table. He shook his head then looked at me again.

"Have you already started looking?"

"No. I'll talk to your mom before I do anything. I'd hate for her to find out from someone else."

The waitress walked over and set our check on the table. J.P. glanced at it then threw down his credit card.

"Not that I don't understand and totally agree with everything you've just said, but I'm just curious." His frown was replaced by a soft smile. "Does a certain former baseball player have anything to do with this decision you've made?"

"Maybe indirectly." I shrugged. "He reminds me of who I am, and that's not Stewart's whipping girl."

J.P., JESS, AND I SAT AT O'TOOLE'S, A SPORTS BAR NOT FAR FROM MY place. Not only is it wing night, but they'll also have the Waves game showing on several screens so no matter where we sit, we should be able to see and hear the game. The latter is important to me since Cal is in the booth tonight.

Hannah had told him yesterday she'd be in touch, and he texted me earlier to say she had and Mr. Hanover wanted him tonight if he was available. The game would be starting in fifteen minutes and we'd just settled at a table when I saw Cal's image on the TV across from me. I looked at the number on the set and clicked the corresponding digit on the speaker that was built into the wall next to us.

Cal looked polished and professional in a navy blazer, crisp white shirt, and a blue tie sporting tiny Waves logos. He also looked sexy as hell as he nodded at what the man next to him was saying. Then it was his turn to speak.

You're right about that, Jay. Jarvis has had to rely on the bullpen too much lately. I know he's looking to Russell to pitch deep into the game tonight. He's been struggling lately, but you know he has the stuff, he just needs to focus and find the zone.

I heard Jess call my name and shifted my eyes to look in her direction.

"So how was your first day back?" she asked.

"Busy," I said. "But I think I'm caught up so tomorrow should be better."

"And how was Stewie?" I glanced at J.P. before looking at Jess again. She shifted her gaze between us and said, "Okay, spill it. You know I hate it when you two keep secrets."

"They're not secrets," J.P. said. "Barb and I discussed a few things at lunch."

He looked at me and nodded, urging me to spill my story. And I did just that starting with my conversation with Stewart just before lunch and ending with my decision to leave Molly Mack Chocolate.

Jess didn't ask questions or interrupt me in any way as I spoke, which was probably a first. When I finished, she stared at me for a few seconds then blinked.

"Well? What do you think?" I asked.

A slow smile crossed her face. "It's about fucking time."

"I knew you'd approve." I finished my beer. "And there's something I didn't share with J.P. at lunch today." I paused for dramatic effect. "I uploaded the paperwork today to legally change back to my maiden name." Of course I'd already mentioned this to Jess but it was news to J.P. "It's just another step toward becoming me again."

Jess tilted her head toward the TV as Cal's image filled the screen.

"I'm thinking if that guy has anything to say about it, you won't be Barbara Murphy for long."

CAL

Being back at First Allegiant Bank Park is always bittersweet. I still feel like I should be down on the field in uniform instead of sitting in this fucking booth in a tie and blazer. Still, I plastered a smile on my face and bantered back and forth with Jay Glasser, the regular play-by-play broadcaster.

In the middle of the sixth inning, Mr. Hanover entered the booth and asked to speak to me. I removed my headphones and followed him into the hall, hoping he wasn't going to try to convince me to work the booth on a regular basis. We've had that conversation more than once. He likes the fact that I can recite baseball facts and stats without needing someone feeding them to me. And while I don't mind doing this occasionally, I can't imagine doing it all the time.

After we got the usual pleasantries out of the way, he got straight to it.

"I've been told that Hadley Stone is talking about retiring again," he said, referring to the infield coach for the organization's Triple A team, the Fayetteville Waves. "His contract is up this year, so I don't know if he's serious or if he just wants to use that to renegotiate."

Mr. Hanover stared at me, as though waiting for me to say something. I'm not sure of the point of this conversation, so I just said, "Stone was a great coach. He taught me a lot."

He nodded at my words, seemingly satisfied.

"When I heard, you're the first person I thought of to replace him.

Besides the fact that you were an all-star player, you're smart, you know the game, and you have the personality for it." I fought to keep a poker face as he stared at me. "Thoughts?"

"I uh, I'm flattered Mr. Hanover. I've never really thought about coaching, but you've made some valid points."

"Like I said, nothing is official yet, I just wanted to have an informal conversation to gauge your interest."

I wasn't lying when I said I'd never thought about coaching. But now that he's put the idea in my head, I can see it being a good fit. I know the game and have a knack for spotting weaknesses. Throughout my career, I've used those skills to improve my game. As a coach, I'd be able to help players get to the next level.

"I'm definitely interested, sir."

"Excellent." He shook my hand. "I'll keep you in the loop."

I stepped back into the booth and put my headphones into place. Not missing a beat, Jay started up our banter again, offering some leading questions so I could add color. Back and forth it went, and I think I did a pretty good job considering I couldn't get my conversation with Mr. Hanover out of my head.

The more I thought about it, the more I liked the idea of coaching in Triple A.

As the game ended in a Waves victory, I couldn't wait to get out of the stadium and call Barb. And that's when my bubble burst.

Because I'm pretty sure she won't be as thrilled about the idea of me getting back onto the field as I am.

Chapter 20

Barbara

"Your clinic is amazing," I said to Sabrina.

Even though I'd called her on Tuesday morning, she'd managed to fit me in for a physical therapy session on Friday. Which I really appreciate because I didn't want to put it off too long.

"Thank you. I opened it a little over a year ago so it's still new and shiny."

"Where did you work before that?"

"The Meyers Rehabilitation Clinic up near Cary," she said. "I was a partner there, but ended up selling out a couple years ago to start my own shop."

"Is that where you lived before you and Dan got together?"

She nodded and sat back as our salads were served. Picking up her knife and fork, she cut the tails off the shrimp in her Caesar salad. I mirrored her actions as I cut up the chicken in mine.

"When I decided to stay down here, I figured I could commute part-time, but it became obvious pretty quickly that wasn't going to work. Especially during the season." She shoved a forkful of salad into her mouth, chewed, and swallowed. "I mean, I could have done it, but it would have been a pain in the ass and wouldn't have been fair to Lexi."

"Looking at you and Lexi, you'd never know you're not her biological mother. Aside from the fact you have the same coloring, you're so natural with her."

"She's an amazing girl and it was easy to fall in love with her." She chuckled. "I'm just lucky she was so willing to share her father with me. Until the day I showed up, she'd had him all to herself."

I was dying to ask what happened to Lexi's mother, but didn't feel comfortable. After all, I'd just met Sabrina.

"So you and Cal," she said before I could think more about that. "He told us you dated in college and broke up a few months after he got drafted, but I'm sure there's more to it than that."

I raised my brow and shrugged as I finished chewing a mouthful of salad. Taking a long drink, I washed it down and figured out what to say.

"We met freshman year and started dating about a month later. I wasn't lying when I told Hannah that he was even sweet back then. Honestly, he was perfect and we dated until I started my senior year."

"So what happened?"

I started off slow, but then in between bites, eventually spilled the whole story. I told her about how thrilled we were when he got drafted even though he had to move out to the West Coast. How my mother died and I just lost it.

"He was there for me as much as he could have been, but you know what things are like during the season," I said. "As the days went on, I felt more and more alone. And while his phone calls made me feel good, they just made me more upset when they were over." I shrugged. "So I broke it off."

She reached over and squeezed my hand.

"I'm so sorry, Barbara. That must have been such a rough time for you."

I nodded, acknowledging her words, then we ate in silence for a few minutes.

"Anyway, I worked hard to forget about him and get on with my life. I got married a few years later and focused on that life. I knew Cal played for the Waves, but even after my divorce, I avoided stories about him. And then he walked into that bank meeting."

I couldn't stop the smile from spreading across my face after that last sentence because this reunion with Cal has been amazing.

"Well I know for a fact that he's thrilled to have this second chance with you. And trust me, if Dan and I can end up together after our history, you and Cal shouldn't have any issues at all."

Then she proceeded to give me the condensed version of her history with Dan. They too had dated in college, but it turns out the relationship hadn't been as perfect as mine and Cal's. He'd cheated on her and she ended things when she found out and managed to hold a grudge against him for more than a decade.

"Then one day I got called into my manager's office and was told that Dan McMullen wanted me to be his physical therapist. I'd immediately refused, but then she said if I accepted the assignment, I'd be made a partner at the clinic." She shrugged. "So I took the job, figuring I'd keep things professional, get him back on his feet, and head home in a new tax bracket with a boost to my resume."

"But then he worked his charm?"

"Between him and Lexi I didn't stand a chance." She looked down at the table, a small smile on her face. It was at least a minute before she spoke again. "I did try to resist, but I'm so glad I gave him a chance." She met my gaze again and changed the subject back to Cal and me. "I met Cal right when he and Marsha split up and honestly, he was a mess back then. But he came back to life little by little over the last few years and despite everything that happened since then, I thought he was back to normal. But then he came over one day and he looked different, happier. A week or so later, he mentioned you. And I was thrilled when I met you and found that you lived up to all his praise."

I smiled at that last sentence, not sure how to respond. Instead of giving some lame response, I focused on what she'd said about Cal looking happier.

"It's been a great few weeks," I said. "And now that I'm back on my feet, I'm looking forward to us being able to do more things together."

Cal

"Where on Earth are you taking me?" Barbara asked as Cal zigged and zagged through a myriad of back roads.

"We're almost there." I slowed down for a sharp curve. "So how did your appointment with Sabrina go today?"

"It went well. I'll be going to see her twice a week for three weeks plus she gave me some exercises to do at home. She said she'll reevaluate things then and we'll take it from there."

"Does she still want you to wear the aircast?"

"Yeah, at least for those three weeks when I'm going to be walking around. She said I can leave it off if I'm just hanging around the house."

"Well that must make you happy. I couldn't wait to get rid of my neck brace after my surgery."

"Oh God, you had to wear one of those things? I think I'd feel claustrophobic in one...like I was choking."

"I didn't mind at first because my neck hurt everytime I moved it and the brace pretty much prevented that. But once I started feeling better, it just drove me crazy."

I saw the sign for The Angler and turned into the parking lot, pulling into a spot right next to J.P.

"Did you have trouble finding the place?" I asked him as we all walked toward the restaurant.

"No, I had an idea where I was going," he said. "I've never been here before, but I've been to Red's Place just down the road."

I held open the door and stepped back so they could all enter ahead of me. As I expected on a Friday night, most of the tables are full. In an hour or so, the foyer will be full of people waiting to be seated. For a place that's hidden on a back road, this restaurant is pretty popular with the locals.

The host stand was empty when we entered but I spotted one of the owners weaving his way through the restaurant coming toward us.

"Cal, it's great to see you again."

The guys and I have been coming here for years so we know Andy and his brother Mark pretty well. Besides the fact that the food is amazing and the place has a great atmosphere, we've always been left alone here. So it's one of our favorite local restaurants to frequent.

After I introduced him to the rest of my party, he led us through the restaurant and to a table in the back corner. I held Barb's chair for her before sitting with my back to the room.

Andy waited until we were settled then handed us menus and said someone would be around for our orders.

"This place is really nice. Do you come here a lot?"

I nodded. "Pretty regularly."

"Do you have issues going out in public?" Jess looked around the room. "I mean, no one is paying attention to you now, but that can't always be the case. Especially when you go out with your baseball friends."

"It depends on where we go, who's there. Like when Barb and I went to the Rat Pack show, the usher recognized me but it didn't seem like anyone else did." I shrugged and looked at Barb. "No one approached anyway."

"Just the guy in the parking lot," she said.

"Right, but that was it. It is harder to blend when we're all together, but through the years, we've found places throughout the country where we can quietly hang out. For the most part, anyway." I shrugged. "It just takes common sense. Obviously if I hung out at Broadway the Beach or at the bars near the stadium, I'd be more likely to be recognized and mobbed. So I stay away from those places unless I have a meet and greet to attend."

The waitress approached to take our drink order which paused our conversation.

Once she left, J.P. turned to Jess and said, "You should probably stop interrogating Cal and check out the menu."

"I'm not interrogating him. But hanging out at Barb's, I forgot that Cal is famous. I'm just curious how he lives his life." Then with barely a pause she added, "What's good here?" It took me a second to catch up.

"I usually get whatever the catch of the day special is," I said then looked at the specials menu. "Which is grouper topped with mango salsa and crabmeat tonight. You can also get the catch of the day blackened or grilled with a lemon butter sauce."

"That special sounds good." Barb closed her menu. "I'm gonna get that."

Jess scrunched up her nose and looked at J.P. "Do I like grouper?"

"I don't think you've ever had it," he said.

"What was that fish I had that time at that place in Virginia Beach? The one I didn't like."

Surprisingly he not only followed that, he answered.

"That was tilapia."

Everyone had decided by the time the waitress came back with our drinks. We'd also agreed to get an order of calamari as well as the baked shrimp dip to share.

"Did you know my mother was going away for the weekend with Bill Robinson?" J.P. asked Barb.

Barb took a sip of her sangria and chuckled. "They're going to a wedding in Maryland. You make it sound like they're having an illicit affair or something."

"She mentioned the wedding to me a few weeks ago, but didn't tell me it was an overnight trip until she was leaving the office this afternoon."

"Would you stop it already," Jess said. "It's no big deal. She's a grown woman."

"She should have at least told me," he said.

Jess said, "Do you also think she should ask your permission?" at the exact same time Barb said, "Do you tell her everything you do?"

He shook his head and looked at me. "I'm not gonna win this one, am I?"

"Probably not."

"Oh-kay then," he said. "Next subject."

We moved on to discuss Barb's appointment with Sabrina earlier. She'd apparently already told Jess the basics over the phone, but went into more detail now.

"Everyone has been asking about you at the studio so hopefully you'll be able to come back soon."

"They're just looking for some comic relief," Barb said.

Jess rolled her eyes. "You're not that bad."

"Not *that* bad." Barb looked at me and smirked. Hitching her thumb toward Jess, she said, "This one can tie herself into a pretzel. And while I managed to keep up in the beginner yoga classes, I either fall over or suffocate myself in the more advanced ones she makes me go to."

"Are you seriously gonna complain about your boobs?" Jess asked.

Before Barb could respond, our appetizers arrived. Everyone's attention turned to the food and soon the calamari and dip were history. Then the conversation turned to favorite out-of-the-way restaurants. I thought I'd hit all the best places within a hundred-mile radius, but my dinner companions mentioned a few I made a mental note to check out.

"So where is your hot date taking you tomorrow night?"

I'd just taken a long drink when J.P. spoke. My beer went down the wrong pipe and I choked and started hacking, fighting for breath between each cough. Three pairs of eyes watched me, frozen in place, unsure what to do to help me. Barb reached over and alternately rubbed and patted my back until things calmed down to a wheeze. I took another quick drink, swallowed, and cleared my throat.

"Are you okay?" Barb asked, but even her adorable frown couldn't distract me from J.P.'s question.

"I'm fine now, thanks." I shifted my gaze between Jess and J.P. several times then asked, "Did you ask where her hot date is taking her?" They both nodded. I shifted my gaze between them again then looked at Barb. "Am I missing something?"

She looked confused by my question at first, then her eyebrows rose when she understood.

"Oh, Jess and J.P. aren't a couple."

"They're not?"

Besides the fact they spend a good portion of their time together, they act like an old married couple. The fish conversation tonight is just one of the many I've heard like that. Most non couples don't act like that.

"Did you ever see the show Will & Grace?" Barb asked. When I nodded, she added, "That's pretty much those two."

I continued to shift my gaze between J.P. and Jess still in shock.

Jess leaned her head on J.P.'s shoulder and patted his chest. "Yes we dated for three wonderful years and then he realized that despite my boyish figure, I don't have a penis and wasn't going to miraculously sprout one."

"But you do have bigger balls than any man I've ever met," J.P. teased.

And it went on like that through dinner and dessert.

Being with Barbara and her friends is no different than being with mine. They're fun, easy to hang out with, and it's pretty obvious they'd do anything for each other. And, over these past few weeks, Jess and J.P. have been accepting and supportive of me being in Barb's life.

It seems our lives are meshing together perfectly in every way.

Chapter 21

Barbara

Cal led me through the stadium corridors toward Hannah's office. I haven't been to a baseball game since my junior year in college and it's been even longer than that since I've been at a professional game. I'm pretty lucky to be at this one, since it's the start of the playoffs.

"It's a good thing I decided to come with you. I never would have found my way to Hannah's office by myself."

"She would have met you out front if you were coming by yourself," Cal said. "But I'm glad you were able to get out of work so we could come together. Besides the fact that I love spending time with you, getting in and out of the stadium is normally crazy. During playoffs, it's even worse."

"It's definitely good to have friends in high places."

He stopped walking and turned to face me. Taking my hands in his, he kissed them one at a time then let them hang between us.

"I wish I was down on that field so you could watch me play like back in the old days."

"I know. Me too."

I've missed so much with him.

"But we're not looking back, we're moving forward," Cal said, reading my mind.

Taking a step closer, he leaned down and kissed me. Our lips had just touched when the door next to us opened and we pulled apart.

"Don't stop on my account." Hannah stood in the doorway of her office with an armful of folders.

Cal stepped to my side and wrapped his arm around my waist.

"Need help?" he asked Hannah.

"Actually, I was gonna ask if you could give this to Jay," she said and held out the folder from the top of the stack.

"Will do," he said, taking it from her. "Am I meeting you here after the game?"

"Here is probably best. You'll get mobbed if you show up on the concourse."

I was about to make a comment about him being kind of a big deal, but before I could say anything, his cell chirped.

"I gotta get up there." He gave me a quick kiss. "I'll see you after the game. See you later, Hannah. Take good care of my girl."

I felt Hannah's eyes on me as I watched Cal walk away. When I looked at her, she fanned herself dramatically and we giggled like school girls.

"Come on. I have a couple places to stop before we head to our seats." We walked further down the hallway and I waited while she went into one office then another and emerged with empty hands. "I'm all yours now."

"Do you watch all the games?"

"I'm usually around somewhere. Although since Jack and I have gotten together, I tend to sit in the stands for at least part of the game."

"Cal told me how you guys got together. It's amazing that you knew each other for so many years and then one day noticed each other and fell in love. What a great story."

"If I'm being honest, I noticed him a long time before he noticed me," she said, drawing out the word *long*. "But, it all worked out."

"I'll say." I followed her through a door and the sounds of the stadium got louder. "Wow, there's a lot of energy out there."

"Waves fever has definitely hit," she said. "Did you want to get something to eat or drink?"

I shook my head. "Cal and I ate before we came here."

"Then follow me."

Hannah led me around the throngs of people in the concourse, through an opening, and down the concrete steps. I followed her about halfway down a row and took the seat next to her.

"These seats are amazing." I looked at the first base line, just a few rows down.

"If Sabrina was here, I would have grabbed seats in the family section, but she couldn't make it because it's back to school night at Lexi's school. There are some other people over there that you'll eventually meet, but I thought it'd be nice if it was just the two of us tonight."

I was going to comment when the crowd got even louder as the Waves took the field and the lineups were announced. The decibel level increased when the first half of the inning ended with three quick outs.

"Off to a good start," I said. "Cal said the Waves' pitching will determine the outcome of this series." `

"Yeah, our starters have been struggling so the bullpen has been getting a workout. When that happens, it just makes it hard all around. The defense has to work harder and so much pressure is put on the offense to score runs."

"You sounded like Cal when you said that. You must be a big baseball fan."

"I am now. I don't think I ever even saw a game before college. My father is from Ireland and is into rugby and soccer. Somehow I got a job with the Waves without having any baseball knowledge or experience. So of course I was determined to learn all about it just so I didn't look like an idiot in meetings," she said around a chuckle. "And now my dad follows baseball too, so I guess you can teach an old dog new tricks. How about you?"

Hannah's attention turned to the field as Jack stepped up to the plate. He looked in our direction before stepping into the batter's box and you could practically feel the sparks zing between them.

I didn't say anything as I watched him take the first pitch, which was called a strike. She tensed beside me as he hit a foul ball behind home plate for strike two. The next pitch was in the dirt and the one after that outside. With a two and two count, Jack fouled off the next three pitches. Hannah's knuckles turned white as they held onto the armrests.

The pitcher released the next pitch and Jack swung, sending it sailing into right-center field. When he stopped at first base, Hannah visibly relaxed.

"Sorry about that. I don't know why I get so nervous when he bats," she said. "So are you a big baseball fan?"

"No, but I was a big Cal Chase fan," I said. "I was raised by a single mom who wouldn't have known a baseball from a football. But when I started dating Cal, I watched with him and went to every game that I could."

"And once you broke up?"

"I avoided it like the plague," I said around a chuckle.

"That's understandable, I guess."

The next batter hit a long fly ball to left field, but it was caught at the wall. It was far enough out that Jack was able to tag up and reach second base before the throw.

Dan was up to bat next and after getting behind in the count, hit a ground ball between third and shortstop. Jack had a big enough lead that he was able to score.

"Well, we're on the board first. Hopefully that's a good sign," Hannah said.

The next batter flew out to center field ending the inning for the Waves.

"I wanted to thank you for being so welcoming on Sunday. It's not always easy being the newcomer to a group, but everyone made me feel like part of the gang."

"You don't have to thank me for that, you fit right in." She tipped her head toward me and smiled. "I'm not sure if that's a compliment or not."

"Well, I'll take it as one," I said around a laugh.

"But seriously, Cal's such a great guy. I'm so happy you found each other again. You're exactly the kind of person I always thought he'd be with, not like—"

I know I shouldn't pry, but I can't help myself. Eventually Cal and I will discuss our divorces, but it will be nice to have another woman's perspective on his ex-wife.

"What *was* she like? His ex?"

"By the time Jack and I got together, they were already divorced, so my only interactions with her were more professional than personal. But she was...." She shook her head and gestured, as if searching for a word. "Cold is the only word that comes to mind, but I'm not sure that's the right one to use. She's from a wealthy Long Island family and just had a certain air about her."

Cal is so warm and giving, I'm surprised he married someone like that. Then again, I married Stewart.

Hannah reached down and took her phone out of her pocket. Over the noise of the crowd, I heard *When Irish Eyes are Smiling.*

"I have to take this. It's my dad."

I turned my attention to the game, giving her some privacy for her call...well as much privacy as she could have in a stadium full of 54,000 people. Dale caught a line drive to end the inning and the Waves ran off the field. I looked at the scoreboard and was surprised to see it was already the bottom of the fourth inning. So far, the Waves pitcher was holding his own and they still had a 1-0 lead.

"Sorry about that," Hannah said as she slid her phone back in her pocket. "We've been playing phone tag for two days. He's on location in Northern Canada and his cell service is terrible."

"On location?"

Her eyes widened and she smiled. "You really don't pay attention to local gossip. My dad is Aaran Diskin. It was all over the news a couple years ago."

I looked at her and blinked, figuring I'd heard wrong. "Your father is Aaran Diskin?" She nodded. "Like Mac Flynn Aaran Diskin?" She nodded again. "Holy hell."

"Well, I'm glad this came up now. I wouldn't want you to be in shock when you see him at the wedding."

"Oh uh, I'm uh not..."

"You will be," she said with a big smile. "I mean, that is if you're not busy that day. Cal mentioned he may have a plus one. I'm sure he just didn't get around to asking you yet. Also, before *I* forget to mention it, I'm doing a spa day in lieu of a traditional bachelorette party, and I'd love it if you could come. It's just my step-mother slash best friend Melanie, my former neighbor Mrs. Button, Sabrina, and me and now you if you're available." I frowned, trying to follow what she said about the first person she named. "Long story short, Melanie was my best friend growing up and now she's married to my dad. And no, I wasn't always as calm and casual about that fact. But we're good now and I'm sure at some point, we'll have a few drinks and I'll bore with the whole story." She took in a deep breath and let it out. "Anyway, we have a suite booked at the Berkman Hotel and will have a whole spa day Saturday then have dinner and some drinks that night and go home Sunday. I'd love it if you could come."

"I'd love to. Thank you for inviting me."

I like how Cal's friends have accepted me as one of them even though we've only met once. But most of all, I love the fact that I'll be meeting Aaran Diskin. It's all I can do to contain the squeal my inner teenager wants to let out.

"Sorry it took us so long to get out of there," Cal said.

"That's okay. I have to expect things like that since you're kind of a—"

"Don't say it." He reached over and tickled my side. When I grabbed his wrist, he interlaced our fingers and rested our joined hands on the center console.

As we drove in comfortable silence toward his house, I thought about how much I'd enjoyed the game. It would have definitely been better if Cal had been playing or if he was sitting with me, but I still had fun. I really enjoy Hannah's company and looked forward to spending more time with her and the rest of Cal's friends. Which reminded me.

"You didn't tell me Hannah's father is Aaran Diskin."

"Sorry, it just never came up. No offense to Hannah, but when I'm with you, I'm not really thinking about her or her father."

I kissed the back of his hand. "I'll forgive you then."

"Speaking of, I've been meaning to ask...would you like to come to Jack and Hannah's wedding with me?" He glanced over at me before looking back at the road. "It's the Saturday before Thanksgiving."

"I'd love to go with you."

"Yeah?"

"Yeah." He shifted in his seat and seemed to relax. "Were you really afraid I'd say no?"

He turned into his driveway, pulled into the garage, and closed the door behind us. After taking his seatbelt off, he turned to face me. Sliding his hand across my jaw to the back of my head, he leaned forward and brushed his lips against mine. It was the briefest of contact, but still made an electric zing spread across my entire body.

Pulling back slightly, he said, "I hoped you'd say yes, but I don't want to take anything for granted. I don't want to take *you* for granted."

He kissed me again, his hands in my hair, and I couldn't get enough of his lips, his tongue, and the sweet hotness of his mouth. His arms wrapped around me, holding me close, and I savored the feel of him, the taste of him.

As he ended the kiss, his chocolate gaze met mine, as if trying to read my thoughts. I'm pretty certain they're obvious, but just in case, I said, "One thing you can take for granted is that once we get inside, you'll see me naked."

A slow smile spread across his face, promising all sorts of naughty things.

CAL

After helping Barb out of the 4Runner, I practically dragged her up the stairs and into the kitchen. Pushing her up against the island, I pressed my lips against hers as her hands slid over my chest and across my shoulders before twisting into my hair. I devoured her mouth and she kissed me back with the same hunger and desperation, and I wanted more. I wanted everything.

I lifted her until she sat on the edge of the granite countertop. Her legs wrapped around my waist and she shifted forward, whimpering as she ground herself against my erection. I groaned against her mouth then pulled back, panting.

"Well, this isn't gonna last long."

Cupping her ass in my hands, I picked her up and walked to the bedroom with her clinging to me, our mouths sipping and nipping at each other. I set her down on the bed and she watched with wide blue eyes as I stood back and removed my shirt, almost ripping all the buttons in my haste to get it off.

Leaning forward, she grabbed the waistband of my pants and pulled me closer. She unbuttoned and unzipped them, then slid her hands inside my boxer briefs and dragged everything down my legs until I stood naked before her. As I toed off my shoes and stepped out of my pants, she grabbed onto my dick and slowly stroked before giving it a long lick.

I grabbed her wrists. "Oh no you don't. This will be over before it starts if you do that."

Like a man possessed, I pulled at her clothes until she was as naked in front of me. She
grabbed my face and kissed me as my hands traveled over her body, hungry to touch every inch of her. Grazing my hand down her stomach, I continued lower and slipped a finger into her slick heat.

"You're always so fucking wet for me I love it."

I added a second finger and she tightened around me and I couldn't wait another minute to be inside her. She whimpered as I pulled back then shifted onto her knees in the middle of the bed as I grabbed a condom.

I climbed back into bed and rested against the pillows. She took the foil packet from me and ripped it open then slowly rolled the condom down onto my length, squeezing and teasing me in the process. Sitting back on her heels, she looked at her handiwork before meeting my gaze with a small smile.

I wrapped my hands around her waist.

"Come here."

She shifted her leg to straddle my lap. Twisting her fingers into my hair, she groaned my name as she thrust forward, and I slid into her wet heat. I lifted my head to lick and suck her nipple into a tight peak before moving to give the other one the same treatment.

Barbara moved against me, eroding my self-control with each long, slow stroke. She picked up her pace, pressing against me with each forward thrust. Resting back against the pillows, I pinched and rolled her nipples enjoying the view as she rode me faster and faster.

She panted my name and fell forward, opening her mouth over mine, kissing me, our tongues thrusting in the same rhythm as her hips. Her movements became more and more frantic and she pulled back, taking in a deep breath before letting it out on a long, low groan as I felt the first ripples of her orgasm. I thrust up, moving my hips in time with hers until I followed her over the edge.

BARB RESTED HER HEAD ON MY SHOULDER AND I HELD HER CLOSE.

"I'm so glad I brought clothes to stay here tonight," she said. "I'm so comfy, I'd hate to have to leave."

"And I'm glad you're staying." I kissed the top of her head. "I like you being here."

I felt her smile against my chest.

"Thanks for coming to the game tonight. It was nice knowing you were there."

"I had a good time with Hannah, but maybe we can go to a game together sometime when you're not in the booth."

"Sounds like a plan."

"Do you like doing that? Announcing?"

I didn't immediately answer, instead I tried to figure out how to explain my feelings to her.

"I enjoy it. It's fun to do every once in a while."

"But?"

Of course she'd know there's a *but*.

I shifted onto my side to face her, looking into her wide blue eyes. I've never shared my true feelings about all this with anyone, not even my parents. But I want to open up to Barb. I want her to understand. Maybe if I do, she'll be able to help me understand.

"You know how much I love the game," I said. "Playing baseball has been part of my life as long as I can remember. I lived it, breathed it, and then one day it was just...gone." I paused to collect my jumbled thoughts. "Watching games on TV isn't too bad, but when I'm at the stadium, I feel like I should be on the field and the fact that I can't be physically hurts." I dragged my fingers through my hair and shifted slightly so I could look at the ceiling. "I know how stupid that sounds. I mean, obviously I'd have to retire someday, but I figured I'd have a few years to prepare for that. And after one stupid dive into the seats, it was all over." I looked back at Barb. "Mr. Hanover and Hannah and the guys all act like I'm still part of the team. I don't want to be one of those guys always hanging around trying to relive his glory days."

I swallowed and closed my eyes then rubbed my hand down my face. Barb rested her hand on my bicep and squeezed, and I looked at her.

"Cal, first of all, no one thinks you're hanging around trying to relive your glory days. From what Hannah said, Mr. Hanover likes you in the booth because you know the game and she likes you at events because you're great with the fans and they love you."

She shifted closer and kissed my chest then tilted her head back to look me in the eye again.

"Your other feelings are totally understandable and don't sound stupid at all. I know how much you love the game and how much it's a part of you. Even if you did retire in the usual way, you'd miss it, but with the way it happened, I can see why you'd feel cheated."

I tucked a stray piece of hair behind her ear then cupped her jaw.

"Thank you."

"For what?"

"For not making me feel like a whining pussy."

She burst out laughing at my words. I knew they'd lighten the mood.

"No one could ever accuse you of that."

She wrapped her arm around my waist and leaned her head against my chest. Her breathing slowed and I thought she had fallen asleep, but then she spoke.

"Can I talk to you about something?" she asked.

"Anything."

"I'm thinking about looking for a new job."

"What? Why?"

If her shit stain of an ex-husband did something to her, I swear I'll break every bone in his body.

She squeezed me closer and nuzzled further into my chest.

"I love my job, but after being away for six weeks, I realize how toxic my relationship with Stewart has become. Right now, Molly is there to mediate things, but once she retires, I don't know exactly what will happen, but I can't imagine it will be good." I felt her warm breath on my skin as she took in a deep breath and slowly let it out. "I know that part of me will miss it. After all, I've been working there for more than a decade. But it's time to move on."

I waited to see if she was going to add anything else. When she didn't, I asked, "Have you spoken to Molly about this?"

She shook her head. "Not yet. I figured I'd tell her when I mention that I'm going back to my maiden name."

We'd had the maiden name discussion a few weeks ago. She told me that me calling her Murphy sparked her decision. I wonder if I'm also part of the catalyst for her job change. But she spoke before I could ask.

Pulling back, she looked me in the eye.

"Can I ask you something?"

"Sure"

"Do you enjoy your job at all?"

I felt like a deer caught in the headlights and I'm sure I looked like one, too. How should I answer that?

I shook my head. This is Barb. Only the truth will do.

"Not really. Why?"

"Then why do it?"

"I have to do something to stay busy and the opportunity kind of fell in my lap." I shrugged. "At the time, I figured that if I couldn't play ball, it didn't really matter what I did."

"And now?"

"Now I'm trying to figure out what to do with the rest of my life."

"You have so much baseball experience and I know you have a ton of contacts. Isn't there *something* you'd want to do that would keep you involved with the game?"

Talk about the perfect segway to tell her about my conversation with Mr. Hanover. But instead of telling her about my potential job offer, I just said, "I'll figure it all out eventually."

So much for always telling the truth.

Chapter 22

Barbara

I found Molly standing beside my patio table when I brought the salad outside.

"I still can't get used to your new hair," I said. "You look like a different person."

For all the years I've known her, Molly had worn her shoulder length hair pulled up into a French twist. A couple weeks ago, she had it cut into a short, sleek bob with a side bang. The new hairstyle makes her look ten years younger.

She patted her hair. "Thank you. I'm so happy I did it. It's so easy to care for and I do really like the way it looks."

"Have a seat and help yourself to some salad. I'm just going to grab a bottle of wine."

Running back inside, I grabbed two glasses off the shelf and a bottle of white out of the refrigerator. After turning the stove off, I headed back out to the patio.

"The table looks lovely," she said as she poured homemade Italian dressing onto her salad.

"I've wanted to have you over to say thank you for all you did for me while I was laid up."

"Oh honey, you don't have to thank me." She patted my hand. "We're family, we take care of each other."

I smiled at her words. Molly has treated me like family since before Stewart and I were married and continues to do so years after our divorce. But instead of letting things get too sappy, I decided to change the subject to her new beau.

"So I haven't really spoken to you since your weekend away. How was it?"

"It was wonderful. The wedding was beautiful," she said. "Bill's family was so welcoming and I really enjoyed being there."

"I'm happy to hear that, and I'm happy you two are getting along so well."

Molly took her time spearing lettuce with her fork.

"And what about your young man? How's that going?"

I couldn't stop the smile from spreading across my face at the thought of Cal.

"Things with Cal are great. It's like…" I shook my head.

"Like?"

"Like we've never been apart," I finished. "Like we picked up right where we left off."

She smiled. "You deserve to be happy."

I swallowed down the lump in my throat and nodded.

We finished our salads and I stood, stacking her dish on top of mine. I told Molly I'd be right back with our dinner. After rinsing the salad plates, I dished out two healthy servings of shrimp scampi over linguini and grabbed the garlic bread out of the oven.

"That smells delicious," Molly said as I set her plate down in front of her. She twirled pasta around her fork then speared a shrimp and took a bite. "Mmm, it tastes even better."

We chatted about what we've been doing the past couple weeks since we hadn't seen much of each other. Molly told me how fond Mr. Robinson is of Cal and how happy he is that he's fitting in so well at the bank. I didn't mention that Cal's banking career may not be a long-term thing.

"Bill has been planning an extended trip to Europe and wants me to go with him," she said. "He doesn't have any dates set in stone, but has a list of places he'd like to visit."

"How long would you be gone?"

"A month, maybe two if he keeps adding to the itinerary."

"That sounds amazing!" I said. "Oh my gosh, what a dream."

She nodded. "I haven't mentioned the trip to J.P. and Stewart yet, so please don't say anything. I'll tell them when I have dates and exact plans."

"Your secret is safe with me."

She picked up a piece of garlic bread and took a bite.

"Mmm, this is so good," she said. After she chewed and swallowed, she asked, "So, what did you want to talk to me about?"

"What do you mean?"

"You don't have much of a poker face, Barbara, and it's obvious there's something on your mind."

I toyed with the remaining pasta on my plate, deciding to start with the name change.

"I filed paperwork a couple weeks ago to change my name back to Murphy." She just looked at me and blinked, so I continued. "It will be finalized this week."

Molly rested her fork on her plate and pushed it toward the center of the table.

"Well, you and Stewart *are* divorced so I shouldn't be surprised, but I guess I am because
you didn't do it immediately."

"It honestly didn't even occur to me back then, and when Stewart brought it up, I dug my heels in. Probably because it was so important to him." I shrugged. "It's not really a huge deal, I just wanted to let you know before you heard from someone at work. I'm sure word will get around once I do the official name change in HR."

"I do appreciate you letting me know." She winked. "I have to keep up the appearance that I still have my finger on the pulse."

Which leads to why I have to share my next news with her. Since making the decision, I've tried to figure out how to tell her, but there's no easy way. So I just have to say it.

"There's something else," I said. Molly took a sip of wine and I waited until she swallowed to speak again. "You know I love my job and I adore working at Molly Mack, but I think it's time for me to start looking for something else."

Her brow furrowed as she stared at me from across the table. After what seemed like forever, she blinked, then picked up her wine glass and drained it before very deliberately setting it down. Toying with the stem, she asked, "Did something happen?"

Even though she didn't add *with Stewart* it still hung in the air between us.

"Nothing specific."

"I do know that you love your job and the company is very lucky to have you. You're smart and level-headed, plus you know the business and you're good with people." Her glistening eyes met mine. "So why?"

"Molly, you know the issues between Stewart and me. I had hoped that they'd go away with time, but that just hasn't happened. In some ways, they've gotten worse." A million things popped into my head, but this conversation isn't about bashing her son or listing all the problems between us, it's about sharing my future plans. "Right now, you're around to mediate, but I can't expect you to be our buffer forever. I know Mr. Robinson is hoping to retire and I imagine with you two spending so much time together, it's in your near future, too. I'm sure this extended trip to Europe is just the first of many you'll want to take. And you deserve that. You've worked hard your whole life and single-handedly made Molly Mack Chocolate what it is today. It's time for you to reap the rewards of that and enjoy yourself." She shook her head and opened her mouth, but I spoke again, before she could. "My work life would be miserable without you there and the tension between Stewart and me wouldn't be good for morale or the company."

Molly blinked then wiped away a tear with her index finger.

"I'm sorry that it's come to this." She sniffed. "Through the years, I've talked to Stewart, I have, but—"

I cut her off.

"It's not your fault. Stewart is a grown man and his actions are his own. The fact that we have issues has *nothing* to do with you."

Molly didn't look convinced, but she let the topic of Stewart drop. She picked up her napkin and dabbed tears from her eyes.

"When will you be leaving?"

"I haven't even started looking yet. I wanted to have this conversation first so you didn't find out I was looking for something else." Her image blurred as I smiled and squeezed her hand. "Molly, I appreciate all you've done for me, how you've been like a mother to me, even after the divorce." I swallowed and wiped the tears from my cheeks, then chuckled. "I don't know why I'm crying. I mean, I'm just getting a new job, it won't change our relationship."

"You've been working at Molly Mack Chocolate your whole adult life. Deciding to change that must be scary, not to mention sad. I know it makes me sad, even though I understand your reasons. And you're right, it won't change our relationship. I'll still consider you my daughter no matter where you work, or live, or who you're married to." She added those last words around a sly smile. "I know that once you put word out that you're looking for a new position, you'll be flooded with offers, but if you need help just let me know."

I couldn't stay in my seat anymore. I stood and gave her a hug, holding on tight until the angle made my ankle hurt and I had to let go.

"Thank you Molly. I don't know what I'd do without you."

"Hopefully you won't find out for a long time," she said.

Chapter 23

Barbara

"This place is so romantic."

Cal and I sat at a table for two on a deck overlooking the ocean. Since I got out of my boot, he's been determined to take me out at least twice a week, under some misguided notion that he has to make up for not being able to "spoil me" when we dated in college.

"Dan and Sabrina said the tuna tartare appetizer is really good and that if they have oysters we should get them." He looked up at me. "That is, if you like oysters."

"I do and I also love tuna tartare."

The waitress brought the bottle of wine we'd ordered and went through the whole opening and tasting ritual. After she filled our glasses, she took our orders and we were once again alone.

"I had so much fun today. It was nice moving around like that again."

Since I got the go ahead from both my doctor and Sabrina, we'd gone hiking at one of the state parks. Just a short hike and I know Cal really slowed down so I could keep up, but I'd still done it.

"How does your ankle feel?"

He looked down and I lifted my foot so he could see it.

"It's a little swollen, but Sabrina said to expect that. But it doesn't really hurt...no more than the rest of my legs anyway."

"I'll rub them later." He bobbed his eyebrows. "And anything else that hurts."

"Hmm, come to think of it, my whole body is feeling a little achy."

Before he could comment, the waitress returned with our appetizers, but it didn't stop his eyes from devouring me. They continued to devour me as I added cocktail sauce and Tabasco to an oyster, then picked it up, held it to my mouth, tipped my head back, and swallowed. I may have added a little more tongue and suction than necessary.

"Good?" he raised his brow and gave me a sexy smirk.

I licked my lips and met his hot gaze. "Real good."

Turnabout is fair play and Cal did a sexy slurp of his own oyster, making my lady parts tingle thinking about his tongue giving them the same treatment.

The food foreplay continued through the oysters, but we let up when we started on the tuna tartare. If we didn't, we probably wouldn't have made it through dinner. As it is, I had to keep my thighs pressed together to ease the throbbing ache between them.

Time to bring the heat level down a few notches.

"I'm sorry about the Waves losing."

After winning the Division Series, the Waves lost the League Championship Series in five games.

"Yeah, it sucks, but without the pitching staff at a hundred percent, their chances of winning weren't great." He shoved a tuna-covered crispy wonton into his mouth and chewed, then smiled. "They did win the game I announced, so no one can blame me for bringing bad luck."

I rolled my eyes. "I'd think you were joking with that last statement, but I know how ridiculously superstitious you guys are."

"I wouldn't say it's ridiculous."

"Do you remember the socks, Cal?"

He threw his head back and laughed. "I can't believe you remember that."

"Cal, I think I'm still scarred by that. Do you know what it was like sitting downwind of you guys?"

Cal's team went undefeated sophomore year and five games into the streak, the entire team stopped washing their socks in order to "keep the luck" in them.

"Hey, it worked, didn't it?"

I laughed at the smug look on his face.

"So spill." I took a sip of wine and placed it back on the table, wrapping my fingers around the base of the stem. "What kind of crazy things have you done in the past fifteen years in the name of good baseball?"

"Nothing is crazy if it works." I raised my eyebrows, prompting an answer. "Okay, me telling you these things is in no way an admission that they're crazy." I nodded and waved my hand in a circular motion urging him along. "I chewed different flavored gum for offense and defense."

"Seriously?" He nodded. "What kind of gum?"

"Grape for defense and original for offense," he said. "But if my batting tanked or I had an error I'd switch it to watermelon for defense and berry for offense. Mixing it up like that for a few days usually restored things back to order."

I had no idea what to say to that, so I just urged him to continue. "What else?"

"What makes you think there's more?"

"Just a hunch."

"I got dressed the same way for every game, which actually may be more of a routine than a superstition."

"What happened if you strayed from your *routine*?" I asked.

"One time I put on my right sock before the left and I went 0-5."

I rounded my eyes. "And putting your socks on in the wrong order caused that?"

"You can't prove it didn't." His eyes crinkled at the corners.

I love that he can laugh at himself, at this. And it's nice to see him talking about his baseball life without having that sad look in his eyes.

"True," I said. "Anything else?"

"One time, Jack's bat was put in my bin by mistake and I hit a walk-off home run with it. After that, I continued to use his bats through a two-week hitting streak. Once the streak ended, I went back to my own." He chuckled. "Later in the season, he had trouble hitting and tried using one of my bats, but it didn't work for him."

"I guess the luck only went one way."

"Guess so." He shrugged as if what I'd said was perfectly logical and took a sip of wine. "Like Yogi said, 'Baseball is 90% mental, the other half is physical.' A player eating the same pregame dinner for twenty years, or tucking four-leaf clovers into the sweatband of his cap, or wearing a gold thong might sound silly, but if he *thinks* it works, that's all that matters. It's a long season," he said, drawing out the long. "You gotta do what you gotta do to keep putting up numbers."

"Makes sense," I said, then had to ask. "A gold thong?"

"Yep, and I'm not telling who."

The waitress brought our entrees, crab cakes for me and New Orleans style catfish for Cal. She'd barely left the table and I had my fork in hand.

"Mmm, this looks amazing." I scraped my fork across the surface of one of the crab

cakes, flaking it apart. "Look at those lumps of crabmeat." I speared a piece and placed it in my mouth. The flavors burst on my tongue, the salty sweetness of the crab enhanced by the more subtle flavors of dijon mustard, hot sauce, lemon juice, and just a hint of Old Bay.

I took another quick bite then filled the fork again and held it out to Cal. He leaned forward, wrapped his mouth around my fork, and slowly slid back. His gaze never left mine as he slowly chewed.

"That's really good. Here, try this," he said, and put together a bite of his catfish for me, being sure to include a piece of the spicy crawfish.

"Ooh, I like that. There's just enough spice."

We also shared bites of our sides...his, dirty rice and sautéed corn and red peppers, and mine, roasted parmesan potatoes and grilled zucchini. It was all very domestic.

"So did you ever have to dye your hair during your professional career?"

"No," he chuckled. "That was so awful. I couldn't wait for that color to grow out."

One of the good luck rituals his college team had was that the freshmen dyed their hair the school colors, teal and gold, the night before their first tournament. So they showed up to the first game of the season showing school spirit, each player's hair in his preferred pattern. Cal had gone with alternating vertical stripes. It looked quite impressive.

"I didn't know if your mother was going to laugh or cry when she saw it."

"Yeah, I'm not sure she knew either," he said. "She alternated between wanting to shave my head and talking about team spirit."

We ate in silence for a few minutes, just enjoying the good food, great atmosphere, and incredible weather. Not to mention each other's company.

I'd just placed the last bite of crab into my mouth, when Cal spoke.

"We had a lot of great times back then."

He raised his voice slightly on the last word turning his sentence into a question. I looked up and found his gaze trained on me, the candlelight flickering in his warm brown eyes.

"Yeah, we did," I admitted around a small smile. "It's funny, I blocked those memories out for years. It was just—" I took a drink of water and cleared the lump from my throat. "It was necessary to move forward. So I took a few weeks to wallow then balled up all those memories and locked them away." I shook my head. "But since you've come back into my life, all those things keep coming back to me too. I'll get little memory flashes at the most random times, and they make me smile." He reached over and laced our fingers together. "You make me smile."

"You make me smile, too." He lifted our joined hands and kissed my knuckles one by

one. "And we're gonna get it right this time."

CAL

I practically dragged Barbara out of the car and into the house. Instead going upstairs, I speed walked into the rec room and flopped onto the leather sofa, pulling her on top of me. I closed my eyes and groaned when she settled her legs on either side of my hips and rubbed against the erection that had been raging since the appetizer course.

Placing my hands on either side of her face, I pulled her down and crashed our lips together. A sigh escaped her as I focused on her bottom lip, nibbling and sucking at it before opening my mouth fully over hers. She tasted like the chocolate soufflé we'd had for dessert and I wanted more. Dragging my hand through her hair, I cupped the back of her head and pulled her closer to get a better taste.

I felt a moan vibrate through my mouth and chest but couldn't say if it came from her or me. It didn't matter. We were a delicious mess of tongues and lips, as our hips ground against each other.

Moving my hands down her back, I cupped her ass and pushed her down onto my dick as she continued to thrust. I ended the kiss and took in a deep breath, allowing her to do the same.

"Christ Barb, you're so fucking perfect." I squeezed my fingers into her hips to keep her still as her moist heat teased me through layers of clothing. "I can't get enough of you."

I held her gaze as I struggled to catch my breath.

"Cal?" She blinked. "What's wrong?"

"This seemed like a good idea, but I just realized I don't have any condoms down here."

A slow, sexy smile spread across her face then the damndest thing happened. She sat back and placed her hands at the bottom of her shirt then slowly dragged it off. After tossing it on the floor, she reached behind and unhooked her bra, giving it the same fate.

My control slipped away with every second that ticked by and I had to keep reminding myself about the condoms hiding all the way upstairs. At this point, I may have to crawl to get them, and it would be so worth it.

Barbara placed her hands on my stomach and eased them up my chest, dragging my shirt up as she moved. With her fingers digging into my pecs, she placed her mouth directly over mine and said, "Today is day number eight of birth control."

It took my sex-fogged brain a second to process the meaning of that sentence.

"Day eight?" She nodded. "So we don't need a condom?" She shook her head. "Thank fuck."

I wrapped my hands around her waist and flipped us over so I was on top. My mind and body were locked in a war, one demanding finesse and the other insisting to get inside her immediately. I'd like to say my big head won out over my little head, but that did not happen. I mentally justified it by telling myself Barb needed relief just as much as me.

I pulled back long enough to remove our clothes, taking some satisfaction in her full-body flush. She shifted, squeezing her thighs together and I smiled down at her, kneeling at the edge of the couch.

"Oh no, for what I have in mind, these need to be apart." Taking her ankles in mine, I separated her legs. "Far apart." I bent her knees back and rested on my elbows, giving me an up-close glimpse of heaven. "So fucking perfect," I whispered and dragged the tip of my finger along her wet folds before learning forward and tracing my tongue along the same path.

Barb thrusted her hips up and let out a long, low groan. Normally I'd slowly tease and savor her, but I think we both need it a little faster than that after all our verbal foreplay.

I licked and laved, loving her taste and sounds. Cupping my hands under her thighs, I held her open with my thumbs then placed my mouth over her clit and alternately sucked and lapped with my tongue.

"Cal," she groaned, then started that sexy chant of my name, letting me know she was close. I opened my mouth wider and sucked, like I was eating the ripest, juiciest peach.

"*Cal.*" Her thighs tightened around my ears. "Oh God Cal, I'm coming."

I continued to feast until her legs loosened and dropped to the side. Pulling back, I kissed her inner thigh and looked at her over the expanse of her body. She reached down and squeezed my shoulders, urging me toward her.

"I want you inside me," she said.

I settled between her thighs and she wrapped her legs around my hips. Our new position put the tip of my erection at her entrance. It wouldn't take much effort on my part to slip right inside. Testing that theory, I slowly shifted forward and found myself sinking into her wet heat inch by slow inch. Once I filled her completely, I rested on my elbows and gave her a soft kiss, then dragged my mouth along her cheek, to her ear.

"Fuck Barb, you feel amazing."

Her inner muscles squeezed me as I nibbled at the spot just behind her earlobe. Pulling out just as slowly, I kissed my way down her neck and across her chest, her sexy sounds urging me on as I pushed back in.

"Hold on, baby."

I moved faster and faster, thrusting deeper and deeper, never wanting it to end. But all too soon, she was squeezing me over the edge. But I didn't want to go without her.

Shifting back onto my knees, I pulled her up against me, the new position dragging the base of my shaft against her clit with every thrust.

She whimpered and I froze. "Are you okay?"

"Please don't stop."

Barbara tightened her legs around my waist, pulling me even deeper inside. She held onto my shoulders and ground against me, her tight nipples rubbing against my chest as she moved up and down.

I was about to give her a thirty second warning when she threw her head back and thrust harder, groaning louder, starting that sexy name chant. She tightened rhythmically around me just as I felt the start of my own orgasm. I closed my eyes, drowning in pure sensation as she continued to move, riding out the wave.

BARB CURLED UP AGAINST ME AND I REACHED BEHIND ME AND GRABBED the quilt from the back of the couch and threw it over us. She tucked it under her chin and snuggled closer. I closed my eyes and enjoyed the feel of her in my arms.

"Cal?"

"Hmm?"

"Is this quilt made of your old baseball jerseys?"

I peeked one eye open and found her beautiful blue eyes looking up at me. I got lost in them for a minute before I realized she was waiting for an answer.

"Yeah," I said. "My mom made it for me when I graduated college."

"She made this?" Barb shifted onto her elbow and skimmed her hand over the individual squares. "It's amazing."

"There's one at my parents' house, too. And I think she still has some shirts left. There were so many. She's been saving them since pony league."

"What a great gift," she said, resting her forearm against my shoulder and leaning her chin against it. "Did she make one for your brothers too?"

I nodded. "Mine is the only one with a theme. Theirs have some old baseball jerseys but she didn't have enough for a whole quilt so she added in some of their favorite T-shirts."

"And I never asked, when did you graduate?"

"Two and a half years after I left. I was able to take online courses and do independent study during the off season."

"That's pretty impressive. Most guys in your position wouldn't have bothered."

"I know, but if you'll remember, I promised my mom I would."

She kissed my shoulder. "You're so sweet."

I shrugged. "Maybe, but I had to graduate. She wouldn't give me this quilt until I did."

Her laugh echoed through the room, the sweetest sound in the world. She settled her head against my chest and wrapped her arm around my waist.

I knew I'd be happy in this house the moment I saw it...and I have been. The location is perfect and I rearranged and remodeled every inch, turning it into the exact space I wanted. But whenever Barb is here, it feels different. Better. More homey. And I want that all the time.

I've been pretty clear about my feelings for her for weeks now, probably since the moment I saw her in that meeting. There were so many times I almost told her, but I held back, not wanting to move too fast. But I can't wait anymore.

"Barb." I kissed the top of her head. "Are you asleep?"

"No."

Her warm breath puffed against my chest. I brushed my lips against her forehead, then rubbed my cheek against her silky hair. She sighed, the contented sound making my heart skip a beat. Things had always been so perfect between us, so right. I hate the term "soul mate" but if I have one, Barbara Murphy is it.

"I love you." She took in a sharp breath then slowly raised her head to meet my gaze. Those adorable lines formed between her brows and I leaned forward to kiss them away. I pulled back and met her watery gaze. "I love you."

"I love you, too." She smiled, then sniffed and reached up to wipe away a tear that had escaped.

I kissed her and pulled back, knowing I must look like a lunatic with a huge smile on my face. Hopefully her answer to my question won't ruin that.

"Will you move in with me?" Her eyes widened. "I know it's only been a couple months, but we didn't need that whole getting-to-know-you period because we already knew each other. So we just had to get reacquainted." I smiled again, giving her the dimples I know she loves so much. "I love you and I love when you're here. Please move in with me."

"Are you sure?" she asked, still looking a little shocked.

"I'm absolutely positive."

"Then yes."

Chapter 24

Barbara

"You weren't that bad," Jess said as we walked out of the studio to our cars.

Since I was given the green light, I decided to jump back into yoga, knowing it was going to be awful. I wasn't great before, and taking a couple months off didn't improve that.

"We'll agree to disagree," I said. "But like you always say in class, at least I'm there doing it which counts for something." I unlocked my car. "I'll see you at my place."

"I'm so sweaty. I can't wait to get in the water."

"I'll see you there."

After starting my car, I pushed the button to open the top. Once there was nothing more than blue sky and fluffy white clouds above me, I shifted the car into drive and followed Jess out of the parking lot.

I'd planned on telling her that I'm moving in with Cal before class, but I didn't get there as early as I'd anticipated. Something uh, came up and I was late getting out of bed.

She's going to be thrilled. She'll also keep me from overthinking it.

I enjoyed the ride home, knowing my top-down days are numbered as winter gets closer. Jess was just getting out of her car when I pulled up. She grabbed her bag from the passenger seat as I put my top up.

Grabbing my towel and yoga mat, I stepped out of the car, my thighs protesting.

"Ugh, after my hike yesterday and today's class, my legs are not happy."

I unlocked the door and Jess followed me inside.

"What are you thinking, strawberry daiquiris or margaritas?" I asked.

"I'd love to say both, but tomorrow *is* Monday," she said. "Do you have whipped cream?"

"I think so. Let me check." I opened the refrigerator and spotted a can of Redi Whip on the door shelf. Picking it up, I shook it, happy to find it mostly full. "Yep."

"Then daiquiris it is," she said. "I'm gonna go change. I'll be right out."

I pulled a bag of frozen strawberries from the freezer and tossed it on the counter. After retrieving the blender and rum from the cabinet, I grabbed the canister of sugar and started playing bartender. I tossed the ingredients into the blender and at the last minute remembered I had bottled lime juice, so I got that from the refrigerator and added a few dashes. I topped off the blender with ice, put on the top, and flipped the switch.

"Oh, is there a sweeter sound than a blender?" Jess asked, walking into the kitchen in her pink bikini. "It's usually either churning out a milkshake, frozen coffee, or fruity concoction sure to give me a buzz."

I flipped off the blender, picked up the pitcher and shook it, then pulled off the top. Grabbing a teaspoon from the drawer, I took a taste.

"Hmm, I think they're good." I filled the spoon again and held it out to Jess. "What do you think?"

"Perfect," she said. "I'll do that. You go get changed."

"Thanks."

I went into my bedroom and got into my suit. It's not as sexy as Jess's, but the high waist hides a multitude of sins and the halter-style, top holds up my DDs. And I love the navy and white polka-dot print.

Jess was already in the pool when I walked outside. She sat on the steps with a drink in her hand. I grabbed drink she'd poured for me and walked over to dip my toe in to test the water. It's been chilly at night, but Molly turned the heater on so the water is perfect.

I walked down the steps and sat next to Jess.

"You look like a freaking pin-up model in that suit." She looked at my chest and made a face. "I am so jealous of your boobs."

She says that every time I wear something that shows cleavage. Meanwhile, I'd love to have her long, lean body that looks amazing in a string bikini.

"Well, the grass is always greener."

"True statement," she said.

I held up my drink and she clinked her glass against mine. I took a drink then licked the whipped cream from my upper lip.

"Cal asked me to move in with him."

"What?" Jess screeched and turned sideways to face me. "We've been together for hours and you're just telling me this? When?"

"Last night," I said. "Or maybe it was this morning. The timing is kind of fuzzy."

"Why didn't you text me?"

I glanced over at her, my brows raised. "Sorry, we were a little busy. And I was going to tell you before class, but ended up getting out of bed later than expected. I couldn't tell you during class and once it was over, I figured I'd just tell you when we got back here." I shrugged. "So here we are."

"When are you moving?" She grabbed my arm stopping me from taking another drink. "You did say yes, right?"

"I did."

"Oh my God!" she squealed again. "I knew it! I knew you were going to end up together the second I met him."

I figured I might as well get all her squeals out at once before we continue the conversation.

"He told me he loves me," I said and was not disappointed with her reaction.

"So again I ask, when are you moving?"

"As soon as possible, I guess. It shouldn't take me long to pack. I really don't have a lot of stuff. None of the furniture or appliances here are mine, not even the dishes or pots and pans. I literally moved in here with nothing but my clothes," I said.

"That's because you walked away from shithead Stewie with nothing."

"I didn't want anything from that house anyway."

"I would have taken stuff just to spite him."

I shook my head and finished my drink. "Once I found out about him and Frances, I just wanted to get out." But Jess knows all this, so there's no reason to bring it up again. "Need a refill?"

She held out her empty glass and I grabbed it as I walked up the three steps out of the pool. I went into the pool house and pulled the pitcher out of the freezer and refilled our glasses then topped both with a healthy dose of whipped cream.

"Here you go." I held out her drink. "What are you feeling for lunch? I should get something in my stomach before I have much more of this."

"Nothing in particular," she said.

I stepped back into the pool and placed my drink on the side, then swam to the center of the shallow end. I bent my knees and lowered into the water until it hit my shoulders then I floated in place while we discussed the local places who would deliver.

We'd just narrowed it down to Chinese and the pub down the road when I noticed Molly standing on her back porch.

"When are you gonna tell her?" Jess asked, putting a halt to the food discussion.

"Again, as soon as possible."

"No time like the present," she said as Molly walked off her porch and toward us.

I followed Jess out of the pool and walked over to the bin of towels and grabbed one for each of us.

"Don't get out on my account," Molly said.

Jess gave her a kiss on the cheek and said, "We were just deciding what to order for lunch. Are you hungry?"

"Oh no, thank you, Bill is picking me up in a little bit. I just came out to say hello."

"Love is in the air." Jess bobbed her eyebrows, making Molly laugh. "So what do you think?" she said to me. "Chinese or pub food?"

"Pub food. I think it will go better with the daiquiris."

"Good point," Jess said. "Just a burger?"

I nodded. "And an order of that cajun shrimp appetizer."

"I'll go place the order," she said, giving me a pointed look before going inside.

Molly took a seat at the table and I sat next to her.

"Bill and I are discussing our Europe trip today," she said. "We're meeting with his travel agent tomorrow so she can tell us our options."

"I'm so excited for you," I said. "You deserve this extended vacation and anything else you two plan."

I added that last sentence because I'm sure Stewart is going to have issues with her being gone for so long. That or he'll use it as an opportunity to take over and rule like a dictator in her absence.

"And you? How is the job search going?" she asked.

"I've contacted a couple places I'd be interested in working, but neither of them have anything available at the moment."

"Do you want to stay in finance?"

I nodded. "You know what a numbers nerd I am."

"If I hear of something, I'll let you know."

"I appreciate that, especially considering the circumstances."

"Barbara, there are no circumstances," she said and squeezed my hand. "You need to do what's best for you. And as much as I'd like to say otherwise, your reasons for leaving are valid."

Talk about a perfect segway.

"Speaking of leaving," I said. "Cal asked me to move in with him."

"Oh Barbara, that's wonderful." Her smile dimmed slightly and she added, "I'll miss you living here, of course, but as with the new job, it's good for you and will make you happy."

"Molly, I can't thank you enough for letting me live here. I've probably overstayed my welcome, but the past three years have seemed to fly by."

"You have not overstayed your welcome. I've enjoyed having you here." She squeezed my hand again. "I'm thrilled to see you moving forward. And just like with the change of jobs, your change of residence will not alter our relationship at all." She chuckled. "I won't be able to pop outside and interrupt your girls' day but not many mothers can do that with their children."

"You are never an interruption and I expect you and Mr. Robinson to come for dinner once I'm settled in at Cal's."

"When do you plan on moving?"

"I'm guessing as soon as I can pack, which shouldn't take me too long."

Mr. Robinson's car pulled up the driveway and Molly lit up at the sight. I'm guessing Cal and I won't be the only ones co-habitating soon.

"That's my ride," She pushed away from the table and stood. "Let me know when you're packing and I'll come help. I'm sure that young man of yours is going to want you out of here as soon as possible." She winked and walked away, detouring a few steps to open the door of the pool house. "Jess, it's safe to come out now."

Cal

"I don't think I've ever had this many people here," Barbara said looking around.

The week after I'd asked her to move in with me, I arrived with Jack and Dan to help move her stuff to my house. Jess and J.P. had come too and Molly was being the perfect hostess, setting out a sandwich platter and pitchers of sweet tea and lemonade.

"It's a good thing Monte couldn't make it, he may have put us over capacity."

Barb didn't have too much to move so after hauling most of the boxes out to the 4Runner and Dan's Escalade, we all decided to take a break. It had started to drizzle so everyone was inside scattered around the kitchen area, with Dan and Jack sitting at the bar chatting with Molly, and J.P. and Jess standing just off to the side listening.

"Let's go grab something to eat before those oafs eat everything," I said.

Barbara walked into the kitchen while I took a seat next to Dan on the other side of the bar. She handed me a plate and picked up one for herself.

"Molly, these look amazing," Barb said. "Thank you for putting this together."

"We can't have these big, strapping men doing all that heavy lifting without some sustenance," she said.

I grabbed two sandwiches and filled the rest of my plate with chips.

"I still can't believe I'm sitting here with *the* Molly Mack," Dan said. "I sold your candy for fundraisers all through school. This is definitely an item checked off my bucket list."

Molly blushed, obviously loving the attention.

"You'll have to make sure to bring Lexi over some day when Molly is at the house," I said. "Does she even realize Molly Mack is a real person?"

"Oh she definitely does. She wrote a paper on the company for school last year."

"What the hell is a ten-year-old doing writing a paper?" Jack asked.

"That's what I said." Dan wadded up his napkin and put it on his empty plate. "But it's a whole new world."

"Lexi has a sweet tooth to rival Cal's," Barb explained to Molly. "You're probably like a rock star to her."

"I understand a sweet tooth. That's how I ended up in the choco-late business," she said. "It was my favorite thing, still is even after all these years." She wiped her hands on a napkin and stepped back to throw it and her plate in the garbage. "Bring Lexi in for a tour some-time. I'll personally show her around," she told Dan. "You and your wife too, of course."

"She'd love that," Dan said. "We all would."

"You can let Barbara know when you're available and we'll set it up." She clapped her hands. "It will be so much fun."

"Barb, I have a class in an hour," Jess said. "Is there anything you need me to do before I leave?"

"I don't think so," she said. "Thank you so much for helping me pack all week. It made it much more fun."

"I'm not sure if that was me as much as it was the wine."

"If you're not doing anything when you're done, come over to the house," I said to Jess, then looked at J.P. and Molly to include them in the invite as well. "We're not doing anything fancy, just unloading boxes and grilling some burgers."

These are the most important people in Barb's life and I want them to feel comfortable coming to the house.

"Thank you," Molly said. "But Bill and I are having dinner with his brother and sister-in-law."

Jess and J.P. both said they'd come, which is good becuase it will give our friends a chance to meet.

I looked around at the empty plates and platters and figured it was a good time to load the rest of the boxes. Everyone agreed. Jess said her goodbyes when I told her we have things all under control.

Molly and Barbara cleaned up the kitchen while the guys and I packed the rest of the boxes into the trucks. I figured they'd probably need a moment or two alone anyway. I'm hoping to get some time alone with Molly as well.

"You guys can head to the house," I said.

"Where do you want these?" Jack asked.

"They're all clothes, so I guess in the bedroom."

They climbed into the Escalade and headed down the driveway.

"What's your cell?" I asked J.P. "I'll text you the address."

He rattled off the number and his phone chirped a few seconds later with my message.

Looking down, he said, "Got it. I'll see you later."

"Thanks for helping.

"Anytime."

I walked back inside once he drove away.

"I'll come back sometime this week to give it a deep clean," Barb said.

"Don't be silly, I'll have a cleaning company come in and do it." Molly looked around and spotted me. She smiled and looked back at Barb. "Looks like you're all ready to go."

Barb nodded then walked over and hugged Molly. "Thank you so much." She pulled back and looked her in the eye. "For everything."

"You are more than welcome." Molly placed a kiss on Barbara's cheek. "But don't think you're going to be rid of me just because you're moving."

"I know." Barb sniffed. "And I'll definitely see you Monday."

Molly nodded and walked toward me. She placed her hand on my arm and said, "You take good care of her." I nodded and she kissed my cheek then walked out the door.

I spotted the garbage bag resting next to the kitchen and figured this was my chance to get Molly alone. Walking across the room, I grabbed it and said to Barb, "Why don't you take one last look around while I put this outside."

Barb nodded and I jogged out the front door, making sure to close it behind me.

"Molly." She turned when I called her name, her foot on the bottom step of her porch. I'm glad we're far enough away so there's no chance of Barb overhearing our conversation.

"I want to talk to you about something," I said as I approached.

"Is everything all right?" she asked. "I was pretty proud of that exit just now."

"It was a pretty sweet exit." I looked over my shoulder to make sure Barbara hadn't followed me out. "But there's something I wanted to tell you. Or ask you." I took a deep breath and let it out in a quick burst of air. "I asked Barb to move in with me because I couldn't stand being away from her. But I don't want you to think that's the only thing I want." Molly's eyes widened, then seemed to fill with understanding.

"I know Barb considers you a second mother and it's pretty obvious you think of her as a daughter. And since her mom isn't here, I wanted to let you know how much I love her and that I plan on spending the rest of my life with her if she'll have me. I bought a ring and plan on proposing to her in a couple weeks." I chuckled. "Hopefully she'll say yes because my whole family will be in town and I won't be able to lick my wounds in private.

"I know it's old-fashioned but it is tradition, and since you're the most important person in Barbara's life, I would really like your blessing."

"Oh Cal." She squeezed my hand and blinked away tears. "*You* are the most important person in Barbara's life now and I know she'll say yes." A slow smile spread across her face. "That girl deserves all the happiness in the world and I have no doubt you'll give it to her."

"Thank you," I said and kissed her cheek.

"You are most welcome," she said.

I held up the bag that was still in my hand. "I better go put this in the bin and get back inside."

Molly nodded and continued on her way up the steps.

I practically floated back toward the pool house, happier than I've been in a long time. After dealing with my divorce and retirement, I finally feel whole again. Happy. Like things are falling into place.

Chapter 25

Barbara

J.P. and I sat across from each other at the table in the small conference room.

"Do you think we should allocate more funds to the local fundraiser promotions?" I asked.

"If we have it to pull from somewhere else, it wouldn't be a bad idea."

A few months ago, Molly Mack Chocolate was approached by a local print shop asking if we'd be interested in working with them to provide custom logo wrappers for our fundraiser candy bars. They'll print a school or organization's logo on a label and we'll wrap it around ours. It's such a great idea, I don't know why we didn't think of it before.

It takes an extra step on our part to add the logo wrappers to the candy bars, but we've tested them with a few local school districts and they've sold really well. So now J.P. is looking to gradually expand marketing on the product. But since this idea popped up out of nowhere, we hadn't planned for the added expense.

I smiled over at him. "You know I always have money tucked away for unexpected things like this."

Clicking into our shared drive, I updated my master spreadsheet to show the change of allocation, then changed it in the main system, noting detailed reasons for the money shift. Those two moves will notify anyone who needs to know what's been done.

"Thank God for that. You've saved my ass a few times with your slush money."

"Anything else we need to discuss?" I asked.

"I think we covered everything on my list."

I looked at the clock on my laptop before shutting it down. I'm taking a half day today and I'll also be off Monday and Tuesday. Tomorrow is the Waves meet and greet at the stadium and Cal's entire family is coming to attend and spend a long weekend.

"Are you all settled in at Cal's place?" J.P. leaned back in his chair.

"For the most part. I have two or three boxes to unpack but they're filled with old photo albums and stuff like that. Nothing that has to be dealt with immediately."

One I haven't unpacked yet is my "Cal box" where I stuck all the items from our relationship. Even through my marriage, I could never bring myself to throw its contents away. Cal and I had a great time looking through it all. Pictures, a few movie stubs, and lots of flattened boxes of Hot Tamales with the little notes he'd written me. I'd put everything back in the box, but had pulled out the T-shirts he'd given me way back when so I could wear them now.

He told me he has a similar box in his bedroom closet at his mother's house. It's amazing, we were apart for fifteen years, had both married, and still couldn't throw our memories away.

"You're living there almost two weeks. How's it going?"

"It's been amazing. If it was a superstitious person, I'd be nervous," I said around a nervous chuckle. "From the moment I saw him again, it's been perfect. Well, since I opened up and really let him in anyway."

"Just so you know, I think you guys are great together. And from what I can see, he treats you the way you deserve to be treated." I nodded, acknowledging his words. "So are you ready for his family to descend on your little bubble of happiness?"

"I think so," I said. "I always loved Cal's family. Being around them was so different from how I grew up. My mom was terrific, but it was always just the two of us so it was pretty quiet and mellow. Cal's house was the total opposite of that. It was loud and there was always something happening. I can't imagine how crazy it's going to be with the addition of his nieces and nephews, but I'm looking forward to finding out."

"I'm sure you're chomping at the bit to get out of here." J.P. stood and shut his laptop then stacked his notebook on top. "All I ask is that you don't forget your old in-laws when you bond with your new ones." He smiled.

"You and Molly will always be family. You're the only good thing that came out of my marriage to Stewart." I stood and gave him a quick hug. The door to the conference room opened just as we pulled apart.

"This is where you're hiding," Stewart said, looking aggravated. "Before you leave, I need the financial report for the expansion. The one with all the costs broken down."

There are at least three other people who can get that report for him, not to mention the fact that he has access to the drives where they're stored. But instead of telling him that, I opened my computer again.

"You okay here?" J.P. asked and I nodded. "Then I'll see you Wednesday."

He left without acknowledging Stewart's presence. They barely speak these days unless it's necessary for business.

Stewart hovered over my shoulder, arms crossed over his chest. As quickly as possible, I found the report and emailed it to him.

"Anything else before I shut down again?"

He shifted to the side and I turned to look up at him.

"I understand you moved out of the pool house," he said.

I swiveled my chair to fully face him. "I did."

"You moved in with Cal Chase?" I nodded. "Neither J.P. nor my mother would tell me where you went at first. I could care less about my fairy of a brother, but don't appreciate you turning my own mother against me. I don't know what kind of stories you've told her through the years, but there's definitely a change in our relationship, not to mention the fact that she doesn't interact with Frances unless I force it."

So many thoughts ran through my head at his tirade. For instance, why does he care where I moved? And stories? I haven't told Molly anything. I didn't even tell her about him and Frances initially. Which brings me to his second wife. Why is her lack of a relationship with Molly my fault?

But I didn't vocalize any of that. I just sat there watching him ramble on, just like I usually do. Eventually he'll run out of steam and then I can leave for my long weekend.

As if he read my thoughts, he said, "And I can't believe you're taking two and a half days off when you were just off for six weeks."

I couldn't *not* comment on that.

"I was on medical leave for six weeks. That has nothing to do with my vacation time."

I thought about mentioning that I've lost more vacation time than I've used through the years, but decided not to.

"Since you insist on working here, you should at least have the decency to show up once in a while." His mouth curled up into a smug smile and I knew he was getting ready to hit me with something good. I braced myself. "Don't get too comfortable where you're living. I can't imagine someone like you keeping someone like Cal Chase's attention for long. And I hope you've been upfront with him about the fact that you can't have children."

For years I've let Stewart verbally run me over, not wanting to engage or make waves. But his last comment felt like a knife to my heart, bringing back all the hurt and disappointment I felt for all those years we tried to conceive. It was a low blow, even for him. That added to the other shots he fired at me was just too much.

I stood, the momentum pushing the chair against the wall. Stewart actually flinched, his beady eyes blinking in shock.

"First of all, I haven't said anything about you to your mother. I studiously avoid speaking about you in any way, shape, or form both in and out of her presence. In fact, I don't talk or think about you at all. And I'd appreciate it if you'd afford me the same courtesy." I took a deep breath and slowly let it out. "I don't *insist* on working here. I'm damn good at my job and the company is lucky to have me." He opened his mouth to say something and I slashed my hand through the air and told him to shut up. "You've had your say for the past twelve years, now it's my turn."

His look of shock was almost comical, but disappeared before I could fully appreciate it.

"I don't know what your problem is with me. You're the one who cheated, and even though that's true, I walked away from our marriage with next to nothing. I've put up with your adolescent behavior and bitter comments through the years but I won't do it anymore. So this is your warning. Don't push me if you don't want to be pushed back."

I picked up my laptop and cell and cradled them against my chest.

"And as far as children, you've been with Frances for almost five years now and have been married for almost three, and there's still no pitter patter of little feet in your house."

I almost felt bad about that last comment, not because he didn't deserve it, but because it means I've stooped to his level. But I'm too fired up to feel remorse. I stormed past him and put my hand on the doorknob, but before opening the door, I remembered one last thing and turned to face him.

"And you call J.P. a fairy and other words meant to emasculate him every chance you get, but he's more of a man than you'll ever be."

That last zing launched, I ripped the door open and stormed out.

CAL

"I still can't believe you're getting married," I said to Jack.

He, Dan, Monte, and I sat eating lunch on the deck of a small restaurant about an hour from home. We'd just been measured and fitted for our bespoke wedding suits. No rentals for us. I don't mind, I can always use a charcoal suit.

He smiled and placed his hand over his heart. "What can I say?"

"First you," Monte looked at Dan. "Then Jack, and I'm thinking wedding bells aren't too far off for you," he said to me. "I'll be the last man standing. What kind of prize do I win?"

"A weekly date with your right hand," Jack said.

We all laughed and Monte tossed his last bite of bread at Jack's head.

Comments and bits of food flew back and forth like we're in high school. I guess it's true that no one grows up in baseball.

Before things got too out of hand, I decided to share my news. It actually links in to what Monte said, so he'd given me a good opening.

"Behave children," I said. "There's something I want to discuss."

After busting my ass for the serious tone, they settled down and continued eating as they waited for me to speak.

I looked at Jack. "I was hoping we could make a stop on the way home."

"Sure, where'd you need to go?" he said.

"Hammond's Jewel Case."

They all froze in place, Monte and Dan in mid-chew. Then like someone waved a magic wand letting them move again, they all reacted at once.

Dan and Monte sat on either side of me and each gave me a side hug. Jack walked around the table and wrapped his arm around my neck and gave me a noogie on the top of my head.

Once they all settled down, Dan asked, "When are you proposing?"

"Sunday morning," I said. "Barb loves watching the sunrise at the house, so I thought I'd take her for a walk and do it then."

"Does your family know?" Jack asked.

"My parents do and my mom is thrilled. She's already asking about wedding dates and plans, as if I have a clue." I took a drink of sweet tea and set my glass down. "But I'm not thinking beyond popping the question at this point and hoping she says yes."

"Like there's a chance that won't happen," Dan said. "But I know what you mean. I was a nervous wreck when I proposed to Sabrina."

"And you know I was so nervous, I changed my whole proposal plan because I was afraid I was just gonna blurt it out on the way to the restaurant," Jack added.

"You guys have faced down hundred-mile an hour fast balls but freaked out about asking the women you lived with to marry you?" Monte shook his head and smirked.

"You'll see," Dan said. "It's not that easy. No matter how secure you feel in your relationship, there's always that doubt in the back of your mind."

"Well, I don't plan on proposing to anyone anytime soon, so I'm good thanks."

"Sounds like he's testing fate with those words," Jack said.

And honest to God, I never thought I'd hear Jack Reagan utter the word *fate*. Love does crazy things.

"Oh no," Monte said. "Do not turn into those married people who insist on finding their single friend a mate. I'm fine on my own and if you start trying to set me up with people I swear, I'll find new friends."

"Promises, promises," Jack said then tossed down his napkin. "Come on, let's get the check and take Cal to get his ring."

THE GUYS DROPPED ME OFF AND, WITH THE RING BURNING IN MY pocket, I let myself into the house through the garage. As soon as I stepped into the rec room, the amazing aroma of garlic and herbs assaulted my senses, making my mouth water and my stomach growl even though I was still stuffed from lunch.

I took the steps two at a time and the comforting smell intensified when I stepped onto the second floor. The soulful sounds of Van Morrison poured from the bluetooth speaker and I spotted Barbara in the kitchen, her hips swaying in rhythm as he joined Van in singing *Have I Told You Lately?* as she stirred a giant pot of saucy goodness.

Coming home to her is one of my favorite things. The home-cooked meal is just a bonus. Still stirring, she looked over her shoulder and smiled.

"How was your day?"

Before I could answer, she turned back around, gave the sauce one last stir then tapped the wooden spoon and set it on the side of the stove. I walked up behind her and wrapped my arms around her waist, interlacing my fingers over her stomach and slowly swayed to the music. Shifting her hair out of the way with my chin, I kissed her behind the ear.

"It was good. Our suits will be ready in a couple weeks." She turned in my arms and I gave her a quick kiss. "How about yours? Did you get out when you planned?"

"I actually left a little early," she said, after a short pause.

There was a whole lot of something packed into that pause. I pulled back slightly and looked her in the eye.

"Did something happen?"

She shook her head and looked at the ceiling before meeting my gaze again.

"Nothing out of the ordinary."

"Stewart?" She nodded. I pulled her closer and kissed the top of her head as she rested her cheek against my chest. "I'm sorry, honey."

"But you would have been proud of me. I kind of freaked out at him before I left."

"Freaked out at him?" She nodded then pulled back to look me in the eye. "This I gotta hear."

Wrapping my arm around her shoulders, I led her to the couch. I sat down and pulled her onto my lap, her legs resting on the cusion next to us.

"Okay, spill."

She told me about how Stewart had searched her out and all the awful things he'd said. I was proud when I heard her response, especially since she'd normally just ignore him. And while I *am* proud and I know Barb can handle herself, I decided that Stewart and I need to have a come-to-Jesus meeting at some point.

"I am proud of you," I said. "I don't know how you've put up with him all these years. I've only met the little pissant a couple times and it took all my willpower to not throat punch him."

"He's not worth bruising your knuckles."

"Maybe not, but it would definitely make me feel better."

She curled her fingers into my hair and pulled me in for a quick kiss.

"I love you," she said.

"I love you, too."

I pressed my lips to hers, intending to give her a slow, soothing kiss to seal my words, but it soon turned wild, frenzied. She shifted to straddle my lap, nudging her heat right up against me.

Things were starting to get really good when I heard voices downstairs. It's times like this I wish I didn't share the passcode to get into my house with my entire family. Of course, before Barbara, it had been a long time since there was a *time like this*. And when I was married to Marsha, my family hadn't come around much.

Barbara jumped off my lap and smoothed her hair. I stood and kissed her forehead then pulled back and smiled down at her.

"Ready or not, here they come."

Chapter 26

Barbara

I leaned against the deck railing, sipping coffee, enjoying the quiet of the morning. I'm definitely more of a morning person than Cal and since I moved in, I've been sneaking out here to watch the sunrise and enjoy my coffee, before slipping back into bed to start the day off right with the man I love.

After being up late last night getting reacquainted with the Chase family, I woke up later than usual and missed the sunrise, but still got up before everyone else. I threw the two French toast casseroles I'd put together last night into the oven. They take an hour to bake, so I have some time before I have to start cooking the bacon.

I heard the patio door open and glanced over my shoulder to find Cal's mom walking onto the deck.

"Mind if I join you?" she asked.

"Not at all."

"It's so peaceful here. I'm so happy Cal found this place. He always wanted to live right on the beach. Since he was a little boy." She set her mug on the railing. "Of course, I wish it was a little closer to home." Smiling over at me, she added, "But now he has you here so I don't have to worry about him not being happy anymore."

I felt a blush spread across my cheeks. Laura Chase had greeted me with open arms when she arrived last night and we picked up as if fifteen years hadn't passed since we last saw each other.

"We are happy," I said. "And I know he's thrilled to have you all here this weekend. So am I."

"Thank you for being so welcoming. Marsha tried to pretend she enjoyed having us around, but it was obvious she didn't. Whenever we visited them in New York, which wasn't often, we stayed at a hotel." She chuckled. "I know we're a lot to handle, but I hated the fact that I didn't get to see him as often."

"I've always loved spending time with your family. You always made me feel welcome, now it's my turn to do the same."

Before she could respond, I heard a noise against the door. We turned in unison and I spotted Cal's two-year-old niece Allie on the other side of the glass waving at us. The little girl is all Chase with her curly black hair and big brown eyes.

Allie's mom Kelsey picked her up and opened the door then stepped on the deck. I knew Jamie's wife Nic from before, but I just met Alex's wife Kelsey and Ben's wife Veronica last night. We all hit it off immediately and I know we're going to be great friends. Which is good because I plan on sticking around.

The little girl tucked her face into her mother's shoulder when I said hello to her. She's still a little shy around me, but I'm sure we'll fix that by the end of the weekend.

"I was so happy when Cal told me he has a couple nieces," I said. "It must be a nice change after being surrounded by boys all those years."

"Don't get me wrong, I love my boys, but it's so much fun shopping for the girls," Laura agreed. "There are so many cute things for them."

We chatted for a little while, mostly about the kids, when my phone alarm sounded. I dismissed it and said, "Time to cook the bacon."

"Barbara, like I told you last night, you don't have to cook for us all weekend," Laura said.

"I don't mind, I love cooking," I said. "But I only planned last night's spaghetti and today's breakfast. Cal plans on grilling later. We have burgers and hot dogs, and he's picking up steaks on the way home. And tomorrow we're doing brunch at Molinaro's and then sandwiches or leftover spaghetti."

An odd look crossed Laura's face, but before I could question it, Cal joined us.

"Is this a girls only party?"

He gave me a quick kiss before taking Allie from Kelsey's arms. The little girl might be shy around me, but she loves her Uncle Cal, whose name she squealed when he walked outside.

"If it was, you just crashed," I said. "But I was actually just going inside to cook some bacon."

"I'll come help," Kelsey said. "You think you two can handle this little munchkin?"

"I think we'll be fine," he said.

Allie had snuggled against Cal's chest and looked content watching the ocean. I felt a squeezing around my heart as Stewart's words came back to me before I could stop them. Cal is so great with his nieces and nephews and I know he always wanted children of his own. I just don't know if I can give them to him. I'd gone on the pill as a precaution, but even when I got the prescription, I wondered if there was any need for it.

Kelsey and I walked into the kitchen and I pulled the bacon from the refrigerator.

"I was just going to put it on sheet pans and throw it in the oven," I said.

"That's the best way to do it. No popping grease and it always comes out perfect."

After turning on the oven, I pulled three sheet pans from the cabinet and placed them on the island. Kelsey already had the bacon unwrapped and she grabbed a pan and started laying the individual strips out.

"Cal is like a different person since you've gotten together," she said.

"You think so?"

I'd started my own pan of bacon, my hands getting greasier as the task went on.

"Mind you, he was already married when Alex and I started dating. Imagine how shocked I was to find out the guy I met on a blind date is Cal Chase's brother." She giggled. "I'm a huge baseball fan and I'll admit that I fan-girled a little when I first met him, not to mention his friends. He's been graceful enough to let me forget that." She gave me a pointed look. "Alex however, has not." She filled up one pan and started on another. "Anyway, he was married and that was whatever it was. He seemed happy at the time, I guess, but not happy and content like he looks now. And then Marsha dragged him through that awful divorce and he got hurt and ended up retiring. It couldn't have been easy." She shrugged. "I never heard him whine about it and he tried to act fine, but we could tell he wasn't really happy."

We'd filled three pans and there was still bacon left in the pack, so I found another sheet pan. I'm sure it will all get eaten and if not, we can either use it for bacon burgers or BLTs later.

I looked across the living room and through the patio doors at Cal and Laura deep in conversation out on the deck. Whatever they were discussing looked pretty serious, but neither looked upset, so I just went back to focusing on my task.

"Alex told me he always thought you and Cal should have ended up together," she said, continuing our discussion. "The whole family is thrilled you found each other again and I can see why."

"We're very lucky to have a second chance."

Voices sounded downstairs and I know it won't be long before the gang comes looking for breakfast. I put the sheet pans into the oven and set the timer.

"I'm going to go grab a quick shower before everyone else wants to," she said. "Tell Cal to knock if he wants a break from Allie."

"Will do."

But Cal didn't look like he was going to want a break anytime soon. I mentally sighed. We've discussed my issues conceiving, but haven't *discussed* it in terms of us. I guess the time has come for that.

WATCHING CAL INTERACT WITH FANS LITERALLY GAVE ME GOOSEBUMPS. It's obvious they love him and he is truly in his element being surrounded by and talking baseball all day. I'd expected something totally different today, something more formal, but this meet and greet is really great. It's not just players sitting behind tables signing autographs for a line of fans. The players are actually mingling with people, having conversations. It's very up close and personal. And there was Hannah, iPad in hand, keeping it all running smoothly.

"She's amazing, isn't she?" Sabrina asked.

We stood on the concourse bridge, watching from above, away from the crowd. Lexi had run off with her friends and Gavin slept peacefully in his stroller, which she pushed back and forth.

"I'm pretty organized, but she makes me look like a novice. Her checklist for the wedding should be patented."

She chuckled at that and leaned down to adjust Gavin's blanket.

"Why don't we head to the conference room? This is ending soon and that's where everyone will end up. And I really just want to sit down."

"Lead the way," I said.

We took the elevator to the fourth floor and turned left when we got off. As we walked down the hallway, Sabrina said, "I'm glad this one is sleeping," she said as she faced me again. "There's something I wanted to talk to you about and this gives me a chance while we're alone."

"Is everything okay?"

There were already some people milling around the conference room when we entered and Sabrina introduced me as we made our way to a couple chairs tucked into the corner.

"Sorry, I didn't mean to make it sound so serious. Cal told Dan that you're looking for a new job."

While she phrased it as a statement, it was definitely a question.

"I am," I said. "Did he tell him why?"

"The abridged version," she said. "I can't imagine how you've worked with your ex for so long considering what a douchebag he is. That's Cal's word, not mine."

"It's a good word for Stewart."

"You haven't met Dan's cousin Jeff yet, but he's a great guy. Before I came along, he was Lexi's manny and also handled Dan's portfolio. Once we got married and I took over the childcare, he opened up to new clients and things have really taken off. He's thinking about taking on a partner. When Cal mentioned your background is in finance and that you're looking for something new, I thought you might be a good fit. I told Jeff I'd talk to you about it and give you his contact information if you're interested."

"Oh wow. This is...wow." I quickly formed a pros and cons list in my head and couldn't think of a reason I shouldn't at least take an initial meeting. "I'd definitely be interested in talking to him."

She pulled out her phone. "I'll text you his information and let him know you'll be in touch."

"Thanks for thinking of me," I said.

She nodded. "So how are you holding up with your full house?"

"Well, it's only been one night, but so far, so good."

Cal's parents had decided to skip the meet and greet and offered to watch Allie. Jamie and Nic and Ben and Veronica were mingling somewhere downstairs with their children. Alex and Kelsey had stopped in for a little while and left to enjoy some child-free time.

More people trickled into the room, including Hannah. She stopped and said something to one of the guys manning the buffet, then walked over to us.

"They're clearing out the fans now so the guys will be up soon," she said.

"This is pretty impressive," I said. "With all that's happening, there should be total chaos but you have it all under control."

"I just do the planning, I have a lot of people to help keep it running smoothly."

"Like your soon-to-be husband always tells me, you're good at what you do, own it," Sabrina said.

Hannah smiled and nodded, a sappy smile on her face at the mention of Jack.

I spotted Penny Montgomery talking to a man as they both made their way through the buffet. Her amazing copper hair flowed behind her as she threw her head back and laughed at something he said. It was beautiful when I saw it in a braid, but hanging around her shoulders, it looks even more fabulous.

They moved over to a corner and continued their conversation.

"Who's Penny talking to?"

"Mr. Hanover's son, Kenny," Hannah said.

"Looks like sparks are flying over there," Sabrina said and bobbed her eyebrows.

And it wasn't just Sabrina who noticed that. Dale Montgomery spotted his sister immediately as he entered the room and walked over to join in the conversation. From the look on Penny's face, she wasn't too pleased about that.

Sabrina chuckled. "Nothing like an over-protective big brother to spoil your fun."

The three of them talked for a few minutes before Kenny excused himself. Penny watched him leave then gave her brother a look that should have dropped him to the floor. He shook his head and said something. She answered through gritted teeth. He spoke again and she rolled her eyes and walked away.

"Well that was interesting," Sabrina said.

But before either Hannah or I could comment, our guys entered the room and we had our own sparks to deal with.

CAL

"It's been a long day," I said.

"But it's been fun." Barbara kissed my chest then settled back into place. "And tomorrow's another full day."

If she only knew.

"Do you do this often? Have your whole family here?"

"This is only the third time they've all been here since I've moved in. My dad and brothers came down a few times to help me remodel," I said. "Before that, I didn't have a big enough place for everyone. Not that it's huge here, but we make it work."

"The kids are having a ball downstairs," she said. "And they sure do love their Uncle Cal."

"Yeah, I don't see them as often as I'd like, but that just means I get to be the fun uncle."

"You're so good with them."

What she said wasn't at all sad, but her tone had a melancholy undertone. I shifted back to look down at her.

"You okay?"

She froze in my arms, seeming to hold her breath. I turned onto my side, resting my head on the pillow so I could face her. I stroked her cheek with my thumb until she lifted her gaze to look at me.

"What's going on in that pretty head of yours?" I asked.

She'd been quiter than usual earlier, but I didn't think much of it. It *has* been a long day, not to mention loud with my whole family here. On top of that, the guys had come over after the meet and greet adding to the insane number. But it's obvious that something is troubling her.

"I'm not sure if I'm bringing this up too soon or if we should have already discussed it," she said. "You're so amazing with your nieces and nephews, Cal. You're a natural. And I know you've always wanted children of your own." Those frown lines appeared between her brows as she picked her next words. "What if I can't give them to you?"

An ache formed in the center of my chest at the pain in her eyes. I was going to answer her question but it was obvious she had more to say, so I stayed silent. She focused on my chest and swallowed, then nibbled at her bottom lip before meeting my gaze again.

"I told you about the issues I had in the past and how the doctors couldn't find anything wrong. But I never got pregnant. Not once in almost ten years. When I called my gynecologist for birth control, I asked if it was even necessary. She reminded me that all of my tests were normal and there was no medical reason why I couldn't conceive. And, she recommended using birth control unless I'm actually trying to get pregnant."

She blinked and a lone tear made its way down her cheek. I wiped it away with my thumb and silently urged her to continue.

"This has been in the back of my mind, but seeing you with the kids just brought it all to the forefront. I planned on bringing it up after this weekend, when everyone left. But as usual, you read me like a book and knew something was wrong," she said around a watery smile. "Again, I guess I should have brought this up before, maybe when you asked me to move in." She shrugged. "I don't know. I just don't want you to feel stuck with me if we eventually start trying to have a baby and it never happens."

She'd covered so much but I wanted to address her last sentence first.

"Let's get one thing straight. I will never feel like I'm *stuck* with you. Please understand that. Yes, I've always wanted children, and if we can't have our own, maybe we'll look into adopting. But if it ends up being the two of us for the rest of our lives, that is more than enough." She watched me with wide blue eyes. "*When* we decide it's time to have a baby, we'll deal with whatever happens. You said none of the tests showed a physical reason why you couldn't conceive. Maybe the universe knew it wasn't the right time for you, that you weren't with the right person."

I leaned forward and kissed away a tear from her cheek, then followed it up with a soft kiss to her mouth.

"But either way, it's you I want. Anything more is just icing on the cake."

Tears flowed down her cheeks and I pulled her close and just held her like that, her soft sobs the only sound in the room. I stared at the ceiling, thankful we'd discussed this now. I'll be asking her a very important question in approximately five hours and I don't want anything else on her mind but the word *yes*.

Her tears slowly subsided and her breathing evened out. She shifted back until her head rested on my bicep instead of my chest. I'm guessing it's partly to look at me and partly to move her cheek from the wet spot her tears had formed on my T-shirt.

She reached out and dragged her index finger along my jaw and down my chin before rubbing it along my bottom lip. I kissed the tip of her finger and she smiled.

"I love you so much," she said.

"That's good, because you're stuck with me."

Taking in a deep breath, she let it out on a chuckle.

"And only you would compare a baby to icing, Mr. Sweet Tooth."

I threw my head back and laughed, the sound echoing through the room.

Tucking her back against my chest, I kissed the top of her head and said, "Get some sleep, tomorrow's a full day."

BARBARA CONKED OUT SHORTLY AFTER OUR CONVERSATION, BUT I SLEPT in starts and stops, worried I'd miss the dawn. I was going to tell her to wake me in case I overslept, but didn't want her to get suspicious. She probably wouldn't even think about it, but I didn't want to take any chances.

I went over everything I wanted to say to her yet again, knowing I'd probably forget half of it anyway and just blurt out the question. But I guess the important thing is that I do ask.

Barb stirred in my arms, rubbing her cheek against my chest in that adorable way she has. A few minutes later, she kissed my chest then shifted away to climb out of bed. Normally I feel her leave and roll over and go back to sleep for a couple hours. Now I grabbed her wrist and pulled her back to me.

"Hey."

I brushed my lips against hers and tucked her back against my chest.

"What are you doing awake?" she asked, settling against me.

I shrugged. She didn't push for more of an answer than that. We held each other like that, dozing for a few more minutes before she pulled back again.

"As much as I'm enjoying this, I need to go to the bathroom," she said.

I released my hold on her and enjoyed the view as she scurried off the bed and walked across the room in a pair of cheeky underwear and one of my old college T-shirts. As soon as she closed the bathroom door, I jumped out of bed. I walked to the closet and pulled on a pair of shorts with pockets and a new shirt. Retrieving the ring box from the suit pocket I'd stashed it in, I slid it in my pocket and looked in the mirror to make sure it wasn't visible. I called it good and stepped back into the bedroom just as Barb was coming out of the bathroom.

Her eyes widened. "Where are you going?"

"Since I'm awake, I thought I'd watch the sunrise with my favorite girl." I kissed her forehead and headed to the bathroom. "I'll be right out."

I realized through my sleepless night that I'm not so much nervous of her rejecting me as I am that I won't make this absolutely perfect for her. After washing my hands and brushing my teeth, I looked in the mirror and gave myself a quick pep talk.

She'd changed into shorts and a tank top and looked absolutely adorable sitting on the edge of the bed. I held out my hand and when she took it, I led her out of the room, through the living room, and out the patio doors.

"I thought we'd watch from the beach today," I said. "Maybe go for a walk, enjoy the quiet."

"That sounds wonderful."

We walked down the stairs and I opened the gate then gestured for her to step through. After closing the gate behind me, I took her hand again and we walked onto the beach toward the water until we hit the wet sand and the more persistent waves tickled our feet. I turned toward the left since there are fewer houses that way.

"It's so perfect here," she said. "I love it."

She'd given me a perfect segway and I looked over my shoulder to make sure we were far enough away from the house. I'm pretty sure my mom was peeking out the window of her bedroom when we were leaving, and I was hoping to do this without an audience.

I stopped walking and stepped behind Barb. Wrapping my arms around her waist, I kissed her behind the ear, then rested my chin against her temple. We watched as the sun peeked up across the ocean, slowly making its way above the water and toward the sky.

"And I love you." I tightened my arms and she leaned back slightly, resting against my chest, placing her hands over mine. "When I bought this place, my life was in a total upheaval. My marriage ended, my career ended, and when I found this house, I tore it apart and put it back together, hoping I'd be happy here. And I was, or at least I thought I was." Barb shifted her head to glance back at me, and I smiled. "When I walked into that bank meeting, it was like every cliché in every romance novel ever written when I spotted you. My heart skipped a beat, colors became brighter, and I felt like someone turned on a light brightening my dark world. And I sat in that meeting, mentally plotting a way to get you into my life again and keep you this time."

Her lips curled up at the corners. "I thought you were soaking up every word of my fascinating presentation."

"Okay, maybe my attention was divided, but by the end of that meeting, I had a plan. Which of course got shot to hell when you broke your ankle, but I'm nothing if not flexible." Sliding my hands along her waist, I stepped around until I stood in front of her. "And with you in a boot, it was actually better for me because you couldn't run away."

She slapped my chest and I placed my hand over hers, holding it in place. I'm sure she could feel my pounding heart. Hell, she could probably hear it, even over the sound of the ocean.

"Somehow, I lucked out and even after you healed, you still didn't run. Then I convinced you to move in here with me and this house finally became the home I'd dreamed it would be." I wrapped my fingers around hers and held our joined hands at our sides, retrieving the ring box from my pocket with my other hand. "And I know it's only been two months...well, eighteen years and two months." I smirked. "But I'm hoping my luck holds out and I can convince you to do one more thing."

Her eyes widened as I dropped to one knee in front of her, then shifted between mine and the open ring box I held up.

"Will you marry me?" She opened and closed her mouth, but no sound came out. So I added, "Please?" and smiled wide, flashing the dimples I know she loves so much.

"Yes." The word came out on a hoarse whisper.

"Yes?"

"Oh Cal, yes." She nodded. "Yes. Yes. Yes." Her voice got louder and stronger with each word.

I stood and she tightened her arms around my neck as I picked her up, spinning us around and around as we alternately laughed and shared deep, wet kisses. I held her tight as she slid down my body until her feet touched the sand.

She looked up at me with smiling eyes and said, "Did you really just ask me to marry you or was that a dream?"

"It wasn't a dream, I really asked." I stepped back and held out the box I still clutched in my hand. "I got a ring and everything."

"Oh Cal, it's..." She reached out but stopped with her hand hovering over the box. "It's gorgeous."

I pulled the ring from its velvet cushion and took her left hand in mine, then slipped it onto her third finger.

"Perfect fit." I raised her newly beringed hand and kissed her knuckles.

Taking her hand back, she turned it this way and that, watching the sunlight play off the diamond. She looked up at me, her eyes glistening with tears.

"I love you, Cal." She sniffed. "I love you so much."

"I love you too, baby." I reached out and wiped a tear that had escaped the corner of her eye. I nudged my head in the direction of *our* house. "Come on, my mom is probably ready to burst onto the beach to find us."

Chapter 27

Barbara

The weeks following our engagement were loud and lively and full of laughter. Cal's mom had greeted us with a big smile when we made our way back to the house right after he proposed. Thankfully she insisted on taking pictures of us because I didn't even think about capturing the moment. Well, after the moment, but Cal and I still beamed like lovesick fools.

The first of our celebrations was during champagne brunch at Molinaro's. Thankfully Cal had reserved a private room because things got pretty loud. Since then, we've been taken out to dinner by his friends, my friends, and Molly and Mr. Robinson. And while it's been fun, it's been exhausting.

Of course, everyone has been asking if we've set a date, but we honestly haven't discussed it. We just got engaged...shouldn't we have time to just enjoy that before jumping into planning a wedding?

Apparently the answer to that is no since everyone keeps asking.

I pulled into the parking lot of my favorite sushi place. I'm meeting Dan's cousin, Jeff Nealon, to discuss working with him some more. We'd already had a phone conversation and I'm definitely interested in what he has to offer so we decided to discuss things more in person.

As I walked through the parking lot, I realized that the last time I was here was with J.P., when I discussed leaving Molly Mack. If I end up deciding to work with Jeff, things will be coming full circle here.

I spotted Jeff in the hostess area as I entered the restaurant. Sabrina had shown me his picture so I'd be able to recognize him. She must have done the same for him because he greeted me immediately.

"Barbara?"

I nodded and held out my hand. "It's so nice to meet you."

His kind hazel eyes met mine as we shook hands.

The hostess was next to us immediately, menus in hand. She led us to a table near the window and took our drink orders.

"So, I hear congratulations are in order," he said.

"Yes, thank you."

"I won't ask if you set a date because I know that drove Sabrina crazy when she and Dan got engaged."

"That's funny because I think it's the first question she asked me when she found out. But the answer is no, we haven't set a date yet."

"Nothing wrong with that," he said.

The waitress brought our drinks and asked if we were ready to order. Even though I hadn't looked at the menu, I knew exactly what I wanted. Apparently Jeff is a regular here as well because he ordered a couple specialty rolls without looking at the menu either. Once she left, Jeff got right to it.

"We've already discussed your professional background, but I wanted to meet in person to explain a few things, dig a little deeper into what you want," he said. "Sabrina mentioned you before your engagement so that can't be the reason you're looking to leave Molly Mack after more than a decade."

Although phrased as a sentence, that was definitely a question. I took a drink, running different answers through my head. As I swallowed, I decided to just go with an abridged version of the truth.

"Did Sabrina mention that I was married to Stewart Mack?"

"She did."

"Since the divorce, it hasn't been easy working with him. He's just not cooperative and it makes getting things done difficult. Right now, Molly keeps him in line and we manage to get things accomplished with her involvement. But, she won't be there forever, and a few things happened recently that made me realize that no matter how much I love Molly, the company, or my job, it's time for me to move on."

"That was a very diplomatic way of summarizing a situation that must be very difficult."

"Thank you for saying so. I was hoping to not come off like a bitter ex-wife."

"Do they know you're looking?"

"Yes. Well, Stewart doesn't, but Molly and her other son, J.P. do."

"And they're supportive of the move?"

"They're not thrilled with it, but understand my decision."

"So they're not going to offer you a salary increase and perks to make you stay?"

"Definitely not."

"Well, I'd say their loss is my gain," he said. "That is, if you decide to make the jump once I explain what I have in mind."

Our sushi arrived and Jeff told me about what he's looking for as we ate our rolls.

"You mentioned that you don't have investment skills or licenses, but you do have a finance background and you know how to analyze numbers. I was thinking that to start, you could just help me keep an eye on the portfolios, making sure there's a good ROI and spotting anything negative. I have software that I'm sure you'll have no problem using, but I still do some things manually."

"So I don't need any licensing immediately?"

He shook his head. "Not for the first few months anyway and that will only be necessary if you really want to get it. Right now I'd just really like someone working with me, who I can trust, and who isn't going to get all googly-eyed when my more famous clients come to the office."

I stopped mid-chew and said, "Please tell me that didn't really happen."

"Oh yes, it did." He chuckled. "I had three assistants before I finally gave up and decided to work solo. And it wasn't just that they'd fangirl when someone came in, I was afraid to give them access to information about certain clients for fear of what they'd do with it."

"That's understandable."

"I have an office, but once you're up to speed, you could work from home a couple days a week if you'd like. That's what I usually do. I started off in my home office, but once I took on clients I wasn't related to and didn't know personally, I figured it was time to get a separate space for meetings."

It took a minute for what he said to sink in. It sounded like a done deal here.

"Are you saying I have the job?"

"If you want it, it's yours. You have great experience, we seem to get along well, and I know I can trust you to not hit on the clients." I laughed at that last point. "You told me your salary requirements and I'm good meeting them. The only question is, when can you start?"

I PUT MY FEET UP ON THE OTTOMAN AND STRETCHED MY LEGS, WIGGLING my newly-painted toes. I'd spent the day with four amazing women being pampered in the swanky spa of the Berkman Hotel for Hannah's bachelorette party. Now the five of us are hanging out in the suite, sipping champagne, with loose muscles, fresh facials, and fresh manis/pedis.

"Thank you so much for wanting something like this instead of a crazy night of bar hopping," Melanie, Hannah's best friend slash stepmother said.

She's not at all what I expected, considering she's married to one of the biggest movie stars in the world. But she's really sweet, which I suppose makes sense considering she's Hannah's bestie. Speaking of

Aaran Diskin...I don't think I made a total fool of myself when I met him for the first time earlier.

"How long have you known me?" Hannah asked. "Bar hopping was never my thing. And honestly, I didn't plan to do anything but when Jack mentioned this, I thought it was a great idea. Besides, my soon-to-be husband and his guys aren't hitting the town, so why should we?"

"If those guys hit the town together with your father, there'd be riots," Hannah's former neighbor, Mrs. Button said. The woman is in her late seventies and reminds me of Betty White. And, she's been very vocal of her appreciation of how the men look. Especially Jack. Apparently she's always had a thing for him.

"And you'd probably find out where they were going and show up with your friends," Hannah said.

"You know me well." Mrs. Button held up her glass as if to toast and took a sip of champagne.

I obviously haven't met Mrs. Button's friends but if they're anything like her, I can't imagine the mischief they'd cause out on the town together. She's so full of life and just a lot of fun to be around, and it seems as though she says whatever pops into her head.

"So Barbara, I was told I could choose whether I wanted to be paired with Dale or Cal and I was torn, but now that you're in the picture, my decision has been made. I'll stick with Dale since he's single." She winked. "Especially since Cal has those adorable curls now. I'm not sure I'd be able to keep my hands off them."

Cal had stopped cutting his hair so short and I'm loving it. Apparently Mrs. Button is, too.

"He is quite adorable," I said.

"Who knew when Hannah and I became friends she'd surround me with such good-looking men? It's definitely a perk to the friendship," Mrs. Button said. "And meeting all you lovely ladies has been wonderful. Thank you for including me in your big day," she said to Hannah.

"It wouldn't be the same without you," Hannah said.

"Thank you for including me, too," I said. The other women are all in the bridal party. I'm just along for the ride.

"Same goes for you," Hannah said. "I'm so happy you and Cal found each other again. You're perfect together and I'm glad to have another friend." She looked at Sabrina. "Now we just have to get Karen Walsh to give Dale a chance."

I've heard Karen mentioned a few times and apparently she's a single mother Dale is interested in down in Florida, but she won't give in to his charms. I'm sure if Hannah is on the case, things will happen. Especially if Sabrina joins forces.

That reminds me.

"Thank you so much for recommending me to work with Jeff," I said to Sabrina. "The job sounds great and I'm happy I won't have to go get used to a whole new set of office politics."

"I think Jeff should give me a finder's fee," Sabrina said. "Because I know you're a perfect fit."

"Thanks for the confidence, but I think he'll probably want to see how this works out before agreeing to pay up," I told her.

"When do you plan on starting?" she asked.

"At the beginning of the year."

"And then you'll have a wedding to plan," Hannah chimed in. "Tell us what's going on with you and Cal. Any plans yet?"

I looked around the room at the four expectant faces.

"Just some vague ideas. Neither of us wants a big wedding and we know it has to happen during the off season so his friends can be there," I said. "Honestly, I think we'd both be happy running off to Vegas, but Cal's mom would be heartbroken. So we'll figure something out."

"If you need help planning things, I'm happy to help," Hannah said.

"I've seen you in action so you can be sure I'll be taking you up on that offer," I said then finished off my champagne. I stood and refilled my glass then walked around the room and topped off the other girls. "But enough about me. This is your night. We should be talking about you and Jack."

"She won't give details of their sex life," Mrs. Button said. "I've tried to get her to share a tidbit or two, but she refuses."

"Especially not with me in the room," Melanie chimed in. "She's afraid I'll share details of my sex life."

Hannah made a gagging noise. "Please stop."

"If you feel the need to discuss, I'm always available," Mrs. Button said, waggling her eyebrows.

"Yeah, go out with Mrs. Button and her friends some night. They love to discuss details."

"We'll need to get Jess and Mrs. Button together sometime," I said. "They'll have a great time together."

"Oh, Jess is so awesome!" Hannah said. "We'll all have to go out after Jack and I get back from Fiji."

"A private jet then three weeks in Fiji with Jack Reagan," Mrs. Button said, fanning her face with her hand. "I expect pictures. Lots and lots of pictures."

Hannah giggled. We just finished our second bottle of champagne here in the room, plus we had a few glasses throughout the day down in the spa. We're all getting giggly. And I know I'll probably have one hell of a headache tomorrow, but tonight will be worth it.

CAL

Barb walked out of the hotel wearing dark sunglasses even though it's an overcast day. I opened the passenger door and took her duffle bag before helping her into the 4Runner.

"You okay?" I asked.

She started to nod, then abruptly stopped. "Just a little headache."

I kissed her forehead then closed the door before running around to get back into the driver's seat.

"You didn't try to keep up with Mrs. Button, did you?"

"Oh God, don't make me laugh," she said. "I think we all drank equal amounts, but now that you mention it, she did look better than the rest of us when she left earlier."

"Despite the headache, did you have fun?"

"I had a great time and I think once I have some greasy hangover food, I'll be fine."

"You want to go to The Diner?"

"Sounds perfect," she said. "How was your night?"

"Nothing out of the ordinary. We had Hannah's dad there, so that was different. Lexi made Jack a T-shirt that said *Groom to Be,* which he of course wore all night. Then once the kids fell asleep, we just hung out and had a few drinks. I took an Uber home just after midnight." I glanced over at her. "Then I tossed and turned most of the night because I missed you."

"I missed you, too." She chuckled. "Oh God, are we one of those annoying couples that can't be away from each other?"

I turned into The Diner's parking lot and pulled into a spot then leaned over the console and kissed her.

"I think we might be."

The Diner was full of hungover college students as well as those looking for a big breakfast for very little money. This is the one place I could afford to bring Barbara back when we were dating because their breakfast specials are ridiculously cheap.

We settled into a booth in the back away from the windows and Barb slid her sunglasses to the top of her head.

The waitress came over immediately and filled our mugs with coffee and placed the carafe in the middle of the table. Barb and I each ordered the skillet special...home fries topped with cheese, sausage, bacon, and two eggs...and a side of biscuits and gravy.

"Hannah offered her services if we need help planning our wedding," she said.

"Now we just have to figure out what we want to do."

She put two creamers and a half teaspoon of sugar into her coffee and stirred.

"I wouldn't mind having it at the house. We could either set every-thing up on the beach or maybe just do the ceremony there and set up tables on the deck and in the living room. We'd have to move the furniture, but if we open all the patio doors, it will flow well," she said. "But then we'd have to worry about the weather and have a backup plan if it rains or if it's really cold." She blew on her coffee and took a sip. "Or that place where we went to see the Rat Pack is really nice. I wouldn't mind having it there."

"Do you have a date in mind?"

"Not really. I know we'll need to do it when your friends can be there, so that narrows it down to November through mid-February."

The waitress brought our breakfast over, still sizzling in personal-sized cast iron skillets. She set one in front of each of us, then placed the plate of biscuits and gravy in the middle of the table.

Barb picked up her fork. "I really want to dig into this but I learned my lesson long ago," she said. Instead she reached out and took a big forkful of biscuit. "Oh my God, this is so good." She took another quick bite.

"You look like you might reenact Meg Ryan's scene from *When Harry Met Sally.*"

"I just might." She laughed and took another bite. "You better dig in Chase, or there won't be any left."

I did just that and had to agree with her. The biscuits and gravy are amazing, just like I remember. I was mid-chew when an idea popped into my head.

"If you had a choice, would you rather a beach wedding?"

"I think that'd be nice. We could keep it casual and I like that idea. But I think I'd be a nervous wreck about the weather. Even with Hannah helping me plan every last detail, I wouldn't be able to control that."

"I'm telling her you said that. She'll be upset that you doubt her powers," I said. "But I have an idea if you want to get married at the beach and aren't opposed to a destination wedding."

"What are you thinking?"

"We could get married in the Keys or somewhere down in Clearwater. We could either do it in February just before spring training starts or figure out a date when the Waves aren't playing. The guys would all be there and we could fly my family and anyone you want to invite down there. "

Barbara blinked then squinted in that way she does when she's thinking about something.

"I'd like that, if you think we can make it work."

"Hannah will know the spring training schedule and once we have that, we can figure a date. We can do your beach wedding without worrying about the weather."

"I think I'd like that."

"Good, now we're closer to a plan than we were before," I said. "You should have a hangover more often."

She laughed. "Speaking of, do you think this skillet is safe to eat yet?"

I dug into my skillet and shoved it into my mouth and thankfully didn't burn a layer of my tongue off.

"It's good," I said around a mouthful.

She batted her eyes. "My hero."

Chapter 28

Cal

Jack and Hannah's wedding isn't until later, and since the ceremony is at Dan's house with the reception directly after, I don't need to be there until late afternoon. The weather is perfect, so Barbara and I took a walk on the beach then spent a lazy day by the pool.

I couldn't tear my eyes off Barb as she stood and adjusted the towel on her lounge chair. She looks absolutely amazing in her navy polka dot bikini and it's taken all my willpower the past few hours to not rip it off her. But we're getting close to the time where we have to go in and start getting ready, so it's now or never.

"We're gonna have to go in soon. Why don't we have one last swim?"

She glanced at the clock. "Oh wow, I didn't realize it was so late."

"Time flies when you're having fun." I stood and jumped into the pool, letting myself sink all the way to the bottom of the deep end, then I pushed off the floor and popped through the surface. Barb stood at the edge of the pool watching me. "Come on in."

"I'm not getting in *that* way," she said and walked toward the steps.

I swear she put an extra swing in her hips, but it could be my imagination after lusting after her all day. She walked down the steps and drifted into the shallow end, meeting me at its edge. Placing my hands on her waist, I pulled her against me, resting my forehead against hers. Looking down, I had a perfect view down her cleavage.

"You know this suit is driving me crazy."

I met her gaze at the same time I reached up and loosened the bow at the base of her neck, the only thing holding her halter top up. I looked down just in time to watch the material fall down until the triangles hung at her stomach, giving me an eyeful of the most perfect breasts I've ever seen.

"And what's beneath it drives me even crazier," I said. I leaned down and took one tight pink nipple into my mouth and feasted, sucking it against my tongue until her hips thrust forward, grinding into my rock hard erection that was trying to pry its way out of my board shorts.

She wrapped her legs around my waist as I picked her up and turned my attention to the other nipple. I needed more. More contact. More of her. Lifting my head, I pressed my mouth against hers and our tongues met and tangled, as she tightened her legs, rubbing harder against me. Even through the water and two layers of clothing I could feel her heat.

I walked over to the side of the pool and leaned her against the wall. She continued to rub against me and I knew I wouldn't last long. Dragging my mouth from hers, I took in a deep breath and backed away just enough to slip my fingers into her bathing suit bottoms.

My finger slipped right over her clit and into her tight, wet heat.

"Christ Barb, you're so fucking wet," I groaned and slipped another finger inside. "I can't wait to get inside you."

Her answering moan was music to my ears. I stepped back and she slumped against the side of the pool as I pulled her bikini bottoms down and off, letting them float away. She watched as I opened my board shorts, letting my dick spring free. It bobbed forward in the water and Barb licked her bottom lip then bit it as she reached out. Before she could touch me, I grabbed her wrist.

"Oh no you don't."

I turned her around and placed her palms flat against the ledge of the pool. Bending my knees, I pulled her hips back just enough and pushed forward, driving home in one swift, sweet thrust.

"Oh God, Cal."

You're telling me. Her muscles clenched and released as she relaxed and adjusted around me.

Buried deep inside her, I leaned forward and nipped at that spot behind her ear that drives her wild, then licked it with my tongue over and over, keeping time with the motion of my hips.

Her answering groan was low and deep and animalistic.

"Cal, I'm so close. So close."

I kept up a steady in and out motion, loving the drag of her walls against me every time I pulled out and her welcoming heat as I pushed back in. The water lapped around us adding to the sensation and I knew I couldn't last much longer. Reaching around, I slipped my index finger between her slick folds and circled it around her tiny bundle of nerves. Twice was all it took before I felt her walls flutter around me. I continued to hammer into her and play with her clit until she clamped down around me. Her elbows bent and I wrapped my arm around her waist to keep her from slamming against the edge of the pool.

My own release was right there, and as she writhed around me, I let go, coming so hard, I thought I might black out and drown right there in the shallow end.

"YOU LOOK SO HANDSOME," BARBARA SAID AS I SLIPPED INTO MY blazer.

I have to admit, the charcoal suit and silver tie does look pretty nice, classic. The bridesmaids are wearing silver dresses from what I understand.

"Take a good look at me because there are gonna be two other guys there dressed just like this. I don't want you to get us mixed up."

Wearing just a pale pink bra and panty set, she looped her arms around my neck.

"Like I could ever mistake anyone else for you." She gave me a quick kiss and pulled away. "I just have to slip into my dress and I'll be ready."

I watched her walk into the closet and a couple minutes later, she walked back out wearing a dress that I called pink, but was pointedly told it's vintage mauve. The neckline plunged just enough to give a hint of her amazing cleavage and the material nipped in at the waist before flowing over her curves and landing just above the knee in the front and ankle in the back. Her feet were encased in a pair of nude com-fuck-me heels that I plan on making her wear as I do just that when we get home later.

"Can you zip me?"

She turned her back and slid her hair to the side, exposing her long neck. It was all I could do to not give her a hickey right there on the side, marking her as mine. Closing my eyes against temptation, I blindly reached out and felt for her zipper and slowly slid it up her back until it wouldn't go anymore. I opened my eyes as she turned around.

My eyes took a lazy tour of her from head to toe. I felt the corner of my mouth kick up. Barb always looks amazing, but dressed up with her hair in soft waves and just enough makeup to enhance her beautiful features, she looks like she belongs in old Hollywood.

"You look absolutely breathtaking," I said.

Her cheeks turned slightly pink and she gave me a shy smile.

"Come on, let's go before we miss the wedding."

BARBARA

Jack and Hannah's wedding was larger than I anticipated but still intimate. She made an absolutely stunning bride, in her classic, off-the-shoulder satin gown. As part of his wedding gift to her, Jack had found a pair of vintage Chanel silver eyeglass frames and had them fitted with her prescription. Eyeglasses are Hannah's favorite accessory and I've been told that since they've been together, Jack searches consignment shops when he's on the road to find vintage frames for her. So sweet.

His other gift to her, a stunning pair of diamond earrings made to match her engagement ring, sparkled in her ears.

The groom hadn't taken his eyes off his bride the entire time she walked down the makeshift aisle on her father's arm. He also hadn't tried to hide the tears that filled them.

As the couple recited their vows, I glanced at my guy looking so freaking sexy standing there. He shifted his gaze and met mine and smiled. In a few short months, we'll be taking the same vows. My body broke out in goosebumps at that thought.

Even six months ago, I had no idea I could be this happy. I was content for sure, but didn't feel this deep down satisfaction with my life that I do now. I'm in love with a wonderful man who loves me just as much and treats me right. I live in a beautiful house right on the ocean. And I'm starting a new job after the holidays.

The happy couple was pronounced man and wife and Jack pulled Hannah in for a long deep kiss, bending her over his arm before letting her come up for air. The attendees clapped and hollered and everyone stood as they made their way back down the aisle. They were followed by Dan and Sabrina, Cal and Melanie, and Dale and Mrs. Button. As Cal had said, the groomsmen were all dressed alike. Jack wore a matching suit, but his tie was ivory instead of silver. The bridesmaids wore silver satin dresses in different styles.

I waited for them all to pass before making my way to the other side of the yard for the reception. There was a band and dance floor off to one side and tables were scattered through the lawn, strewn with white twinkle lights that would provide illumination once the sun set.

Cal walked up behind me as I set my purse down at our table.

"You're next, Ms. Murphy."

"So are you, Mr. Chase."

"I wouldn't have it any other way," he said.

I DON'T THINK I'VE EVER HAD SO MUCH FUN AT A WEDDING. SINCE Melanie was Cal's partner in the wedding and her husband is Hannah's father, the two of them danced when the bridal party was called up and I danced with my guy. And we stayed on the dance floor for a good part of the night, through fast and slow songs.

"I need to go to the ladies room," I told him in between songs and he escorted me off the floor.

I made my way to the downstairs powder room and when I was done and heading back outside, Hannah and Sabrina commandeered me to help the bride, who also needed a bathroom break. We went upstairs to a larger bathroom and held the dress up as Hannah did her business, thanking us and laughing through the whole embarrassing process.

"Jack offered to help, but if that happened, we'd ever come back down," she said.

When she was done, we stepped back and brushed our hands down her dress to remove some of the wrinkles.

"This is such a great wedding, Hannah," I said. "I'm really having a great time."

Jack waited for us...well for Hannah...at the bottom of the stairs. Sabrina and I chuckled.

"Come on, let's go find our guys," she said.

They didn't even notice when we left and walked outside. Sabrina spotted Dan over by the bar and went in that direction. Cal was over by our table talking to Mr. Hanover. I walked over toward them and caught bits and pieces of their conversation as I approached. I was just about to let Cal know I was behind him when the topic of their conversation became apparent and I froze in place, three feet from the two men.

"Like I said, I think you'll be perfect for the job," Mr. Hanover said. "Hadley Stone was a great coach and he will be missed, but you'll fill his shoes just fine."

"Thank you, sir. I appreciate you thinking of me. It does sound like a good fit and I know I'll enjoy getting back on the field again instead of staring at four walls all day," Cal said.

"We'll send an offer over to your agent and I promise we'll be generous. You know I'm not afraid to go in with my best offer. It just saves time giving everybody exactly what they want."

My stomach twisted and I was afraid I was going to throw up on the spot. I must have made a noise because Cal turned in my direction. The smile that was on his face when he first saw me faded when he saw the look on mine. I can only imagine all the upset and anger and betrayal are right there for him to see.

"Uh Barbara, you remember Mr. Hanover."

I pulled myself together enough to smile and say, "Of course, I do. Nice to see you again."

"You too. I understand congratulations are in order," he said.

"Yes," I said, without much conviction. I'm trying to give Cal the benefit of the doubt, but from what I heard of his conversation with the owner of the Waves, he's been offered some sort of coaching position with the organization and he's basically accepted it without talking to me. The last time he abandoned me for baseball, I had understood it was the path he'd been working toward. This new career has totally blindsided me.

"Love is definitely in the air for the Waves," Mr. Hanover said. "Enjoy the rest of your night."

I watched the man walk away and waited until he was out of earshot before looking over at Cal.

"When were you going to tell me?" I asked.

"It wasn't...I didn't..." Cal dragged his hand through his hair and looked up at the sky before meeting my gaze again. "He mentioned this a while ago, but it wasn't a done deal. Hadley Stone is the infield coach for the Fayetteville Waves, and through the years, whenever his contract came up, he mentioned retirement, hoping to use it as a negotiating tool."

"Fayetteville?" I fought to keep the screech out of my voice but don't think I was very successful.

"When Mr. Hanover mentioned the opportunity to me, he wasn't sure if Coach Stone was crying wolf again or if he was really out this time. But based on his history, I figured he'd be signing his contract at the eleventh hour and there'd be nothing to discuss. So I didn't even mention it. But Mr. Hanover found out a couple days ago that he's really retiring."

"So where does that leave us?"

He blinked. "What do you mean?"

"Are we back where we were fifteen years ago?" I chuckled and held up my left hand, flashing my diamond. "Actually we're further along than we were back then."

Cal looked around with panicked eyes.

"Can we talk about this at home?" he asked. "We have a lot to discuss and I really don't want to do it with an audience."

I nodded and used the knuckle of my index finger to dab at my right eye. I blinked and looked at Cal.

"Is my mascara okay?" I asked.

"It's perfect, just like you."

I gave him a sad smile, my head spinning with my newfound knowledge. He reached out and took my hand, then pulled it to his lips and kissed my knuckles.

"Come on," he said. "Let's dance."

He led me to the dance floor and I settled into his arms as the band played *A Thousand Years* by Christina Perri.

I fought to push the last ten minutes from my mind and just enjoy the song and the dance and the feel of being held by the man I love.

Chapter 29

Cal

Since we got home late, Barb and I decided to talk in the morning. She turned her back to me when we got into bed, but I took it as a good sign that she didn't shift away when I pulled her against me and spooned her from behind. I held onto her through the night, kicking myself in the ass for not telling her about the job when Mr. Hanover first mentioned it to me. She probably wouldn't have been so hurt and upset if she'd heard it directly from me. It was near dawn when I fell asleep and I still hadn't figured out a way to make things right between us.

I woke up alone, clutching a pillow to my chest. Rolling onto my back, I stared at the ceiling and rubbed my eyes. I'm not sure if the dull ache in my head is because I had too much to drink last night, a lack of sleep, or guilt over the fact that I have no idea how to fix things with Barb.

Oh well, time to face the music.

I got dressed and walked out of the bedroom. Barb sat at the table out on the deck, coffee in hand. Her small smile didn't reach her eyes as I stepped outside and sat across from her. We sat in silence for several minutes while I collected my thoughts, trying to figure out what to say. But there's really only one thing I can say.

"I'm sorry." She shifted her gaze from the ocean view to me, but didn't speak. "I should have told you about the coaching job when Mr. Hanover mentioned it, but I honestly didn't think it was gonna go anywhere. And—" I dragged my fingers through my hair.

"You were afraid I'd freak out," she finished for me. I nodded. "So what's your plan? What would this job entail?"

"I'd be the infield coach, which is exactly what it sounds like. I'd coach the infielders, help them perfect their game."

"And you'd have to live in Fayetteville, travel with the team?"

"I would. But it's only two hours away and there'd be days off, plus the off season," I said, grasping at straws. She didn't want that life fifteen years ago. I have no delusions she'd want it now, when we're getting ready to plan a wedding and possibly start a family.

Barb took a sip of coffee then placed her mug on the table, her movements, slow, precise, and deliberate. That can't be good.

"Cal, I love you," she said, the frown lines appearing between her eyes as she concentrated on her index finger tracing the rim of the mug. "But I really need to figure out how I feel about all this, what I want to do." She looked up at me, her blue eyes full of pain. "I'm going to stay with Jess so I can think."

I shook my head as she spoke that last sentence. "Please don't go, Barb. We can make this work, I know we can."

"I'm hoping that's true, but right now, it seems impossible. I just need some space to think." She wiped a stray tear off her cheek and sniffed. "Please give that to me."

BARBARA

"You'd think I'd be cried out by now," I said around a sad, sarcastic chuckle. "If nothing else, I should be dehydrated."

"The human body is an amazing thing."

"I'm sorry, Jess. I know you didn't plan on spending your Sunday watching me cry while I whine about my relationship."

"Hey, you know I'm always here for you," she said. "I'm not gonna lie though, you did dilute the positive energy in class earlier."

"I'm sorry about that, too. I'd hoped yoga would help me clear my mind but it didn't work. I didn't mean to sob the whole time."

"You're forgiven."

Jess got up from the couch and walked into the kitchen and returned, handing me a pint of Ben & Jerry's Phish Food and a spoon, plus a bottle of water.

"There you go," she said. "You can drown your sorrows in sugary goodness and rehydrate while we discuss this again."

I peeled the lid off the ice cream and dug in. After several spoonfuls, the only thing I could think of is how much Cal would love this. The chocolate ice cream is generously swirled with marshmallow and caramel and an abundance of fudge fish. The room blurred and I blinked, trying to clear the tears before they could fall. My cheeks and the skin around my eyes feel chapped and sore and I don't want that to get worse.

"So Cal basically took this job offer without talking to you about it, and it's a huge deal because he'd be away at least half the time."

"Pretty much," I said around a mouthful of ice cream.

"Okay, tell me what you're thinking."

"I'm wondering how we'll make a marriage work when he's not home half the time," I said then scooped another spoonful of ice cream, making sure to grab a fish. "I'm thinking that if we start a family, I'll basically be a single mother a good portion of the time." I shoved the spoon into my mouth. "And on top of those things, I'm pissed that he didn't tell me about the job, that I had to find out about it by eavesdropping on a conversation between him and the owner of the Waves. As if it wouldn't affect me, affect us."

"Don't bite my head off for saying this, but considering your history, I can kind of understand why Cal didn't tell you." My eyes bugged out of my head at her words and she held her hands out, palms up. "Just listen. From what you've said, the only reason you broke up before was because of his career. So why get you all upset this time when he didn't even have a definite job offer?"

I shrugged and put the lid back on the ice cream and placed the pint on the end table next to me. Cal had said as much, and logically it makes sense, but I'm not ready to be rational.

"That may be the case but it doesn't help me figure out how I'll build a life with a man who's not around a good portion of the time." I grabbed the bottle of water and took a long drink. "We'd even have to change our wedding plans. Which isn't a huge deal, but we just figured out what we want to do. But he'd have to be at spring training so we'd either be squeezing it in before his games or doing it ahead of time and then he'd be off coaching right away. Unless we change it to this time next year like we'd originally planned." I rubbed my temples and groaned. "It's just complicated."

"It can get complicated, for sure," Jess said. "But essentially this all comes down to two questions. Do you love him? And are you willing to make it work this time?"

CAL

"She left Sunday morning," I said to Dan after telling him my whole fucked up tale of woe. "I know I screwed up big time not telling her about the job but I can't go back and change that. I need to figure out how to fix things."

I asked Dan to come over because he's been in my shoes. Considering their history, the whole perceived baseball lifestyle freaked Sabrina out and she left to think about things, too. Not that there aren't ballplayers who are players off the field too, regardless of their marital status, but Dan was never like that.

"Have you spoken to her?" he asked.

"No. I've texted to tell her I miss her and say good night, but we haven't spoken." I took a long drink of beer then rested the bottle on my knee. "When we got back together, I couldn't help but play the what if game. What if I'd pulled out of the draft and stayed in college?

I could have been there for her after her mother died and maybe we would have ended up together. And what if I had to do it all over again, would I make a different decision? Up until Mr. Hanover offered me that job, I thought that maybe I would. Yet here I am, basically faced with the same scenario, and my first instinct was to choose baseball."

"It's tough having two loves," he said. "I was lucky, Sabrina came back. I have no idea what I would have done if she didn't."

"Even though we haven't really talked about it, I'm sure you and the guys know how adrift I've felt since I had to retire," I said.

Dan nodded and I recognized the look that crossed his face all too well. It's the one most of my former teammates have given me at one time or another. As a ballplayer, you obviously know your days on the field are limited, but it's not something you want to think about. And then something happens to put that fact front and center...like one of your best friends being forced out of the game because of an injury.

"You know how much I love the game. I've spent my life analyzing it, perfecting my play. Coach Stone helped me so much when I was in Triple A, and I know I have a lot to offer young players."

"I agree. You'd be a great asset to the organization and I know you'd love being back on the field again, even if it's as a coach. But let me ask you this," he said. "If Barbara decides she just can't handle that life and leaves again, will it be enough?"

"I'd hoped it wouldn't be an either-or thing," I said, then finished my beer in one long gulp.

"I could have Sabrina talk to her."

"I'll give her one more day before calling in the big guns." I stood. "Want another beer?"

"Sure."

In the kitchen, I grabbed two bottles from the refrigerator and twisted off the tops. I walked back into the living room and handed one to Dan before flopping back onto the recliner.

"I can't work at the bank much longer," I said. "When I took the job, I promised myself I'd give it at least a year, but even if Mr.

Hanover didn't offer me the coaching position, I'm not sure that would have happened."

"Have you considered doing something that would get you back in the game but wouldn't require you to move two hours away and be on the road?" he asked.

"Honestly I wasn't thinking of anything until Mr. Hanover brought it up."

"Did you have a plan for when you retired?"

"I figured I'd be married and have a few kids by then and would spend time with them." Dan raised his brow, as I realized the obvious. "And that's what I could have now if I turn down this job."

"Look, since I'm still playing, I'm not gonna begin to pretend I understand what it's like not being involved in the game you've dedicated your whole life to," Dan said. "But I don't imagine it feels any worse than you do now." He tipped his bottle at me in a mock toast. "And feeling like shit after the woman you love walks out the door is something I do know."

The man has a point.

"When Mr. Hanover mentioned the job, I wasn't thinking of anything beyond getting involved in the game again. I figured if the offer happened, I'd make it work with Barbara, but the look on her face..." I swallowed and shook my head. "Even if she came back, I know she wouldn't be really happy living like that."

"You guys are great together. I'm sure you'll figure it out, but if you want me to get Sabrina involved, just say the word." Dan finished his beer. "In the meantime, I thought you might be interested in hearing what I plan on doing once I retire."

Chapter 30

Barbara

I look like shit.

After three nights of crying myself to sleep, no amount of concealer can hide the bags under my bloodshot eyes or my red, chapped cheeks. When I arrived this morning, a coworker had asked if my allergies are acting up. It's as good an excuse as any. I'm glad she gave it to me to use because I have three meetings with Stewart today.

I glanced at the clock. Speaking of...it's time to head to the first one. Grabbing my computer and cell, I headed to the conference room.

J.P.'s eyes widened as I entered. He'd seen me last night, so as I thought, I'm even more of a mess today.

Stewart walked in and sat across from me. "I have a hard stop at ten so we have to start on time."

"We'll get started as soon as mom gets here," J.P. said.

Stewart started to roll his eyes but stopped midway when he spotted me. "What is wrong with you?"

"Be nice, Stewart," Molly said as she breezed into the room, closing the door behind her.

With Molly in the room, Stewart was *nice* but I wasn't as lucky for the other two meetings. In meeting number two, he'd assured the other attendees that I wasn't contagious, drawing more attention to me than I would have had otherwise.

J.P. popped into my office just after lunch carrying two boxes. "Charlie asked me to give these to you." He set them on the desk and sat across from me. "How are you doing?"

I shrugged and grabbed a box cutter from my top drawer.

"Put it this way, I look better than I feel."

He cringed, the look on his face making me laugh for the first time in four days. I opened the box and pulled out the bubble wrap. I sucked in a sharp breath when I spotted the contents, then dropped back into my chair, my hands shaking.

"Barb?" J.P. jumped up and came over to kneel beside my chair. "What's wrong?"

I shook my head as tears rolled down my cheeks. "I'm fine," I said between sobs. "Really, I'm fine, J.P."

He went back to the other side of the desk and sat. I grabbed a tissue and dabbed under my eyes then blew my nose. Taking in a deep breath, I let it out slowly, getting myself back under control. I picked up the box cutter and opened the second box, then picked up its contents as well as the item from the first box and held them up for him to see.

"I ordered these for the house a few weeks ago."

After going through my Cal and Barbara memory box, I'd taken the pictures to a frame shop to have custom collage frames made for them. In the middle of each collage was a new photo...one a picture from our first official date when we went to see the Rat Pack show and the other was the photo Laura had taken of us right after we got engaged.

"What do you want to do, Barb?" J.P. asked.

And suddenly everything became clear.

"I can't lose him again, J.P." I blinked away happy tears. "I love him and I can't live without him again wondering *what if*. We'll make it work. Whatever it takes, we'll make it work."

He stood and walked around the desk then pulled me into his

arms for a tight hug. Kissing the top of my head, he pulled back and said, "It's about time you figured that out."

My phone chirped, signaling meeting number three. This meeting is in Stewart's office, a definite power play on his part. He loves to sit in his huge chair behind his giant desk and act like he's important. The man definitely has a Napoleon complex.

After placing the frames back in their boxes, I grabbed my computer and said, "Come on, let's go get this over with."

J.P. opened the door and stepped aside for me to walk into the hallway.

"Look at the bright side, your meetings like this are numbered."

"True."

We walked down the hall and stepped into Stewart's lair. He hung up his desk phone just as we entered and glared at me.

"You're lucky I double-checked the numbers you gave me before I met with Herbert's ice cream, because they were wrong," he said.

"That's not possible." I opened my computer and waited for it to boot up then clicked into the shared drive and retrieved the file. Setting my laptop on the edge of his desk, I pointed to the open spreadsheet. "There's nothing wrong with those numbers."

His gaze shifted between my screen and the paper on his desk then pointed at my screen, looking like it had offended him. "That is not the file that was out there."

I picked the paper off his desk and looked at the numbers.

"Stewart, this is the old spreadsheet." I turned my computer and clicked on the drive again then shifted it so he could see. "It's in the folder titled *old* for a reason. The correct file had last week's date in the name. I told you that in the meeting."

His face turned bright red and he slammed my laptop closed, making me jump back. J.P. shifted to the edge of his seat.

"Oh, sit back," Stewart spat out. Literally. Spit landed right in the middle of the folder in front of him. He turned his cold eyes on me. "Your job is to make sure the numbers are correct."

"The numbers were correct. You printed the wrong file."

He blinked at me, then rounded his eyes.

"This was your screw up, not mine." He let out a cold chuckle. "Instead of fixing your mistake, I should have gone in with the wrong numbers so my mother can finally see you're not as great as she thinks you are."

My heart pounded and I flexed my fingers. From the corner of my eye, I saw J.P. shifting his gaze between Stewart and me.

I've stood up to my ex-husband more in the past couple weeks than I have in years. No matter how he blamed his mistakes on me or berated me, I just took it because I didn't want to deal with him. But now I really don't care. In another couple months, I won't have to put up with him ever again. Plus, now that I know what I want to do about Cal and me, I just want to get the hell out of here.

"You know what, Stewart?" I met his flat brown eyes. "In another couple months, you won't have to put up with my so-called incompetence anymore. Then you might have to actually pay attention to what you're doing because you won't have me as your scapegoat anymore." I picked up my laptop and walked to the door then turned to add, "I'm going home now."

CAL

I pulled into the driveway and nearly ran into the mailbox when I spotted Barb's car. My heart pounded and I barely put the car in park before I jumped out of the 4Runner. I didn't even put it in the garage because I didn't want to wait for the door to open.

Running through the gate, I took the deck stairs two at a time. Thankfully she had the patio doors open because otherwise, I may have run through the glass. I stopped short when I spotted her in the kitchen, using a spatula to flip something in the pan in front of her. She looked over at me then turned off the stove and moved the pan to another burner.

I watched her slowly walk toward me and ran to meet her in the middle because I couldn't wait another second to touch her. I reached out and pulled her against me. She wrapped her arms around my neck and held on tight.

"I'm so sorry I left, Cal," she sobbed against my chest.

"It's not your fault, it's mine." I pulled back and wiped her tears with my thumbs. "I should have told you about the job. Whatever I said my reasons were for not saying anything, I was just kidding myself. I knew you'd have an issue with a job like that."

She shook her head and wrapped her fingers around my wrists.

"Cal, I just want to be with you," she said. "We can figure every-thing else out as we go along."

With my hands cupping her cheeks, I pulled her in and brushed my lips against hers...once, twice...before pressing my open mouth against hers to get a better taste. I tangled my tongue with hers and shifted my hands to her waist, desperate to get closer. She must have felt the same because she twisted her fingers into my scalp, holding me in place.

We really need to talk, but it seems like forever since we've been together, even though it's only been four days. If she didn't seem interested, I'd pull back, but with the way her hips are pistoning against mine, I'd say she wants this as much as I do.

Our mouths never lost contact as I walked us over to the couch and sat, pulling her onto my lap. She pulsed her hips against me and I reached between us to open my pants before I get a zipper imprint on my dick. I groaned deep in my throat as she shifted back and wrapped her hand around my shaft and stroked. Up and down. Up and down. Then she got fancy and twisted her hand around the tip on the upstroke, dragging the head against her palm before stroking down again.

She let go just long enough for me to drag her shirt off, then she grabbed him again. It was the sweetest torture and I wanted her to stop and keep going in equal measures. When she looked down and licked her lips, I knew I had to take control.

I pulled my shirt off and scooted Barb off my lap so I could remove her pants and mine. She settled back over me, her knees on either side of my hips, and sank down my entire length inch by slow fucking inch.

Digging my fingers into her ass, I grit my teeth and closed my eyes and mentally recited baseball stats. In times like this, you gotta go with what works.

"Cal," she moaned, then started that breathless chant of my name that I love so much.

I opened my eyes and looked down, watching my dick appear and disappear and she rode him, moving up and down, faster and faster.

"Barb." Her name sounded like a warning, which it was. I let out a garbled groan as I lost control. At the same time, her inner walls clamped down as she milked me dry and rode out her own release.

HAVING RECONNECTED PHYSICALLY, WE WERE BOTH MUCH MORE relaxed than when I got home. Which is good, because we have some serious things to talk about.

Barb had made crab cakes and a salad for dinner and we decided to open a bottle of wine and eat out on the deck. We decided to enjoy the delicious meal she'd prepared before starting our discussion. She told me about her day and I couldn't be more proud that she finally told off her asshat of an ex-husband. Thankfully she won't have to see him again once she starts her new job.

Once we both finished our meals, I topped off our drinks and sat back in my chair. I opened my mouth to speak but she beat me to it.

"So, I was thinking. With my new job, I would only have to be in the office half the week and for important client meetings, so I'd be able to come up to Fayetteville, maybe go on some close road trips. That way, we wouldn't be apart so much."

"I'm not taking the job, Barb."

She looked at me and blinked, then took a sip of wine.

"Cal, I know how much you love baseball and this job really is perfect for you. We'll work it out."

I leaned forward and took her hand in mine.

"I do love baseball, but I love you more." I kissed her fingertips one at a time. "I've had that life, but what I missed out on is our life. The one we should have had, the one we would have had if things didn't get so messed up at the end. I can't lose you again." I let out a sad chuckle. "Hell, you were gone four days and it felt like an eternity. I don't want to do that on a regular basis. I won't survive being without you."

"So what are you going to do?" she asked. "You can't keep working at the bank. It will eventually suck the life out of you."

"Dan was here the other night and shared his retirement plan with me. He wants to open a baseball training facility that will eventually host its own travel ball teams." I smirked. "You know that superstitious thing baseball players have? Well it extends to their careers. No one wants to talk about retirement, because if you don't mention it hopefully the day will never come."

"So you never knew this is what he had planned?"

I shook my head. "He asked me if I'd be his partner. Eventually we might even be able to bring Jack in. And since we're all kind of big deals, our names should pull people in." I bobbed my eyebrows as I used her phrase.

"And you'd be happy doing that?"

"I think I will and it will give me the opportunity to help kids develop their skills just like so many coaches did for me. And we'd have a staff to run things so I wouldn't have to be there all the time. I think it will be perfect."

"You really are an amazing man," she said.

"No, you're the amazing one. You have no idea what it means to me that you were willing to come back, even when you thought I was taking the coaching job."

"Cal, I gave you up once. I won't do it again." She stood and stepped next to my chair then climbed into my lap, wrapping her arms around my neck. "When I overheard your conversation with Mr. Hanover, I freaked out. All those memories from when my mom died and you were gone and I felt so alone came rushing back and just took over. And I felt so scared, just like I did back then. " She kissed me then rested her head on my shoulder. "But then I realized that with you, I don't have anything to be afraid of. I'm just sorry it took me four days to come to my senses."

I rubbed my hand up and down her back in slow, soothing strokes.

"Just so you know, I planned on going to see you to get this all straightened out tonight. I couldn't face sleeping without you one more night."

She sat back and smiled up at me, then her eyes rounded and she jumped up.

"Oh, I almost forgot. I have something to show you."

She ran into the house and came back out carrying two boxes. Placing them on the table next to each other, she opened one then the other and reached inside. She held up a picture frame in each hand. My eyes shifted between the two, taking in all the wonderful memories we'd managed to capture on film so many years ago.

I reached out and took one from her to get a closer look.

"I ordered these a couple weeks ago," she said, setting the other frame down in front of me. "For the past couple days, I knew I wanted to make this work, I just hadn't figured how. Then these came today, and I knew I couldn't wait one more day to come home. I also realized that I didn't have to figure it out, we'd make it work together."

She stepped behind me and rested her hands on my shoulders.

"If I'd done that back in college instead of letting the depression and heartache from losing my mom cloud my decisions, those kids would have been fine." She kissed the back of my neck and rested her cheek against mine. "And we will be too. No matter what."

I carefully placed the frame on the table then stood. Pulling Barbara into my arms, I kissed her. Softly, sweetly at first promising the future the kids in those pictures were too young to appreciate, to hold on to. But we're older now, wiser and I know we'll never take what we have for granted again.

Slowly ending the kiss, I looked down at her and smiled.

"Come on, let's go find a place to hang those pictures where we can see them every single day and those kids can watch us living their happily ever after."

THE END

Made in the USA
Monee, IL
08 November 2020

47018319R00166